W0391233

NOT A PENNY MORE, NOT A PENNY LESS

JEFFREY ARCHER, whose novels and short stories include *Kane and Abel, A Prisoner of Birth* and *Cat O' Nine Tales,* has topped the bestseller lists around the world, with sales of over 270 million copies.

He is the only author ever to have been a number one bestseller in fiction (sixteen times), short stories (four times) and non-fiction (*The Prison Diaries*).

The author is married with two sons, and lives in London and Cambridge.

www.jeffreyarcher.com

ALSO BY JEFFREY ARCHER

NOVELS

Shall We Tell the President? Kane and Abel
The Prodigal Daughter First Among Equals
A Matter of Honour As the Crow Flies
Honour Among Thieves
The Fourth Estate The Eleventh Commandment
Sons of Fortune False Impression
The Gospel According to Judas
(with the assistance of Professor Francis J. Moloney)
A Prisoner of Birth Paths of Glory
Only Time Will Tell The Sins of the Father

SHORT STORIES

A Quiver Full of Arrows A Twist in the Tale
Twelve Red Herrings The Collected Short Stories
To Cut a Long Story Short Cat O' Nine Tales
And Thereby Hangs a Tale

PLAYS

Beyond Reasonable Doubt Exclusive The Accused

PRISON DIARIES

Volume One – Belmarsh: Hell
Volume Two – Wayland: Purgatory
Volume Three – North Sea Camp: Heaven

SCREENPLAYS

Mallory: Walking Off the Map False Impression

JEFFREY ARCHER

NOT A PENNY MORE, NOT A PENNY LESS

PAN BOOKS

First published 1976 by Jonathan Cape Ltd

This edition published 2009 by Pan Books
an imprint of Pan Macmillan, a division of Macmillan Publishers Limited
Pan Macmillan, 20 New Wharf Road, London N1 9RR
Basingstoke and Oxford
Associated companies throughout the world
www.panmacmillan.com

ISBN 978-1-4472-2823-3

Copyright © Jeffrey Archer 1976

The right of Jeffrey Archer to be identified as the author of this work has been asserted by him in accordance with the Copyright, Designs and Patents Act 1988.

The Macmillan Group has no responsibility for the information provided by any author websites whose address you obtain from this book ('author websites'). The inclusion of author website addresses in this book does not constitute an endorsement by or association with us of such sites or the content, products, advertising or other materials presented on such sites.

All rights reserved. No part of this publication may be reproduced, stored in or introduced into a retrieval system, or transmitted, in any form, or by any means (electronic, mechanical, photocopying, recording or otherwise) without the prior written permission of the publisher. Any person who does any unauthorized act in relation to this publication may be liable to criminal prosecution and civil claims for damages.

1 3 5 7 9 8 6 4 2

A CIP catalogue record for this book is available from the British Library.

Typeset by SetSystems Ltd, Saffron Walden, Essex
Printed and bound by CPI Group (UK) Ltd, Croydon, CR0 4YY

This book is sold subject to the condition that it shall not, by way of trade or otherwise, be lent, re-sold, hired out, or otherwise circulated without the publisher's prior consent in any form of binding or cover other than that in which it is published and without a similar condition including this condition being imposed on the subsequent purchaser.

Visit **www.panmacmillan.com** to read more about all our books and to buy them. You will also find features, author interviews and news of any author events, and you can sign up for e-newsletters so that you're always first to hear about our new releases.

To Mary

and the Fat Men

Author's Note

I acknowledge all the help I received from so many people in writing this book and wish to thank them: David Niven, Jr, who made me do it, Sir Noel and Lady Hall who made it possible, Adrian Metcalfe, Anthony Rentoul, Colin Emson, Ted Francis, Godfrey Barker, Willy West, Madame Tellegen, David Stein, Christian Neffe, Dr John Vance, Dr David Weeden, the Rev. Leslie Styler, Robert Gasser, Professor Jim Bolton, and Jamie Clark; Gail and Jo for putting it together; and my wife, Mary, for the hours spent correcting and editing.

PROLOGUE

'JÖRG EXPECT $7 million from Crédit Parisien in the No. 2 account by 6 pm tonight, Central European time, and place it with first-class banks and triple "A" commercial names. Otherwise, invest it in the overnight Euro-dollar market. Understood?'

'Yes, Harvey.'

'Place $1 million in the Banco do Minas Gerais, Rio de Janeiro, in the names of Silverman and Elliott and cancel the call loan at Barclays Bank, Lombard Street. Understood?'

'Yes, Harvey.'

'Buy gold on my commodity account until it reaches $10 million and then hold until you receive further instructions. Try and buy in the troughs and don't rush – be patient. Understood?'

'Yes, Harvey.'

Harvey Metcalfe realised that the last instruction was unnecessary. Jörg Birrer was one of the most conservative bankers in Zürich and, more important to Harvey, had over the past twenty-five years proved to be one of the shrewdest.

'Can you join me at Wimbledon on Tuesday, June

25th at 2 pm, Centre Court, my usual debenture seat?'

'Yes, Harvey.'

The telephone clicked into place. Harvey never said goodbye. He had never understood the niceties of life and it was too late to start learning now. He picked up the phone, dialled the seven digits which would give him the Lincoln Trust in Boston, and asked for his secretary.

'Miss Fish?'

'Yes, sir.'

'Remove the file on Prospecta Oil and destroy it. Destroy any correspondence connected with it and leave absolutely no trace. Understood?'

'Yes, sir.'

The telephone clicked again. Harvey Metcalfe had given similar orders three times in the last twenty-five years and by now Miss Fish had learnt not to question him.

Harvey breathed deeply, almost a sigh, a quiet exhalation of triumph. He was now worth at least $25 million, and nothing could stop him. He opened a bottle of Krug champagne 1964, imported from Hedges & Butler of London. He sipped it slowly and lit a Romeo y Julieta Churchill, which an Italian immigrant smuggled in for him in boxes of two hundred and fifty once a month from Cuba. He settled back for a mild celebration. In Boston, Massachusetts, it was 12.20 pm – nearly time for lunch.

*

In Harley Street, Bond Street, the King's Road and Magdalen College, Oxford, it was 6.20 pm. Four men, unknown to each other, checked the market price of Prospecta Oil in the final edition of the London *Evening Standard*. It was £3.70. All four of them were rich men, looking forward to consolidating their already successful careers.

Tomorrow they would be penniless.

1

Making a million legally has always been difficult. Making a million illegally has always been a little easier. Keeping a million when you have made it is perhaps the most difficult of all. Henryk Metelski was one of those rare men who had managed all three. Even if the million he had made legally came after the million he had made illegally, Metelski was still a yard ahead of the others: he had managed to keep it all.

Henryk Metelski was born on the Lower East Side of New York on May 17th, 1909, in a small room that already slept four children. He grew up through the Depression, believing in God and one meal a day. His parents were from Warsaw and had emigrated from Poland at the turn of the century. Henryk's father was a baker by trade and had soon found a job in New York, where immigrant Poles specialised in baking black rye bread and running small restaurants for their countrymen. Both parents would have liked Henryk to be an academic success, but he was never destined to become an outstanding pupil at his high school. His natural gifts lay elsewhere. A cunning, smart little boy, he was far more interested in the control of the underground school market in cigarettes and liquor than in stirring tales of the American Revolution and the Liberty Bell. Little Henryk never believed for one moment that the best things in life were free, and the pursuit of money and power came as naturally to him as the pursuit of a mouse to a cat.

When Henryk was a pimply and flourishing fourteen-year-old, his father died of what we now know to be cancer. His mother outlived her husband by no more than a few months, leaving the five children to fend for themselves. Henryk, like the other four, should have gone into the district orphanage for destitute children, but in the mid-1920s it was not hard for a boy to disappear in New York – though it was harder to survive. Henryk became a master of survival, a schooling which was to prove very useful to him in later life.

He knocked around the Lower East Side with his belt tightened and his eyes open, shining shoes here, washing dishes there, always looking for an entrance to the maze at the heart of which lay wealth and prestige. His first chance came when his room-mate Jan Pelnik, a messenger boy on the New York Stock Exchange, put himself temporarily out of action with a sausage garnished with salmonella. Henryk, deputed to report his friend's mishap to the Chief Messenger, upgraded food-poisoning to tuberculosis, and talked himself into the ensuing vacancy. He then changed his room, donned a new uniform, lost a friend, and gained a job.

Most of the messages Henryk delivered during the early twenties read 'Buy'. Many of them were quickly acted upon, for this was a boom era. He watched men of little ability make fortunes while he remained nothing more than an observer. His instincts directed him towards those individuals who made more money in a week on the Stock Exchange than he could hope to make in a lifetime on his salary.

He set about learning how to master the way the Stock Exchange operated, he listened to private conversations, opened sealed messages and found out which closed company reports to study. By the age of eighteen he had four years' experience of Wall Street: four years which most messenger boys would have spent simply walking across crowded floors, delivering little pink pieces of paper; four years which to Henryk Metelski were the equivalent of a Master's Degree from the Harvard Business School. He was not to know that one day he would lecture to that august body.

One morning in July 1927 he was delivering a message from Halgarten & Co, a well-established brokerage house, making his usual detour via the washroom. He had perfected a system whereby he could lock himself into a cubicle, study the message he was carrying, decide whether the information was of any value to him and, if it was, immediately telephone Witold Gronowich, an old Pole who managed a small insurance firm for his fellow countrymen. Henryk reckoned to pick up an extra $20 to $25 a week for the inside knowledge he supplied. Gronowich, in no position to place large sums on the market; never let any of the leaks lead back to his young informant.

Sitting on the lavatory seat, Henryk began to realise that this time he was reading a message of considerable importance. The Governor of Texas was about to grant the Standard Oil Company permission to complete a pipeline from Chicago to Mexico, all other public bodies involved having already agreed to the proposal. The market was aware that the company had been trying to obtain this final permission for nearly a year, but the general view was that the Governor would turn it down. The message was to be passed direct to John D. Rockefeller's broker, Tucker Anthony, immediately. The granting of this permission to build a pipeline would open up the entire North to a ready supply of oil, and that could only mean increased profits. It was obvious to Henryk that Standard Oil stock must rise steadily on the market once the news had broken, especially as Standard Oil already controlled 90 per cent of the oil refineries in America.

In normal circumstances Henryk would have sent on this information direct to Mr Gronowich, and was about to do so when he noticed a rather overweight man, who was also leaving the washroom, drop a piece of paper. As there was no one else about at the time, Henryk picked it up and retreated back into his private cubicle, thinking that at best it would reveal another piece of information. In fact, it was a cheque for $50,000 made out to cash from a Mrs Rose Rennick.

Henryk thought quickly, and not on his feet. He left the washroom at speed and was soon standing outside on Wall Street itself. He made his way to a small coffee-shop on Rector Street and sat there pretending to drink a Coca-Cola while he carefully worked out his plan. He then proceeded to act on it.

First, he cashed the cheque at a branch of the Morgan Bank on the south-west side of Wall Street, knowing that in his smart uniform as a messenger at the Exchange he would easily pass as a carrier for some distinguished firm. He then returned to the Exchange and acquired from a floor broker 2,500 Standard Oil shares at $19⅞, leaving himself $126.61 change after brokerage charges. He placed the $126.61 in a Checking Account with the Morgan Bank. Then, waiting in tense anticipation for an announcement from the Governor's office, he put himself through the motions of a normal day's work, too preoccupied with Standard Oil even to make a detour via the washroom with the messages he carried.

No announcement came. Henryk could not know that the news was being held up until the Exchange had officially closed at 3 pm in order to allow the

Governor himself to buy shares anywhere and everywhere he could lay his grubby hands on them. Henryk went home that night petrified that he had made a disastrous mistake. He had visions of losing his job and everything he had built up over the past four years. Perhaps he would even end up in jail.

He was unable to sleep that night and became steadily more restless in his small open-windowed but airless room. At 1 am he could stand the uncertainty no longer, so he jumped out of bed, shaved, dressed and took a subway to Grand Central Station. From there he walked to Times Square where with trembling hands he bought the first edition of the *Wall Street Journal*. For a moment he couldn't take in the news, although it was shrieking at him in banner headlines:

GOVERNOR GRANTS OIL PIPELINE RIGHTS
TO ROCKEFELLER

and a secondary headline:

HEAVY TRADING EXPECTED IN STANDARD OIL SHARES

Dazed, Henryk walked to the nearest all-night café, on West 42nd Street, and ordered a large hamburger and French fries, which he covered in ketchup and nibbled at like a man eating his last breakfast before facing the electric chair, rather than his first on the way to fortune. He read the full details of Rockefeller's coup on page one, which spread over to page fourteen, and by 4 am he had bought the first three editions of the *New York Times* and the first two editions of the *Herald Tribune*. The lead story was the same in each. Henryk hurried home, giddy and elated, and changed into his uniform. He arrived at the Stock Exchange at 8 am and went through the motions of a day's work, thinking only of how to carry out the second part of his plan.

When the Stock Exchange opened officially, Henryk went over to the Morgan Bank and requested a loan of $50,000 against the security of his 2,500 Standard Oil shares, which had opened that morning at $21¼. He placed the loan in his Checking Account and instructed the bank to issue him a draft for the $50,000 to be made out to Mrs Rose Rennick. He left the bank and looked up the address and telephone number of his unwitting benefactor.

Mrs Rennick, a widow who lived off the investments left by her late husband, lived in a small apartment on 62nd Street, which Henryk knew to be one of the most fashionable parts of New York. The call from a Henryk Metelski, asking to see her on an urgent private matter, came as something of a surprise to her, but a final mention of Halgarten & Co. gave her a little more confidence and she agreed to see him at the Waldorf-Astoria at 4 pm that afteroon.

Henryk had never been inside the Waldorf-Astoria, but after four years on the Stock Exchange there were few prominent hotels or restaurants he had not heard mentioned in other people's conversations. He realised that Mrs Rennick was more likely to have tea with him there than to see a man with a name like Henryk Metelski in her own apartment, especially as his Polish accent was more pronounced over the telephone than it was face to face.

As Henryk stood in the thickly carpeted lobby of the Waldorf, he blushed at his sartorial naïveté. Imagining that everybody was staring at him, he buried his short, amply-covered frame in an elegant chair in the Jefferson Room. Some of the other patrons of the Waldorf were amply covered too, but Henryk felt that *Pommes de Terre Maître d'Hôtel* were more likely to have caused their obesity than French fries. Vainly wishing he had put a little less grease on his black wavy hair and a little more on his down-at-heel shoes, he scratched nervously at an irritating pustule on the side of his mouth and waited. His suit, in which he felt so assured and prosperous among his friends, was shiny, skimpy, cheap and loud. He did not blend in with the décor, still less with the patrons of the hotel, and, feeling inadequate for the first time in his life, he picked up a copy of the *New Yorker*, hid behind it, and prayed for his guest to arrive quickly. Waiters fluttered deferentially with instinctive superciliousness. One, he noticed, did nothing more than circle the tearoom delicately proffering lump sugar from silver tongs in a white-gloved hand: Henryk was enormously impressed.

Rose Rennick arrived a few minutes after four, accompanied by two small dogs and wearing an outrageously large hat. Henryk thought she looked over sixty, overweight, overmade-up and overdressed, but she had a warm smile and appeared to know everyone, as she moved from table to table, chatting to the regular Waldorf-Astoria set. Eventually reaching what she had rightly assumed to be Henryk's table, she was rather taken aback, not only to find him so strangely dressed, but also looking even younger than his eighteen years.

Mrs Rennick ordered tea while Henryk recited his well-rehearsed story: there had been an unfortunate mistake with her cheque, which had been wrongly credited to his firm at the Stock Exchange on the previous day; his boss had instructed him to return the cheque immediately and to say how much they regretted the unfortunate error. Henryk then passed over the draft for $50,000, and added that he would lose his job if she insisted on taking the matter any further, as he had been entirely responsible for the mistake. Mrs Rennick had, in fact, only been informed of the missing cheque that morning and did not realise that it had been cashed, as it would have taken a few days to clear her account. Henryk's perfectly genuine anxiety as he stumbled through his tale would have convinced a far more critical observer of human nature than Mrs Rennick. Readily she agreed to let the matter drop, only too pleased to have her money returned; as it was in the form of a draft from the Morgan Bank, she had lost nothing. Henryk breathed a sigh of relief and for the first time that day began to relax and enjoy himself. He even called for the waiter with the sugar and silver tongs.

After a respectable period of time had passed, Henryk explained that he must return to work, thanked Mrs Rennick for her co-operation, paid the bill and left. Outside on the street he whistled with relief. His new shirt was soaked in sweat (Mrs Rennick would have called it perspiration), but he was out in the open and could breathe freely again. His first major operation had been a success.

He stood on Park Avenue, amused that the venue for his confrontation with Mrs Rennick had been the Waldorf, the very hotel where John D. Rockefeller, the President of Standard Oil, had a suite. Henryk had arrived on foot and used the main entrance, while Mr Rockefeller had earlier arrived by subway and taken his private lift to the Waldorf Towers. Although few New Yorkers were aware of it, Rockefeller had had his own private station built fifty feet below the Waldorf-Astoria to save him travelling the eight blocks to Grand Central Station, there being no stop between there and 125th Street. (The station remains to this day, but as no Rockefellers live at the Waldorf-Astoria, the train never stops there.) While Henryk had been discussing his $50,000 with Mrs Rennick, Rockefeller had been considering an investment of $5,000,000 with Andrew W. Mellon, President Coolidge's Secretary of the Treasury, fifty-seven floors above him.

The next morning Henryk returned to work as usual. He knew he had only five days' grace to sell the shares and clear his debt with the Morgan Bank and the stockbroker, as an account on the New York Stock Exchange runs for five business days or seven calendar days. On the last day of the account the shares were standing at $23¼. He sold at $23⅛, and cleared his overdraft of $49,625 and, after expenses, realised a profit of $7,490 which he left deposited with the Morgan Bank.

Over the next three years, Henryk stopped ringing Mr Gronowich, and started dealing for himself, in small amounts to begin with, but growing larger as he gained in experience and confidence. Times were still good, and while he didn't always make a profit, he had learnt to master the occasional bear market as well as the more common bull. His system in the bear market was to sell short – not a practice considered to be entirely ethical in business. He soon mastered the art of selling shares he didn't own in expectation of a subsequent fall in their price. His instinct for market trends refined as rapidly as did his taste for clothes, and the guile learnt in the backstreets of the Lower East Side always stood him in good stead. Henryk soon discovered that the whole world was a jungle – sometimes the lions and tigers wore suits.

When the stock market collapsed in 1929 Henryk had turned his $7,490 into $51,000 of liquid assets, having sold on every share he possessed the day after the Chairman of Halgarten & Co jumped out of one of the Stock Exchange windows. Henryk had got the message. With his newly acquired income he had moved into a smart apartment in Brooklyn and started driving a rather ostentatious red Stutz. Henryk realised at an early age that he had come into the world with three main disadvantages – his name, background and impecunity. The money problem was solving itself, and now the time had come to expunge the other two. To that end, he had made an application to change his name by court order to Harvey David Metcalfe. When the application was granted, he ceased all further contact with his friends from the Polish community, and in May 1930 he came of age with a new name, new background, and very new money.

It was later that year at a football game that he first met Roger Sharpley and discovered that the rich have their problems too. Sharpley, a young man from Boston, had inherited his father's company, which specialised in the import of whisky and the export of furs. Educated at Choate and later in Dartmouth College, Sharpley had all the assurance and charm of the Boston set, so often envied by his fellow countrymen. He was tall and fair, looked as if he came from Viking stock, and with his air of the gifted amateur, found most things came easily to him – especially women. He was in every way a total contrast to Harvey. Although they were poles apart, the contrast acted like a magnet and attracted the one to the other.

Roger's only ambition in life was to become an

officer in the Navy, but after graduating from Dartmouth he had had to return to the family business because of his father's ill-health. He had only been with the firm a few months when his father died. Roger would have liked to have sold Sharpley & Son to the first bidder, but his father had made a codicil to his will to the effect that if the firm were sold before Roger's fortieth birthday (that being the last day one can enlist for the US Navy), the money gained from the sale would be divided equally among his other relatives.

Harvey gave Roger's problem considerable thought, and after two lengthy sessions with a skilful New York lawyer, suggested a course of action to Roger: Harvey would purchase 49 per cent of Sharpley & Son for $100,000 and the first $20,000 profit each year. At the age of forty, Roger could relinquish the remaining 51 per cent for a further $100,000. The Board would consist of three voting members – Harvey, Roger and one nominated by Harvey, giving him overall control. As far as Harvey was concerned, Roger could join the Navy and need only attend the annual shareholders' meeting.

Roger could not believe his luck. He did not even consult anyone at Sharpley & Son, knowing only too well that they would try to talk him out of it. Harvey had counted on this and had assessed his quarry accurately. Roger gave the proposition only a few days' consideration before allowing the legal papers to be drawn up in New York, far enough away from

Boston to be sure the firm did not learn what was going on. Meanwhile, Harvey returned to the Morgan Bank, where he was now looked upon as a man with a future. Since banks deal in futures, the manager agreed to help him in his new enterprise with a loan of $50,000 to add to his own $50,000, enabling Harvey to acquire 49 per cent of Sharpley & Son, and become its fifth President. The legal documents were signed in New York on October 28th, 1930.

Roger left speedily for Newport, Rhode Island, to commence his Officers Training programme in the US Navy. Harvey left for Grand Central Station to catch the train for Boston. His days as a messenger boy on the New York Stock Exchange were over. He was twenty-one years of age and the President of his own company.

What looked like disaster to most, Harvey could always turn into triumph. The American people were still suffering under Prohibition, and although Harvey could export furs, he could no longer import whisky. This had been the main reason for the fall in the company profits over the past decade. But Harvey soon found that with a little bribery, involving the Mayor of Boston, the Chief of Police and the Customs officials on the Canadian border, plus a payment to the Mafia to ensure that his products reached the restaurants and speak-easies, somehow the whisky imports went up rather than down. Sharpley & Son lost its more respectable and long-serving staff, and replaced them with animals better-suited to Harvey Metcalfe's particular jungle.

From 1930 to 1933 Harvey went from strength to strength, but when Prohibition was finally lifted by President Roosevelt after overwhelming public demand, the excitement went with it, Harvey allowed the company to continue to deal in whisky and furs while he branched out into new fields. In 1933 Sharpley & Son celebrated a hundred years in business. In three years Harvey had lost 97 years of goodwill and doubled the profits. It took him five years to reach his first million and only another four to double the sum again, which was when he decided the time had come for Harvey Metcalfe and Sharpley & Son to part company. In twelve years from 1930 to 1942, he had built up the profits from $30,000 to $910,000. He sold the company in January 1944 for $7,000,000, paying $100,000 to the widow of Captain Roger Sharpley of the US Navy and keeping $6,900,000 for himself.

Harvey celebrated his thirty-fifth birthday by buying at a cost of $4 million a small, ailing bank in Boston called the Lincoln Trust. At the time it boasted a profit of approximately $500,000 a year, a prestigious building in the centre of Boston and an unblemished and somewhat boring reputation. Harvey intended to change both its reputation and its balance sheet. He enjoyed being the President of a bank – but it did nothing to improve his honesty. Every dubious deal in the Boston area seemed to emanate from the

Lincoln Trust, and although Harvey increased the bank's profits to $2 million per annum during the next five years, his personal reputation was never in credit.

Harvey met Arlene Hunter in the winter of 1949. She was the only daughter of the President of the First City Bank of Boston. Until then Harvey had never taken any real interest in women. His driving force had always been making money, and although he considered the opposite sex a useful relaxation in his free time, on balance he found them an inconvenience. But having now reached what the glossy magazines referred to as middle age and having no heir to leave his fortune to, he calculated that it was time to find a wife who would present him with a son. As with everything else that he had wanted in his life, he considered the problem very carefully.

Harvey had first run into Arlene when she was thirty-one: quite literally, when she had backed her car into his new Lincoln. She could not have been a greater contrast to the short, uneducated, overweight Pole. She was nearly six feet tall, slim and although not unattractive, she lacked confidence and was beginning to think that marriage had passed her by. Most of her school friends were already on their second divorces and felt rather sorry for her. Harvey's extravagant ways came as a welcome change after her parents' prudish discipline, which she often felt was to blame for her awkwardness with men of her own age. She had only had one affair – a disastrous failure, thanks to her total innocence – and until Harvey arrived, no one had seemed to be willing to give her a second chance. Arlene's father did not approve of Harvey, and showed it, which only made him more attractive to her. Her father had not approved of any of the men she had associated with, but on this occasion he was right. Harvey on the other hand realised that to marry the First City Bank of Boston with the Lincoln Trust could only be of long-term benefit to him, and with that in mind he set out, as he always did, to conquer. Arlene didn't put up much of a battle.

Arlene and Harvey were married in 1951 at a wedding more memorable for those who were absent than those who attended. They settled into Harvey's Lincoln home outside of Boston and very shortly afterwards Arlene announced she was pregnant. She gave Harvey a daughter almost a year to the day after their marriage.

They christened her Rosalie, and she became the centre of Harvey's attention; his only disappointment came when a prolapse closely followed by a hysterectomy prevented Arlene from bearing him any more children. He sent Rosalie to Bennetts, the most expensive girls' school in Washington, and from there she was accepted at Vassar to major in English. This even pleased old man Hunter, who had grown to tolerate Harvey and adore hs granddaughter. On gaining her degree, Rosalie continued her education at the

Sorbonne, after a fierce disagreement with her father concerning the type of friends she was keeping, particularly the ones with long hair who didn't want to go to Vietnam – not that Harvey had done much during the Second World War, except to cash in on every shortage. The final crunch came when Rosalie dared to suggest that morals were not to be decided only by length of hair or political views. Harvey missed her, but refused to admit the fact to Arlene.

Harvey had three loves in his life: the first was still Rosalie, the second was his paintings, and the third his orchids. The first had started the moment his daughter was born. The second was a love that had developed over many years and had been kindled in the strangest way. A client of Sharpley & Son was about to go bankrupt while still owing a fairly large sum of money to the company. Harvey got wind of it and went round to confront him, but the rot had already set in and there was no longer any hope of securing cash. Determined not to leave empty-handed, Harvey took with him the man's only tangible asset – a Renoir valued at $10,000.

Harvey's intention was to sell the picture quickly before it could be proved that he was a preferred creditor, but he became so entranced with the fine brushwork and the delicate pastel shades that his only desire was to own more. When he realised that pictures were not only a good investment, but that he actually liked them as well, his collection and his love grew hand in hand. By the early 1970s, Harvey had a Manet, two Monets, a Renoir, two Picassos, a Pissarro, a Utrillo, a Cézanne, as well as most of the recognised lesser names, and he had become quite a connoisseur of the Impressionist period. His one remaining desire was to possess a Van Gogh, and only recently he had failed to acquire *L'Hôpital de St Paul à St Remy* at the Sotheby-Parke Bernet Gallery in New York, when Dr Armand Hammer of Occidental Petroleum had outbid him – $1,200,000 had been just a little too much for Harvey.

Earlier, in 1966, he had failed to acquire Lot 49, *Mademoiselle Ravoux*, from Christie, Manson & Woods, the London art dealers; although the Rev. Theodore Pitcairn, representing the Lord's New Church in Bryn Athyn, Pennsylvania, had pushed him over the top, he had only whetted his appetite further. The Lord giveth, and on that occasion the Lord had taken away. Although it was not fully appreciated in Boston, it was already recognised in the art world that Harvey had one of the finest Impressionist collections in the world, almost as widely admired as that of Walter Annenberg, President Nixon's Ambassador to London who, like Harvey, had been one of the few people to build up a major collection since the Second World War.

Harvey's third love was his prize collection of orchids, and he had three times been a winner at the New England Spring Flower Show in Boston, twice beating old man Hunter into second place.

*

Harvey now travelled to Europe once a year. He had established a successful stud in Kentucky and liked to see his horses run at Longchamp and Ascot. He also enjoyed watching Wimbledon, which he considered was still the greatest tennis tournament in the world. It amused him to do a little business in Europe at the same time, giving him the opportunity to make some more money for his Swiss bank account in Zürich. He did not need a Swiss account, but somehow he got a kick out of doing Uncle Sam. Although Harvey had mellowed over the years and cut down on his more dubious deals, he could never resist the chance to take a risk if he thought the reward was likely to be big enough. One such golden opportunity presented itself in 1964 when Her Majesty's Government invited applications for exploration and production licences in the North Sea. At that time neither the British Government nor the civil servants involved had any idea of the future significance of North Sea oil, or the role it would eventually play in British politics. If the Government had known that in 1978 the Arabs would be holding a pistol to the heads of the rest of the world, and the British House of Commons would have eleven Scottish Nationalist Members of Parliament, it would surely have reacted in a totally different way.

On May 13th, 1964, the Secretary of State for Power laid before Parliament 'Statutory Instrument – No. 708 – Continental Shelf – Petroteum'. Harvey read this particular document with great interest, thinking that it might well be a means of making an exceptional killing. He was particularly fascinated by Paragraph 4 of the document, which read:

> Persons who are citizens of the United Kingdom and Colonies and are resident in the United Kingdom or who are bodies corporate incorporated in the United Kingdom may apply in accordance with these Regulations for:
>
> (a) production licence; or,
> (b) an exploration licence.

When he had studied the Regulations in their entirety, he had to sit back and think hard. Only a small amount of money was required to secure a production and exploration licence. As Paragraph 6 went on to point out:

> (1) With every application for a production licence there shall be paid a fee of two hundred pounds with an additional fee of five pounds for every block after the first ten in respect whereof that application is made.
>
> (2) With every application for an exploration licence there shall be paid a fee of twenty pounds.

Harvey couldn't believe it. How easy it would be to use such a licence to create an impression of a vast enterprise! For a few hundred dollars he could be alongside such names as Shell, BP, Total, Gulf and Occidental.

Harvey went over the Regulations again and again, hardly believing that the British Government could release such potential for so small an investment. Only the application form, an elaborate and exacting document, now stood in his way. Harvey was not a British subject, none of his companies was British and he realised he would have problems of presentation. He decided that his application must therefore be backed by a British bank and that he would set up a company whose directors would win the confidence of the British Government.

With this in mind, early in 1964, he registered at Companies House in England a firm called Prospecta Oil, using Malcolm, Bottnick and Davis as his solicitors and Barclays Bank, who were already the Lincoln Trust's representative in Europe, as his bankers. Lord Hunnisett became Chairman of the company and several distinguished public figures joined the Board, including two ex-Members of Parliament who had lost their seats when the Labour Party won the 1964 Election. Prospecta Oil issued 2,000,000 10-pence shares at one pound, which were all taken up for Harvey by nominees. He also deposited $500,000 in the Lombard Street branch of Barclays Bank.

Having thus created the front, Harvey then used Lord Hunnisett to apply for the licence from the British Government. The new Labour Government elected in October 1964 was no more aware of the significance of North Sea oil than the earlier Conservative administration. The Government's requirements for a licence were a rent of £12,000 a year for the first six years, 12½ per cent revenue tax, and a further Capital Gains tax on profits; but as Harvey's plan was to reap profits for himself rather than the company that presented no problems.

On May 22nd, 1965, the Minister of Power published in the *London Gazette* the name of Prospecta Oil among the fifty-two companies granted production licences. On August 3rd, 1965, Statutory Instrument No. 1531 allocated the actual areas. Prospecta Oil's was 51° 50′ 00″ N: 2° 30′ 20″ E, a site adjacent to one of BP's holdings.

Then Harvey sat back, waiting for one of the companies which had acquired North Sea sites to strike oil. It was a longish wait but Harvey was in no hurry, and not until June 1970 did BP make a big commercial strike in their Forties Field. BP had already spent over $1 billion in the North Sea and Harvey was determined to be one of the main beneficiaries. He was now on to another winner, and immediately set the second part of his plan in motion.

Early in 1972 he hired an oil rig which, with much flourish and advance publicity, he had towed out to the Prospecta Oil site. Having hired the rig on the basis of being able to renew the contract if he made a successful strike, he engaged the minimum number of workers allowed by the Government Regulations, and then proceeded to drill to 6,000 feet. After this drilling had been completed he released from the company's employment all those involved, but told Reading &

Bates, from whom he had rented the rig, that he would be requiring it again in the near future and therefore would continue to pay the rental.

Harvey then released Prospecta Oil shares on to the market at the rate of a few thousand a day for the next two months, all from his own stock, and whenever the financial journalists of the British Press rang to ask why these shares were steadily rising, the young public relations officer at Prospecta Oil's city office would say, as briefed, that he had no comment to make at present but there would be a press statement in the near future; some newspapers put two and two together and made about fifteen. The shares climbed steadily from 10 pence to nearly £2 under the guidance of Harvey's chief executive in Britain, Bernie Silverman, who, with his long experience of this kind of operation, was only too aware of what his boss was up to. Silverman's main task was to ensure that nobody could show a direct connection between Metcalfe and Prospecta Oil.

In January 1974 the shares stood at £3. It was then that Harvey was ready to move on to the third part of his plan, using Prospecta Oil's enthusiastic new recruit, a young Harvard graduate called David Kesler, as the fall-guy.

2

DAVID PUSHED his glasses back on to the bridge of his nose and read the advertisement in the Business Section of the *Boston Globe* again, to make sure he was not dreaming. It could have been tailor-made for him:

> Oil Company based in Great Britain, carrying out extensive work in the North Sea off Scotland, requires a young executive with experience in the stock market and/or financial marketing. Salary $25,000 a year. Accommodation supplied. Based in London. Apply Box No. 217A.

Knowing it could lead to other openings in an expanding industry, David thought it sounded like a challenge and wondered if they would consider him experienced enough. He recalled what his tutor in European affairs used to say: 'If you must work in Great Britain, better make it the North Sea. With their union problems, there's nothing else great about the country.'

David Kesler was a lean, clean-shaven young American, with a crew cut which would have been better suited to a lieutenant in the Marines, a fresh complexion and an unquenchable earnestness. David wanted to succeed in business with all the fervour of the new Harvard Business School graduate. He had spent six years in all at Harvard, the first four studying mathematics for his Bachelor degree, and the last two across the Charles River at the Business School. Recently graduated and armed with a BA and an MBA, he was looking for a job that would reward him for the exceptional capacity for hard work he knew he possessed. Never a brilliant scholar, he envied those natural academics among his classmates who mastered post-Keynesian economic theories like children learning their multiplication tables. David had worked ferociously for six years, only lifting his nose far enough from the grindstone to fit in a daily workout at the gymnasium and the occasional weekend watching Harvard Jocks defending the honour of the university on the football field or on the basketball court. He would have enjoyed playing himself, but that would have meant less time for study.

He read the advertisement again, and then typed a carefully prepared letter to the box number. A few days passed before a reply came, summoning him for an interview at a local hotel on the following Wednesday at 3.00.

David arrived at 2.45 pm at the Copley Hotel on Huntingdon Avenue, the adrenalin pumping through his body. He repeated the Harvard Business School motto to himself as he was ushered into a small private room: look British, think Yiddish.

Three men, who introduced themselves as Silverman, Cooper and Elliott, interviewed him. Bernie Silverman, a short, grey-haired, check-tied New Yorker with a solid aura of success, was in charge. Cooper and Elliott sat and watched David silently.

Silverman spent a considerable time giving David an enticing description of the company's background and its future aims. Harvey had trained Silverman carefully and he had at his well-manicured fingertips all the glib expertise needed by the right-hand man in a Metcalfe coup.

'So there you have it, Mr Kesler. We're involved in one of the biggest commercial opportunities in the world, drilling for oil in the North Sea off Scotland. Our company, Prospecta Oil, has the backing of a group of banks in America. We have been granted licences from the British Government and we have the financing. But companies are made not by money, Mr Kesler, but by people – it's as simple as that. We're looking for a man who will work night and day to help put Prospecta Oil on the map, and we'll pay the right man a top salary to do just that. If we offer you the position, you'll be working in our London office under the immediate direction of our Managing Director, Mr Elliott.'

'Where are the company headquarters?'

'New York, but we have offices in Montreal, San Francisco, London, Aberdeen, Paris and Brussels.'

'Is the company looking for oil anywhere else?'

'Not at the moment,' answered Silverman. 'We're

sinking millions into the North Sea after BP's successful strike, and the fields around us have so far had a one-in-five success ratio, which is very high in our business.'

'When would you want the successful applicant to start?'

'Some time in January, when he's completed a government training course on management in oil,' said Richard Elliott. The slim, sallow No. 2 sounded as if he was from Georgia. The government course was a typical Harvey Metcalfe touch – maximum credibility for minimum expense.

'And the company apartment,' said David, 'where's that?'

Cooper spoke:

'You'll have one of the company flats in the Barbican, a few hundred yards away from our London City office.'

David had no more questions – Silverman had covered everything and seemed to know exactly what he wanted.

Ten days later David received a telegram inviting him to join Silverman for lunch at the 21 Club in New York. When David arrived at the restaurant, he recognised a host of well-known faces at nearby tables and felt new confidence: his host obviously knew what he was about. Their table was in one of the small alcoves selected by businessmen who prefer their conversations to remain confidential.

Silverman was genial and relaxed. He stretched

the conversation out a little, discussing irrelevancies, but finally, over a brandy, offered David the position in London. David was delighted: $25,000 a year, and the chance to be involved with a company which obviously had such an exciting future. He did not hesitate in agreeing to start his new appointment in London on January 1st.

David Kesler had never been to England before: how green the grass was, how narrow the roads, how closed in by hedges and fences were the houses! It felt like Toy Town after the vast highways and large automobiles of New York. The small flat in the Barbican was clean and impersonal and, as Mr Cooper had said, convenient for the office a few hundred yards away in Threadneedle Street.

Prospecta's offices consisted of seven rooms on one floor of a large Victorian building; Silverman's was the only office with a prestigious air about it. There was a tiny reception area, a telex room, two rooms for secretaries, a larger room for Mr Elliott and another small one for himself. It seemed very poky to David, but as Silverman was quick to point out, office rent in the City of London was $30 a square foot compared with $10 in New York.

Bernie Silverman's secetary, Judith Lampson, ushered David through to the well appointed office of the Chief Executive. Silverman sat in a large black swivel chair behind a massive desk, which made him look like a midget. By his side were positioned four telephones, three white and one red. David was later to learn that the important-looking red telephone was directly connected to a number in the States, but he never actually discovered to whom.

'Good morning, Mr Silverman. Where would you like me to start?'

'Bernie, please call me Bernie. Take a seat. Notice the change in the price of the company's shares in the last few days?'

'Oh, yes,' enthused David. 'Up a half to nearly $6. I suppose it's because of our new bank backing and the other companies' successful strikes?'

'No,' said Silverman in a low tone designed to give the impression that no one else must hear this part of the conversation, 'the truth is that we've made a big strike ourselves, but we haven't yet decided when to announce it. It's all in this geologist's report.' He threw a smart, colourful document over his desk.

David whistled under his breath. 'What are the company's plans at the moment?'

'We'll announce the strike,' said Silverman quietly, picking at his India rubber as he talked, 'in about three weeks' time, when we're certain of the full extent and capacity of the hole. We want to make some plans for coping with the publicity and the sudden inflow of money. The shares will go through the roof, of course.'

'The shares have already climbed steadily. Perhaps some people already know?'

'I guess that's right,' said Silverman. 'The trouble with that black stuff is once it comes out of the ground you can't hide it.' Silverman laughed.

'Is there any harm in getting in on the act?' asked David.

'No, as long as it doesn't harm the company in any way. Just let me know if anyone wants to invest. We don't have the problems of inside information in England – none of the restrictive laws we have in America.'

'How high do you think the shares will go?'

Silverman looked him straight in the eye and then said casually, '$20.'

Back in his own office, David carefully read the geologist's report that Silverman had given him: it certainly looked as if Prospecta Oil had made a successful strike, but the extent of the find was not, as yet, entirely certain. When he had completed the report, he glanced at his watch and cursed. The geologist's file had totally absorbed him. He threw the report into his briefcase and took a taxi to Paddington Station, only just making the 6.15 train. He was due in Oxford for dinner with an old classmate from Harvard.

On the train down to the university city he thought about Stephen Bradley, who had been a friend in his Harvard days and had generously helped David and other students in mathematics classes that year. Stephen, now a visiting Fellow at Magdalen College, was undoubtedly one of the most brilliant scholars of

David's generation. He had won the Kennedy Memorial Scholarship to Harvard and later in 1970 the Wister Prize for Mathematics, the most sought-after award in the mathematical faculty. Although in monetary terms this award was a derisory $80 and a medal, it was the reputation and job offers it brought with it that made the competition so keen. Stephen had won it with consummate ease and nobody was surprised when he was successful in his application for a Fellowship at Oxford. He was now in his third year of research at Magdalen. His papers on Boolean algebra appeared at short intervals in the *Proceedings of the London Mathematical Society*, and it had just been announced that he had been elected to a Chair in Mathematics back at his alma mater, Harvard, to commence in the fall.

The 6.15 train from Paddington arrived in Oxford an hour later and the short taxi ride from the station down New College Lane brought him to Magdalen at 7.30. One of the College porters escorted David to Stephen's rooms, which were spacious, ancient, and comfortably cluttered with books, cushions and prints. How unlike the antiseptic walls of Harvard, thought David. Stephen was there to greet him. He didn't seem to have changed one iota. His suit seemed to hang off his tall, thin, ungainly body; no tailor would ever have employed him as a dummy. His heavy eyebrows protruded over his out-of-date round-rimmed spectacles, which he almost seemed to hide behind in his shyness. He ambled over to David and welcomed him, one minute an old man, the next younger than his thirty years. Stephen poured David a Jack Daniels and they settled down to chat. Although Stephen never looked upon David as a close friend at Harvard, he had enjoyed coaching him and always found him eager to learn; besides, he always welcomed an excuse to entertain Americans at Oxford.

'It's been a memorable three years, David,' said Stephen, pouring him a second drink. 'The only sad event was the death of my father last winter. He took such an interest in my life at Oxford and gave my academic work so much support. He's left me rather well off, actually . . . Bath plugs were obviously more in demand than I realised. You might be kind enough to advise me on how to invest some of the money, because at the moment it's just sitting on deposit in the bank. I never seem to have the time to do anything about it, and when it comes to investments I haven't a clue.'

That started David off about his demanding new job with Prospecta Oil.

'Why don't you invest your money in my company, Stephen. We've had a fantastic strike in the North Sea, and when they announce it the shares are going to go through the roof. The whole operation would only take a month or so and you could make the killing of a lifetime. I only wish I had some of my own money to put into it.'

'Have you had the full details of the strike?'

'No, but I've seen the geologist's report, and that makes pretty good reading. The shares are already going up fast and I'm convinced they'll reach $20. The problem is that time is already running out.'

Stephen glanced at the geologist's report, thinking he would study it carefully later.

'How does one go about an investment of this sort?' he asked.

'Well, you find a respectable stockbroker, buy as many shares as you can afford and then wait for the strike to be announced. I'll keep you informed on how things are going and advise you when I feel is the best time to sell.'

'That would be extremely thoughtful of you, David.'

'It's the least I can do after all the help you gave me with maths at Harvard.'

'Oh, that was nothing. Let's go and have some dinner.'

Stephen led David to the college dining hall, an oblong, oak-panelled room covered in pictures of past Presidents of Magdalen, bishops and academics. The long wooden tables at which the undergraduates were eating filled the body of the hall, but Stephen shuffled up to the High Table and offered David a more comfortable seat. The students were a noisy, enthusiastic bunch – Stephen didn't notice them, but David was enjoying the whole experience.

The seven-course meal was formidable and David wondered how Stephen kept so thin with such daily temptations. When they reached the port, Stephen suggested they return to his rooms rather than join the crusty old dons in the Senior Common Room.

Late into the night, over the rubicund Magdalen port, they talked about North Sea oil and Boolean algebra, each admiring the other for his mastery of his subject. Stephen, like most academics, was fairly credulous outside the bounds of his own discipline. He began to think that an investment in Prospecta Oil would be a very astute move on his part.

In the morning, they strolled down Addison's Walk near Magdalen Bridge, where the grass grows green and lush by the Cherwell. Reluctantly, David caught a taxi at 9.45 leaving Magdalen behind him and passing New College, Trinity, Balliol and finally Worcester, where he saw scrawled across the college wall, '*c'est magnifique mais ce n'est pas la gare*'. He caught the 10.00 am train back to London. He had enjoyed his stay at Oxford and hoped he had been able to help his old Harvard friend, who had done so much for him in the past.

'Good morning, David.'

'Good morning, Bernie. I thought I ought to let you know I spent the evening with a friend at Oxford, and he may invest some money in the company. It might be as much as $250,000.'

'That's fine, David, keep up the good work. You're doing a great job.'

Silverman showed no surprise at David's news, but once back in his own office he picked up the red telephone.

'Harvey?'

'Yes.'

'Kesler seems to have been the right choice. He may have talked a friend of his into investing $250,000 in the company.'

'Good. Now listen carefully. Brief my broker to put 40,000 shares on the market at just over $6 a share. If Kesler's friend does decide to invest in the company, mine will be the only large block of shares immediately available.'

After a further day's consideration, Stephen noticed that the shares of Prospecta Oil moved from £2.75 to £3.05 and decided the time had come to invest in what he was now convinced must be a winner. He trusted David, and had been impressed by the glossy geologist's report. He rang Kitcat & Aitken, a firm of stockbrokers in the City, and instructed them to buy $250,000-worth of shares in Prospecta Oil. Harvey Metcalfe's broker released 40,000 shares when Stephen's request came on to the floor of the stock exchange and the transaction was quickly completed. Stephen's purchase price was £3.10.

After investing his father's inheritance, Stephen spent the next few days happily watching the shares climb to £3.50, even before the expected announcement. Though Stephen didn't realise it, it was his own investment that had caused the shares to rise. He began to wonder what he would spend the profit on even before he had realised it. He decided not to cash in immediately, but hold on; David thought the shares would reach $20, and in any case he had promised to tell him when to sell.

Meanwhile, Harvey Metcalfe began to release a few more shares on to the market, because of the interest created by Stephen's investment. He was beginning to agree with Silverman that David Kesler, young, honest, and with all the enthusiasm of a man in his first appointment, had been an excellent choice. It was not the first time Harvey had used this ploy, keeping himself well away from the action while placing the responsibility on inexperienced, innocent shoulders.

At the same time, Richard Elliott, acting as the company spokesman, leaked stories to the press about large buyers coming into the market, which in itself occasioned a flood of small investors and kept the price steady.

One lesson a man learns in the Harvard Business School is that an executive is only as good as his health. David never felt happy without a regular medical check-up; he rather enjoyed being told he was in good shape, but perhaps should take things a little easier. His secretary, Miss Rentoul, had therefore made an appointment for him with a Harley Street doctor.

Dr Robin Oakley was by anyone's standards a successful man. At thirty-seven he was tall and handsome, with a head of dark hair that looked as if it would never recede. He had a classic strong face and the self-assurance that came from proven success. He still played squash twice a week, which helped him look enviably younger than his contemporaries. Robin had remained fit since his Cambridge days, which he left with a Rugby Blue and an upper-second-class degree. He had gone on to complete his medical training at St Thomas's, where once again his Rugby football rather than his medical skill brought him into prominence with those who decide the future careers of young men. When he qualified, he went to work as an assistant to a highly successful Harley Street practitioner, Dr Eugene Moffat. Dr Moffat was successful not so much in curing the sick as in charming the rich, especially middle-aged women, who came to see him again and again however little seemed to be wrong with them. At fifty guineas a visit that had to be regarded as success.

Moffat had chosen Robin Oakley as his assistant for exactly those qualities which he himself displayed, and which had made him so sought-after. Robin Oakley was unquestionably good-looking, personable, well-educated – and just clever enough. Robin settled very well into Harley Street and the Moffat system, and when the older man died suddenly in his early sixties, he took over his mantle with the ease with which a crown prince would take over a throne. Robin continued to build up the practice, losing none of Moffat's ladies other than by natural causes, and did remarkably well for himself. He had a wife and two sons, a comfortable country house a few miles outside Newbury in Berkshire, and a considerable saving in blue chip securities. He never complained at his good fortune and enjoyed life, at the same time being, he had to confess, a little bored with it all. He was beginning to find that the bland role of sympathetic doctor was almost intolerably cloying. Would the world come to an end if he admitted that he neither knew nor cared just what was causing the minute patches of dermatitis on Lady Fiona Fisher's diamond-studded hands? Would the Heavens descend if he told the dreaded Mrs Page-Stanley that she was a malodorous old woman in need of nothing more medically taxing than a new set of dentures? And would he be struck off if he personally administered to the nubile Miss Lydia de Villiers a good dose of what she so clearly indicated she desired?

David Kesler arrived on time for his appointment. He had been warned by Miss Rentoul that in England doctors and dentists cancel if you are late and still charge you.

He stripped and lay on Robin Oakley's couch. The doctor took his blood pressure, listened to his heart, and made him put out his tongue, an organ that seldom stands up well to public scrutiny. As he tapped and poked his way over David's body, they chatted.

'What brings you to work in London, Mr Kesler?'

'I'm with an oil company in the City. I expect you've heard of us – Prospecta Oil?'

'No,' said Robin. 'Can't say I have. Bend your legs up, please.' He hit David's knee-caps smartly, one after the other, with a patella hammer. The legs jumped wildly.

'Nothing wrong with those reflexes.'

'You will, Dr Oakley, you will. Things are going very well for us. Watch out for our progress in the papers.'

'Why?' said Robin, smiling, 'Struck oil, have you?'

'Yes,' said David quietly, pleased with the impression he was creating, 'as a matter of fact we've done just that.'

Robin prodded David's abdomen for a few seconds. 'Good muscular wall, not fat, no sign of an enlarged liver. Young man, you're in good physical shape.'

Robin left him in the examination room to get dressed and thoughtfully wrote out a brief report on Kesler for his records, while his mind dwelt on deeper things. An oil strike.

Harley Street doctors, although they routinely keep private patients waiting for three-quarters of an hour in a gas-fired waiting-room equipped with one out-of-date copy of *Punch*, never let them feel rushed once they are in the consulting room. Robin had no intention of rushing Mr Kesler.

'There's very little wrong with you, Mr Kesler. Some signs of anaemia, which I suspect are caused by nothing more than overwork and your recent rushing about. I'm going to give you some iron tablets which should quickly take care of that. Take two a day, morning and night.' He scribbled an illegible prescription for the tablets and handed it to David.

'Many thanks. It's kind of you to give me so much of your time.'

'Not at all. How are you finding London?' asked Robin. 'Very different from America, I expect.'

'Sure – the pace is much slower. Once I've mastered how long it takes to get something done here I'll be halfway to victory.'

'Do you have many friends in London?'

'No,' replied David, 'I have one or two buddies at Oxford from my Harvard days, but I haven't yet made contact with many people in London.'

Good, thought Robin, here is a chance for me to find out a little more about the oil game, and spend some time with a man who makes most of his patients look as if they had both feet in the grave. It might even shake me out of my lethargy. He continued, 'Would you care to join me for lunch later in the week? You might like to see one of our antique London clubs.'

'How very kind of you.'

'Excellent. Will Friday suit you?'

'It certainly will.'

'Then let's say one o'clock at the Athenaeum Club in Pall Mall.'

David returned to his City desk, picking up his tablets on the way. He took one immediately. He was beginning to enjoy his stay in London. Silverman seemed pleased with him, Prospecta Oil was doing well and he was already meeting some interesting people. Yes, he felt this was going to be a very happy period in his life.

On Friday at 12.45 pm, David arrived at the Athenaeum, a massive white building on the corner of Pall Mall, overlooked by a statue of the Duke of York. David was amazed by the size of the rooms and his commercial mind could not help wondering what price they would fetch as office space. The place appeared to be full of moving waxworks who, Robin later assured him, were in fact distinguished generals and diplomats.

They lunched in the Coffee Room, dominated by a Rubens of Charles II, and talked about Boston, London, squash, and their shared passion for Katharine Hepburn. Over coffee, David readily told Robin the details of the geologist's findings on the Prospecta Oil site. The shares had now climbed to £3.60 on the London Stock Exchange, and were still going up.

'Sounds like a good investment,' said Robin, 'and as it's your own company, it might be worth the risk.'

'I don't think there's much of a risk,' said David, 'as long as the oil is actually there.'

'Well, I'll certainly consider it most seriously over the weekend.'

They parted on the steps of the Athenaeum, David to a conference on the Energy Crisis organised by the *Financial Times*, Robin to his home in Berkshire. His two young sons were back from prep school for the weekend and he was looking forward to seeing them again. How quickly they had passed from babies to toddlers, to boys; soon they would be young men, he thought. And how reassuring to know their future was secure. Perhaps he should make that future a little more secure by investing in David Kesler's company. He could always put the money back into blue chip shares once the strike had been announced.

Bernie Silverman was also pleased to hear the possibility of a further investment.

'Congratulations, my boy. We're going to need a lot of capital to finance the pipe-laying operations, you know. Pipe-laying can cost $2 million per mile. Still, you're playing your part. I've just had word from head office that we are to give you a $5,000 bonus for your efforts. Keep up the good work.'

David smiled. This was business in the proper Harvard tradition. If you bring home the results, you get the rewards.

'When will the strike be officially announced?' he asked.

'Some time in the next few days.'

David left Silverman's office with a glow of pride.

Silverman immediately contacted Harvey Metcalfe on the red phone, and he set the routine in motion once again. Metcalfe's brokers released on to the market 35,000 shares at £3.73 and approximately 5,000 each day on to the open market, always being able to feel when the market had taken enough and thus keeping the price steady. Once again, the shares climbed when Dr Oakley invested heavily in the market, this time to £3.90, keeping David, Robin and Stephen all happy. They were not to know that Harvey was releasing more shares each day because of the interest they had caused, and that this was now creating a market of its own.

David decided to spend some of his bonus on a painting for his little flat in the Barbican, which he felt was rather grey. About $2,000, he thought, something that was going to appreciate in value. David quite enjoyed art for art's sake, but he liked it even more for business's sake. He spent Friday afternoon tramping around Bond Street, Cork Steet and Bruton Street, the home of the London art galleries. The Wildenstein was too expensive for his pocket and the Marlborough too modern for his taste. The painting he finally picked out was at the Lamanns Gallery in Bond Street.

The gallery, just three doors away from Sotheby's,

consisted of one vast room with a worn grey carpet and red faded wallpaper. As David was later to learn, the more worn the carpet, the more faded the walls, the greater the success and reputation of the gallery. There was a staircase at the far end of the room, against which some unregarded paintings were stacked, backs to the world. David sorted through them on a whim and found, to his delight, something that appealed to him.

It was an oil by Leon Underwood called *Venus in the Park*. The large, rather sombre canvas contained about six men and women sitting on metal chairs at circular tea-tables. Among them, in the foreground, was a comely naked woman with generous breasts and long hair. Nobody was paying her the slightest attention and she sat gazing out of the picture, face inscrutable, a symbol of warmth and love in indifferent surroundings. David found her utterly compelling.

The gallery proprietor, Jean-Pierre Lamanns, advanced on him, adorned in an elegantly tailored suit, as befitted a man who rarely received cheques for less than a thousand pounds. At thirty-five, he could afford the little extravagances of life, and his Gucci shoes, Yves St Laurent tie, Turnbull & Asser shirt and Piaget watch left no one, especially women, in any doubt that he knew what he was about. He was an Englishman's vision of a Frenchman, slim and neat with longish, dark wavy hair and deep brown eyes that hinted at being a little sharp. He was capable of being pernickety and demanding, with a wit that was often as cruel as it was amusing, which may have been one of the reasons why he had not married. There certainly had been no shortage of applicants. Customers, however, saw only his charming side. As David wrote out his cheque, Jean-Pierre rubbed his forefinger backwards and forwards over his fashionable moustache, only too happy to discuss the picture.

'Underwood is one of the greatest sculptors and artists in England today. He even tutored Henry Moore, you know. I believe he is underestimated because of his dislike of journalists and the press, whom he describes as nothing more than drunken scribblers.'

'Hardly the way to endear oneself to the media,' murmured David, as he handed over the cheque for £850, feeling agreeably prosperous. Although it was the most expensive purchase he had ever made, he felt the picture was a good investment and, more important, he liked it.

Jean-Pierre took David downstairs to show him the Impressionist and Modern collection he had built up over many years, continuing to enthuse about Underwood. They celebrated David's first acquisition over a whisky in Jean-Pierre's office.

'What line of business are you in, Mr Kesler?'

'I work with a small oil company called Prospecta Oil, who are exploring prospects in the North Sea.'

'Had any success?' enquired Jean-Pierre, a little too innocently.

'Well, between the two of us, we're rather excited

about the future. It's no secret that the company shares have gone from £2 to nearly £4 in the last few weeks, but no one knows the real reason.'

'Would it be a good investment for a poor little art dealer like myself?' asked Jean-Pierre.

'I'll tell you how good an investment I think it is,' said David. 'I am putting $3,000 in the company on Monday, which is all I have left in the world – now that I've captured Venus, that is. We'll shortly be making a rather important announcement.'

A twinkle came into Jean-Pierre's eye. To one of his Gallic subtlety, a nod was as good as a wink. He did not pursue the line of conversation any further.

'When's the strike going to be announced, Bernie?'

'I'm expecting it early next week. We've had a few problems. Nothing we can't lick, though.'

That gave David some relief, as he had taken up 500 shares himself that morning, investing the remaining $3,000 from his bonus. Like the others, he was hoping for a quick profit.

'Rowe Rudd.'

'Frank Watts, please. Jean-Pierre Lamanns.'

'Good morning, Jean-Pierre. What can we do for you?'

'I want to buy 25,000 Prospecta Oil.'

'Never heard of them. Hold on a minute . . . New

company, very low capital. A bit risky, J.-P. I wouldn't recommend it.'

'It's all right, Frank, I only want them for two or three weeks, then you can sell. I've no intention of holding on to them. When did the account start?'

'Yesterday.'

'Right. Buy this morning and sell them before the end of the account, or earlier. I'm expecting an announcement next week, so once they go over £5 you can get rid of them. No need to be greedy, but buy them in my company name, I don't want the deal traced back to me – it might embarrass the informant.'

'Right, sir. Buy 25,000 Prospecta Oil at market price and sell before the last day of the account, or sooner if instructed.'

'Correct, I'll be in Paris all next week looking at pictures, so don't hesitate to sell once they go over £5.'

'Right, J.-P. Have a good trip.'

The red telephone rang.

'Rowe Rudd are looking for a substantial block of shares. Do you know anything about it?'

'No idea, Harvey. It must be David Kesler again. Do you want me to speak to him?'

'No, say nothing. I've released another 25,000 shares at £3.90. Kesler's only got to do one more big one and I'll be out. Prepare our plan for seven days before the end of this Stock Exchange account.'

'Right, boss. You know quite a few people are also buying in small amounts.'

'Yes, just as before, they all have to tell their friends they're on to a good thing. Say nothing to Kesler.'

'You know, David,' said Richard Elliott, 'you work too hard. Relax. We're going to have enough work on our hands when the announcement's made.'

'I guess so,' said David. 'Work's just a habit with me now.'

'Well, why don't you take tonight off and join me for a spot of something at Annabel's?'

David was flattered by the invitation to London's most exclusive nightclub and accepted enthusiastically.

David's hired Ford Cortina looked somewhat out of place that evening in Berkeley Square among the double-parked Rolls Royces and Mercedes. He made his way down the little iron staircase into the basement, which at one time must have been no more than the servants' quarters for the elegant town house above. Now it was a splendid club, with a restaurant, discothèque and a small elegant bar, the walls covered in old prints and pictures. The main dining-room was dimly lit and crowded with small tables, most of them already occupied. The décor was Regency and extravagant. Mark Birley, the owner, had in the short period of ten years made Annabel's the most sought-after club in London, with a waiting list for membership of well over a thousand. The discothèque was playing in the far corner of a crowded dance floor, on which you couldn't have parked two Cadillacs. Most of the couples were dancing very close to each other – they had little choice. David was somewhat surprised to observe that nearly all of the men on the floor were about twenty years older than the girls they held in their arms. The head waiter, Louis, showed David to Richard Elliott's table, realising it was David's first visit to the club by the way he stared at all the personalities of the day. Oh well, thought David, perhaps one day they'll be staring at me.

After an exceptionally good dinner Richard Elliott and his wife joined the crowd on the dance floor, while David returned to the little bar surrounded by comfortable red settees and struck up a conversation with someone who introduced himself as James Brigsley. Even if he did not treat the whole world as such, Mr Brigsley certainly treated Annabel's as a stage. Tall, blond and aristocratic, his eyes alight with good humour, he seemed at ease with everyone around him. David admired his assured manner, something he had never acquired and feared he never would. His accent, even to David's untutored ears, was resonantly upper-class.

David's new acquaintance talked of his visits to the States, flattering him by remarking how much he had always liked the Americans. After some time, David was able quietly to ask the head waiter who the Englishman was.

'He's Lord Brigsley, the eldest son of the Earl of Louth, sir.'

What do you know, thought David, lords look like anyone else, especially when they've had a few drinks. Lord Brigsley was tapping David's glass.

'Would you care for another?'

'Thank you very much, my lord,' said David.

'Don't bother with all that nonsense. The name's James. What are you doing in London?'

'I work for an oil company. You probably know my Chairman, Lord Hunnisett. I've never met him myself, to tell you the truth.'

'Sweet old buffer,' said James. 'His son and I were at Harrow together. If you're in oil, perhaps you can tell me what to do with my Shell and BP shares.'

'Hold on to them,' said David. 'It's sensible to remain in any commodities, especially oil, as long as the British Government doesn't get greedy and try to take control of the assets themselves.'

Another double whisky arrived. David was beginning to feel just slightly tipsy.

'What about your own company?' enquired James.

'We're rather small,' said David, 'but our shares have gone up more than any other oil company in the last three months. Even so, I suspect they've nowhere near reached their zenith.'

'Why?' demanded James.

David glanced round and lowered his voice to a confidential whisper.

'Well, I expect you realise that if you make an oil strike in a big company it can only put the percentage of your profits up by a tiny amount. But if you make a strike in a small company, naturally that profit will be reflected as a considerably larger percentage of the whole.'

'Are you telling me you've made a strike?'

'Perhaps I shouldn't have said that,' said David. 'I'd be obliged if you'd treat that remark in confidence.'

David could not remember how he arrived home or who put him to bed, and he appeared rather late in the office the next morning.

'I am sorry, Bernie, I overslept after a very good evening with Richard at Annabel's.'

'Doesn't matter a bit. Glad you enjoyed yourself.'

'I hope I wasn't indiscreet, but I told some lord, whose name I can't even remember, that he ought to invest in the company. I may have been a little too enthusiastic.'

'Don't worry, David, we're not going to let anyone down and you need the rest. You've been working your ass off.'

James Brigsley left his London flat in Chelsea and took a taxi to his bank, Williams & Glyn's. James was an extrovert by nature and at Harrow his only real love had been acting; but when he had left school, his father had refused to allow him to go on the stage and insisted that he complete his education at Christ Church, Oxford, where again he took a greater interest in the Dramatic Society than in gaining a degree in his chosen subjects of Politics, Philosophy and Economics. James had never mentioned to anyone since leaving Oxford the class of degree he managed to secure, but for better or worse the fourth-class Honours degree was later abolished. After Oxford he joined the Grenadier Guards, which gave him considerable scope for his histrionic talent. This was indeed to be James's introduction to society life in London, and he succeeded as well as a personable, rich young viscount might be expected to do in the circumstances.

When he had completed his two years in the Guards, the earl gave him a 250-acre farm in Hampshire to occupy his time, but James did not care for the coarser country life. He left the running of the farm to a manager and once again concentrated on his social life in London. He would dearly have liked to go on the stage, but he knew the old man still considered Mrs Worthington's daughter's ambition an improper one for a future peer of the realm. The fifth earl didn't think a great deal of his eldest son one way and another, and James did not find it easy to persuade his father that he was shrewder than he was given credit for. Perhaps the inside information David Kesler had let slip after a few drinks would give him the opportunity to prove his old dad wrong.

In Williams & Glyn's fine old building in Birchin Lane, James was ushered into the manager's office.

'I should like to borrow some money against my farm in Hampshire,' said Lord Brigsley.

Philip Izard, the manager, knew Lord Brigsley well and was also acquainted with his father. Although he had respect for the earl's judgment, he did not have a great deal of time for the young lord. Nevertheless, it was not for him to query a customer's request, especially when the customer's family was one of the longest-standing in the bank's history.

'Yes, my lord, what sum do you have in mind?'

'Well, it seems that farmland in Hampshire is worth about £1,000 an acre and is still climbing. Why don't we say £150,000? I should then like to invest the money in shares.'

'Will you agree to leave the deeds with the bank as security?' enquired Izard.

'Yes, of course. What difference does it make to me where they are?'

'Then I am sure we will find it acceptable to advance you a loan of £150,000 at 2 per cent above base rate.'

James was not at all sure what base rate was, but he knew that Williams & Glyn's were as competitive as everyone else in such matters and that their reputation was beyond dispute.

'Thank you,' said James. 'Please acquire for me 35,000 shares in a company called Prospecta Oil.'

'Have you checked carefully into this company, my lord?' enquired Izard.

'Yes, of course I have,' said Lord Brigsley, very sharply. He was not in awe of the bank-managerial class.

In Boston, Harvey Metcalfe was briefed over the telephone by Silverman of the meeting in Annabel's between David Kesler and a nameless peer who seemed to have more money than sense. Harvey released 40,000 shares on to the market at £4.80. Williams & Glyn's acquired 35,000 of them and, once again, the remainder was taken up by small investors. The shares rose a little. Harvey Metcalfe was now left with only 30,000 shares of his own, and over the next four days he was able to dispose of them all. It had taken him fourteen weeks to off-load his entire stock in Prospecta Oil at a profit of just over $6 million.

On the Friday morning, the shares stood at £4.90 and Kesler had, in all innocence, occasioned four large investments: Harvey Metcalfe studied them in detail before putting through a call to Jörg Birrer.

Stephen Bradley had bought 40,000 shares at $6.10

Dr Robin Oakley had bought 35,000 shares at $7.23

Jean-Pierre Lamanns had bought 25,000 shares at $7.80
James Brigsley had bought 35,000 shares at $8.80
David Kesler himself had bought 500 shares at $7.25.

Among them they had purchased 135,500 shares at a cost of just over $1 million. They had also kept the price rising, giving Harvey the chance to off-load all his own stock on to a natural market.

Harvey Metalfe had done it again. His name was not on the letterhead and now he possessed no shares. Nobody would be able to place any blame on him. He had done nothing illegal; even the geologist's report contained enough ifs and buts to pass in a court of law. As for David Kesler, Harvey could not be blamed for his youthful over-enthusiasm. He had never even met the man. Harvey Metcalfe opened the bottle of Krug Privée Cuvée 1964, imported from Hedges & Butler of London. He sipped it slowly, then lit a Romeo y Julieta Churchill, and settled back for a mild celebration.

David, Stephen, Robin, Jean-Pierre and James celebrated at the weekend as well. Why not? Their shares were at £4.90 and David had assured them all that they would reach £10. On Saturday morning David ordered his first bespoke suit from Aquascutum, Stephen tut-tutted his way through the end-of-vacation examination papers he had set his freshmen students, Robin attended his sons' prep school Sports Day, Jean-Pierre re-framed a Renoir, and James Brigsley went shooting, convinced that at last he had one in the eye for his father.

3

David arrived at the office at 9 am on Monday to find that the front door was locked. He could not understand it. The secretaries were supposed to be in by 8.45.

After waiting around for over an hour, he walked to the nearest telephone box and dialled Bernie Silverman's home number. There was no reply. He then rang Richard Elliott at home: the ringing tone continued. He rang the Aberdeen office with the same result. He decided to return to the office. There must be a simple explanation, he thought. Was he daydreaming? Or was it Sunday? No – the streets were jammed with people and cars.

When he arrived back at the office a young man was nailing up a board. '2,500 sq ft to let. Apply Conrad Ritblat.'

'What do you think you are doing?' David demanded.

'The old tenants have given notice and left. We're looking for new ones. Are you interested in looking over the property?'

'No,' said David, backing away in panic. 'No, thank you.'

He raced down the street, sweat beginning to show on his forehead, praying that the telephone box would still be empty.

He flicked quickly through the L–R directory and looked up Bernie Silverman's secretary, Judith Lampson. This time there was a reply.

'Judith, in God's name, what's going on?' His voice would have left her in no doubt how anxious he was.

'No idea,' replied Judith. 'I was given my notice on Friday night with a month's pay in advance and no explanation.'

David dropped the telephone. The truth was slowly beginning to dawn on him although he still wanted to believe there was some simple explanation. Whom could he turn to? What should he do?

He returned in a daze to his flat in the Barbican. The morning post had arrived in his absence. It included a letter from the landlords of his flat:

Corporation of London,
Barbican Estate Office,
London EC2
01–628–4341

Dear Sir,

We are sorry to learn you will be leaving at the end of the month, and would like to take this opportunity of thanking you for the payment of rent in advance.

We should be pleased if you would kindly deposit the keys at this office at your earliest covenience.

Yours faithfully,

C. J. Caselton,
Estate Manager

David stood frozen in the middle of the room, gazing at his new Underwood with sudden loathing.

Finally, fearfully, he dialled his stockbrokers.

'What price are Prospecta Oil this morning?'

'They've dipped to £3.80,' replied the broker.

'Why have they fallen?'

'I've no idea, but I'll make some enquiries and ring you back.'

'Please put my 500 shares on the market immediately.'

'500 Prospecta Oil at market price. Yes, sir.'

David put the phone down. It rang a few minutes later. It was his broker.

'They've only made £3.50 – exactly what you paid for them.'

'Would you credit the sum to my account at Lloyd's Bank, Moorgate Branch?'

'Of course, sir.'

David did not leave the flat for the rest of the day or night. He lay on his bed chain-smoking, wondering what he ought to do next, sometimes looking out of his little window over a rain-drenched City of banks, insurance companies, stockbrokers and public companies – his own world, but for how much longer? In the morning, as soon as the market opened, he rang his broker again, in the hope that they would have some new information.

'Can you give me any more news on Prospecta Oil?' His voice was tense and weary now.

'The news is bad, sir. There's been a spate of heavy selling and the shares have dropped to £2.80 on the opening of business this morning.'

'Why? What the hell's going on?' His voice rose with every word.

'I've no idea, sir,' replied a calm voice that always made one per cent, win or lose.

David replaced the receiver. All those years at Harvard were about to be blown away in a puff of smoke. An hour passed, but he did not notice it.

He ate lunch in an inconspicuous restaurant and read a disturbing report in the *London Evening Standard* by its City Editor, David Malbert, headlined 'The Mystery of Prospecta Oil'. By the close of the Stock Exchange at 4 pm the shares had fallen to £1.60.

David spent another restless night. He thought with pain and humiliation of how easily two months of good salary, a quick bonus and a good deal of smooth talk had bought his unquestioning belief in an enterprise that should have excited all business suspicion. He felt sick as he recalled his man-to-man tips on Prospecta Oil, whispered confidentially into willing ears.

On Wednesday morning, dreading what he knew he was bound to hear, David once again rang the broker. The shares had collapsed to £1 and there was no longer a market for them. He left the flat and walked over to Lloyd's Bank where he closed his account and drew out the remaining £1,345. The cashier smiled at him as she passed over the notes, thinking what a successful young man he must be.

David picked up the final edition of the *Evening Standard* (the one marked '7RR' in the right-hand corner). Prospecta Oil had dropped again, this time to 25 pence. Numbed, he returned to his flat. The housekeeper was on the stairs.

'The police have been round enquiring after you, young man,' she said haughtily.

David climbed the stairs, trying to look unperturbed.

'Thank you, Mrs Pearson. I guess it's another parking fine I forgot to pay.'

Panic had now taken over completely: David never felt so small, so lonely and so sick in his life. He packed everything he owned into a suitcase, except the painting, which he left hanging on the wall, and booked a one-way ticket to New York.

4

STEPHEN BRADLEY was delivering a lecture on group theory at the Mathematics Institute in Oxford to a class of third-year undergraduates the morning David left. Over breakfast he had read with horror in the *Daily Telegraph* of the collapse of Prospecta Oil. He had immediately rung his broker, who was still trying to find out the full facts for him. He then phoned David Kesler, who seemed to have vanished without trace.

The lecture Stephen was delivering was not going well. He was preoccupied, to say the least. He could only hope that the undergraduates would misconstrue his absentmindedness as brilliance, rather than recognise it for what it was – total despair. He was at least thankful that it was his final lecture of the Hilary term.

Stephen looked at the clock at the back of the lecture theatre every few minutes, until at last it pointed to the hour and he was able to return to his rooms in Magdalen College. He sat in his old leather chair wondering where to start. Why the hell had he put everything into one basket? How could he, normally so logical, so calculating, have been so recklessly stupid and greedy? He had trusted David, and still found it hard to believe that his friend was in any way involved with the collapse. Perhaps he shouldn't have taken for granted that someone he had befriended at Harvard must automatically be right. There had to be a simple explanation. Surely he must be able to get all his money back. The telephone rang. Perhaps it was his broker with more concrete news.

As he picked up the phone, he realised for the first time that the palms of his hands were slippery with sweat.

'Stephen Bradley.'

'Good morning, sir. I am sorry to bother you. My name is Detective Inspector Clifford Smith of the Fraud Squad, Scotland Yard. I was wondering if you would be kind enough to see me this afternoon?'

Stephen hesitated, thinking wildly for a minute that he might have done something criminal by investing in Prospecta Oil.

'Certainly, Inspector,' he replied uncertainly, 'would you like me to travel to London?'

'No, sir,' replied the Inspector, 'we'll come to you. We can be in Oxford by 4 pm, if that's convenient.'

'I'll expect you then. Goodbye, Inspector.'

Stephen replaced the receiver. What could they want? He knew little of English law and hoped he was not going to be involved with the police as well. All this just six months before he was due to return to

Harvard as a professor. Stephen was even beginning to wonder if that would materialise.

The Detective Inspector was about 5 ft 11 in in height, and somewhere between forty-five and fifty. His hair was turning grey at the sides, but brilliantine toned it in with the original black. His shabby suit, Stephen suspected, was more indicative of a policeman's pay than of the Inspector's personal taste. His heavy frame would have fooled most people into thinking he was rather slow. In fact, Stephen was in the presence of one of the few men in England who fully understood the criminal mind. Time and time again he had been the man behind the arrest of international defrauders. He had a tired look that came from years of putting men behind bars for major crimes, only to see them freed again shortly after and living comfortably off the spoils of their shady transactions. In his opinion, crime did pay. The department was so understaffed that some of the smaller fry even got away scot-free; often the office of the Director of Public Prosecutions would decide it would be too expensive to follow the case through to a proper conclusion. On other occasions. the Fraud Squad simply did not have the back-up staff to finish the job properly.

The Detective Inspector was accompanied by Detective Sergeant Ryder, a considerably younger man – 6 ft 1 in, thin in body and face. His large brown eyes had a more innocent look against his sallow skin. He was at least a little better dressed than the Inspector, but then, thought Stephen, he probably wasn't married.

'I'm sorry about this intrusion, sir,' began the Inspector, after he had settled himself comfortably in the large armchair usually occupied by Stephen, 'but I'm making enquiries into a company called Prospecta Oil. Now before you say anything, sir, we realise that you had no personal involvement in the running of this company or indeed its subsequent collapse. But we do need your help, and I would prefer to ask you a series of questions which will bring out the points I need answered, rather than have you just give me a general assessment. I must tell you, sir, you don't have to answer any of my questions if you don't want to.'

Stephen nodded.

'First, sir, what made you invest such a large amount in Prospecta Oil?'

The Inspector had in front of him a sheet of paper with a list of all the investments made in the company over the past four months.

'The advice of a friend,' replied Stephen.

'Mr David Kesler, no doubt?'

'Yes.'

'How do you know Mr Kesler?'

'We were students at Harvard together and when he took up his appointment in England to work for an oil company, I invited him down to Oxford for old times' sake.'

Stephen went on to detail the full background of his association with David, and the reason he had been willing to invest such a large amount. He ended his explanation by asking if the Inspector thought that David was criminally involved in the rise and fall of Prospecta Oil.

'No, sir. My own view is that Kesler, who incidentally has made a run for it and left the country, is no more than the dupe of bigger men. But we would still like to question him, so if he contacts you, please let me know immediately. Now, sir,' the Inspector continued, 'I'm going to read you a list of names and I would be obliged if you could tell me whether you have ever met, spoken to or heard of any of them . . . Harvey Metcalfe?'

'No,' said Stephen.

'Bernie Silverman?'

'I've never met or spoken to him, but David did mention his name in conversation when he dined with me here in college.'

The Detective Sergeant was writing down everything Stephen said, slowly and methodically.

'Richard Elliott?'

'The same applies to him as Silverman.'

'Alvin Cooper?'

'No,' said Stephen.

'Have you had any contact with anyone else who was involved in the company?'

'No.'

For well over an hour the Inspector quizzed

Stephen on minor points, but he was unable to give him very much help, although he had kept a copy of the geologist's report.

'Yes, we are in possession of one of those documents, sir,' said the Inspector, 'but it's cleverly worded. I doubt if we'll be able to rely much on that for evidence.'

Stephen sighed and offered the two men some whisky and poured himself a donnish dry sherry.

'Evidence against whom or for what, Inspector?' he said as he returned to his chair. 'It's clear to me that I've been taken for a sucker. I probably don't need to tell you what a fool I've made of myself. I put my shirt on Prospecta Oil because it sounded like a sure-fire winner, and ended up losing everything I had without having a clue what to do about it. What in heaven's name has been going on in Prospecta Oil?'

'Well, sir,' said the Inspector, 'you'll appreciate there are aspects of the case I'm not at liberty to discuss with you. Indeed, there are some things that aren't very clear to us yet. But the game isn't a new one, and this time it's been played by an old pro, a very cunning old pro. It works something like this: a company is set up or taken over by a bunch of villains who acquire the majority of the shares. They invent a plausible story about a new discovery or super product that will send the shares up, whisper it in a few willing ears, release their own shares on to the market and let them be snapped up by the likes of you, sir, at a higher price. Then they clear off with the profit they have made, after which the shares collapse because the company has no real substance. As often as not, it ends with dealings in the shares being suspended on the stock market, and finally in the compulsory liquidation of the company. That hasn't happened yet in this case, and it may not. The London Stock Exchange is only just recovering from the Caplan fiasco and they don't want another scandal on their hands. I'm sorry to say that we can hardly ever recover the money, even if we produce enough evidence to nail the villains. They have it all stashed away all over the world before you can say Dow-Jones Index.'

Stephen groaned. 'My God, you make it all sound so appallingly simple, Inspector. The geologist's report was a fake, then?'

'Not exactly, sir. Very impressively worded and well presented, but with plenty of ifs and buts; and one thing is for certain; the DPP's office is hardly likely to spend millions finding out if there *is* any oil in that part of the North Sea.'

Stephen buried his head in his hands and mentally cursed the day he met David Kesler.

'Tell me, Inspector, who put Kesler up to this? Who was the real brains behind it all?'

The Inspector realised only too well the terrible agony Stephen was going through. During his career he had faced many men in the same position, and he was grateful for Stephen's co-operation.

'I'll answer any questions I feel cannot harm my

own enquiry,' said the Inspector. 'But it's no secret that the man we'd like to nail is Harvey Metcalfe.'

'Who's Harvey Metcalfe, for God's sake?'

'He's a first-generation American who's had his fingers in more dubious deals in Boston than you've had hot dinners. Made himself a multi-millionaire and a lot of other people bankrupt on the way. His style is so professional and predictable now we can smell the man a mile off. It will not amuse you to learn that he is a great benefactor of Harvard – does it to ease his conscience, no doubt. We've never been able to pin anything on him in the past, and I doubt if we'll be able to this time either. He was never a director of Prospecta Oil, and he only bought and sold shares on the open market. He never, as far as we know, even met David Kesler. He hired Silverman, Cooper and Elliott to do the dirty work, and they found a bright enthusiastic young man all freshly washed behind the ears to sell their story for them. I'm afraid it was a bit unlucky for you, sir, that the young man in question was your friend, David Kesler.'

'Never mind him, poor sod,' said Stephen. 'What about Harvey Metcalfe? Is he going to get away with it again?'

'I fear so,' said the Inspector. 'We have warrants out for the arrest of Silverman, Elliott and Cooper. They all beat it off to South America. After the Ronald Biggs fiasco I doubt if we'll ever get an extradition order to bring them back, even though the American and Canadian police also have warrants out for them. They were fairly cunning too. They closed the London office of Prospecta Oil, surrendered the lease and returned it to Conrad Ritblat, the estate agents, and gave notice to both secretaries with one month's pay in advance. They cleared the bill on the oil rig with Reading & Bates. They paid off their hired hands, Mark Stewart in Aberdeen, and took the Sunday morning flight to Rio de Janeiro, where there was $1 million in a private account waiting for them. Another two or three years, after they've spent all the money, and they'll undoubtedly turn up again with different names and a different company. Harvey Metcalfe rewarded them well and left David Kesler holding the baby.'

'Clever boys,' said Stephen.

'Oh, yes,' said the Inspector, 'it was a neat little operation. Worthy of the talents of Harvey Metcalfe.'

'Are you trying to arrest David Kesler?'

'No, but as I said we would like to question him. He bought and sold 500 shares, but we think that was only because he believed in the oil strike story himself. In fact, if he was wise, he would return to England and help the police with their enquiries, but I fear the poor man has panicked under pressure and made a bolt for it. The American police are keeping an eye out for him.'

'One last question,' said Stephen. 'Are there any other people who made such fools of themselves as I did!'

The Inspector gave this question long consideration. He had not had as much success with the other big investors as he had had with Stephen. They had all been evasive about their involvement with Kesler and Prospecta Oil. Perhaps if he released their names it might bring them out in some way.

'Yes, sir, but . . . you must understand that you never heard about them from me.'

Stephen nodded.

'For your own interest you could find out what you need to know by making some discreet enquiries through the Stock Exchange. There were four main punters, of whom you were one. Between the four of you you lost approximately $1 million. The others were a Harley Street doctor, Robin Oakley, a London art dealer called Jean-Pierre Lamanns, and a farmer, the unluckiest of all, really. As far as I can gather, he mortgaged his farm to put up the money. Titled young gentleman: Viscount Brigsley. Metcalfe's snatched the silver spoon out of his mouth, all right.'

'No other big investors?'

'Two or three banks burnt their fingers badly, but there were no other private investors above £10,000. What you, the banks and the other big investors did was to keep the market buoyant long enough for Metcalfe to off-load his entire holding.'

'I know, and worse, I foolishly advised some of my friends to invest in the company as well.'

'Er . . . there are two or three small investors from Oxford, yes sir,' said the Inspector, looking down at the sheet of paper in front of him, 'but don't worry –

we won't be approaching them. Well, that seems to be all. It only leaves me to thank you for your co-operation and say we may be in touch again some time in the future. In any case, we'll keep you informed of developments, and I hope you'll do the same for us.'

'Of course, Inspector. I do hope you have a safe journey back to town.' The two policemen downed their drinks and left.

Stephen could never recall if it was while sitting in his armchair looking out at the Cloisters, or later in bed that night, that he decided to employ his academic mind to carry out a little research on Harvey Metcalfe and his fellow dupers. His grandfather's advice to him, when as a small child he failed to win their nightly game of chess, floated across his mind: Stevie, don't get cross, get even. He was pleased he had given his final lecture and finished work for the term, and as he fell asleep at 3 am only one name was on his lips: Harvey Metcalfe.

5

Stephen awoke at about 5.30 am. He seemed to have been heavily, dreamlessly asleep, but as soon as he came to, the nightmare started again. He forced himself to use his mind constructively, to put the past firmly behind him and see what could be done about the future. He washed, shaved, dressed and missed college breakfast, occasionally murmuring to himself 'Harvey Metcalfe'. He then pedalled to Oxford station on an ancient bicycle, his preferred mode of transport in a city blocked solid with juggernaut lorries and full of unintelligible one-way systems. He left Ethelred the Unsteady padlocked to the station railings. There were as many bicycles standing in the ranks as there are cars in other railway stations.

He caught the 8.17 train so favoured by those who commute from Oxford to London every day. All the people at breakfast seemed to know each other and Stephen felt like an uninvited guest at someone else's party. The ticket collector bustled through the buffet car and clipped Stephen's first-class ticket. The man opposite Stephen produced a second-class ticket from behind his copy of the *Financial Times*. The collector clipped it grudgingly.

'You'll have to return to a second-class compartment when you've finished your breakfast, sir. The restaurant car is first-class, you know.'

Stephen considered the implication of these remarks as he watched the flat Berkshire countryside jolt past, and his coffee cup lurched unsampled in its saucer before he turned his mind to the morning papers. *The Times* carried no news of Prospecta Oil that morning. It was, he supposed, an insignificant story, even a dull one. Not kidnap, not arson, not even rape; just another shady business enterprise collapsing – nothing there to hold the attention of the front page for more than one day. Not a story he would have given a second thought to himself but for his own involvement, which gave it all the makings of a personal tragedy.

At Paddington he pushed through the ants rushing round the forecourt, glad that he had chosen the closeted life of a university or, more accurately, that it had chosen him. Stephen had never come to terms with London – he found the city large and impersonal, and he always took a taxi everywhere for fear of getting lost on the buses or the underground. Why didn't the English number their streets so Americans would know where they were?

'*The Times* office, Printing House Square.'

The cabby nodded and moved his black Austin deftly down the Bayswater Road, alongside a rain-sodden Hyde Park. The crocuses at Marble Arch looked sullen and battered, splayed wetly on the close grass. Stephen was impressed by London cabs: they never had a scrape or mark on them. He had once been told that cab-drivers are not allowed to pick up fares unless their vehicles are in perfect condition. How different from New York's battered yellow monsters, he thought. The cabby proceeded to swing down Park Lane to Hyde Park Corner, past the House of Commons and along the Embankment. The flags were out in Parliament Square. Stephen frowned. What was the lead story he had read over so inattentively in the train? Ah yes, a meeting of Commonwealth leaders. He supposed he must allow the world to go about its daily business as usual.

Stephen was unsure how to tackle the problem of checking Harvey Metcalfe out. Back at Harvard he would have had no trouble, first making a bee-line for his father's old friend Hank Swaltz, the business correspondent of the *Herald American*. Hank would be sure to have supplied him with the inside dope. The diary correspondent of *The Times*, Richard Compton-Miller, was by no means as appropriate a contact, but he was the only British press man Stephen had ever met. Compton-Miller had been visiting Magdalen the previous spring to write a feature on the time-honoured observance of May Day in Oxford. The choristers on the top of the College tower had sung the Miltonian salute as the sun peeped over the horizon on May 1st:

Hail, bounteous May, that doth inspire
Mirth and youth and warm desire.

On the banks of the river beneath Magdalen bridge where Compton-Miller and Stephen had stood, several couples had clearly been inspired.

Later, Stephen had been more embarrassed than flattered by his appearance in the resulting piece written by Compton-Miller for *The Times* diary: academics are sparing with the word brilliant, but journalists are not. The more self-important of Stephen's Senior Common Room colleagues had not been amused to see him described as the brightest star in a firmament of moderate luminescence.

The taxi pulled into the forecourt and came to a stop by the side of a massive hunk of sculpture by Henry Moore. *The Times* and the *Observer* shared a building with separate entrances, *The Times*'s by far the more prestigious. Stephen asked the sergeant behind the desk for Richard Compton-Miller, and was directed to the fifth floor and then to his little private cubicle at the end of the corridor.

It was only a little after 10 am when Stephen arrived, and the building was practically deserted. Compton-Miller later explained that a national newspaper does not begin to wake up until 11 am and generally indulges itself in a long lunch hour until about 3. Between then and putting the paper to bed, about 8.30 pm for all but the front page, the real work is done. There is usually a complete change of staff, staggered from 5 pm onwards, whose job it is to watch for major news stories breaking during the night. They always have to keep a wary eye on what is happening in America, because if the President makes an important statement in the afternoon in Washington they are already going to press in London. Sometimes the front page can change as often as five times during the night; in the case of the assassination of President Kennedy, news of which first reached England about 7 pm on the evening of November 22nd, 1963, the entire front page had to be scrapped to make way for the tragedy.

'Richard, it was kind of you to come in early for me. I didn't realise that you started work so late. I rather take my daily paper for granted.'

Richard laughed. 'That's OK. We must seem a lazy bunch to you, but this place will be buzzing at midnight when you're tucked up in bed and sound asleep. Now, how can I help you?'

'I'm trying to do a little research on a fellow countryman of mine called Harvey Metcalfe. He's a substantial benefactor of Harvard, and I want to flatter the old boy by knowing all about him when I return.' Stephen didn't care very much for the lie, but these were strange circumstances he now found himself in.

'Hang on here and I'll go and see if we have anything in the cutting room on him.'

Stephen amused himself by reading the headlines pinned up on Compton-Miller's board – obviously stories he had taken some pride in: 'Prime Minister to Conduct Orchestra at Royal Festival Hall', 'Miss World loves Tom Jones', 'Muhammad Ali says "I will be Champion Again"'.

Richard returned fifteen minutes later, carrying a thickish file.

'Have a go at that, Descartes. I'll be back in an hour and we can have some coffee.'

Stephen nodded and smiled gratefully. Descartes never had to solve the problems he was facing.

Everything Harvey Metcalfe wanted the world to know was in that file, and a little bit he didn't want the world to know. Stephen learned of his yearly trips to Europe to visit Wimbledon, of the success of his horses at Ascot and of his pursuit of Impressionist pictures for his private art collection. William Hickey of the *Daily Express* had on one occasion titillated his readers with a plump Harvey clad in Bermuda shorts and a report that he spent two or three weeks a year on his private yacht at Monte Carlo, gambling at the Casino. The Metcalfe fortune was in his opinion too new to be respectable. Stephen wrote down meticulously all the facts he thought relevant and was studying the photographs when Richard returned.

He took Stephen off to have some coffee in the canteen on the same floor. Cigarette smoke swirled mistily round the girl at the cashier's desk at the end of the self-service counter.

'Richard, I don't quite have all the information I might need. Harvard want to touch this man for quite a large sum: I believe they are thinking in terms of about $1 million. Where could I find out some more about him?'

'*New York Times*, I should imagine,' said Compton-Miller. 'Come on, we'll give Terry Robards a visit.'

The *New York Times* office in London was also on the fifth floor of *The Times* building in Printing House Square. Stephen thought of the vast *New York Times* building on 43rd Street and wondered if the London *Times* had a reciprocal arrangement, and was secreted away in their basement. Terry Robards turned out to be a wiry American wearing a perpetual smile. Terry immediately made Stephen feel at ease, a knack he had developed almost subconsciously over the years and which was a great asset when digging a little deeper for stories.

Stephen repeated his piece about Metcalfe. Terry laughed.

'Harvard aren't too fussy where they get their money from, are they? That guy has discovered more legal ways of stealing money than the Internal Revenue Service.'

'You don't say,' said Stephen innocently.

The *New York Times* file on Harvey was voluminous. 'Metcalfe's rise from Messenger Boy to Millionaire', as one headline put it, was documented admirably. Stephen took further careful notes. The details of Sharpley & Son fascinated him, as did the facts on some war-time arms dealing and the background of his wife Arlene and their daughter Rosalie. There was a picture of both of them, but the daughter was only fifteen at the time. There were also long reports of two court cases some twenty-five years past, in which Harvey had been charged with fraud but never convicted, and a more recent case in 1956 concerning a share transfer scheme in Boston. Again Harvey had escaped the law, but the District Attorney had left the jury in little doubt of his views on Mr Metcalfe. The most recent press stories were all in the gossip columns: Metcalfe's paintings, his horses, his orchids, his daughter's success at Vassar and his trips to Europe. Of Prospecta Oil there was not a word. Stephen had to admire Harvey's ability to conceal his more dubious activities from the press.

Terry invited his fellow expatriate to lunch. Newsmen always like new contacts and Stephen looked like a promising one. He asked the cabby to go to Whitfield Street. As they inched their way out of the City into the West End, Stephen hoped that the meal would be worth the journey. He was not disappointed.

Lacy's restaurant was airy and bedecked with clean linen and young daffodils. Terry said it was greatly favoured by press men. Margaret Costa, the cookery writer and her chef husband, Bill Lacy, certainly knew their onions. Over delicious watercress soup followed by *Médaillons de veau à crême au calvados* and a bottle of *Château de Péronne 1972*, Terry became quite expansive on the subject of Harvey Metcalfe. He had interviewed him once at Harvard on the occasion of the opening of Metcalfe Hall, which included a gymnasium and four indoor tennis courts.

'Hoping to get himself an honorary degree one day,' said Terry cynically, 'but not much hope, even if he gives a billion.'

Stephen noted the words thoughtfully.

'I guess you could get some more facts on the guy at the American Embassy,' said Terry. He glanced at his watch. 'No, hell, the library closes at 4 pm. Too late today. Time I got back to the office now America's awake.'

Stephen wondered if press men ate and drank like that every day. They made University dons look positively celibate – and however did they manage to get a paper out?

Stephen fought his way on to the 5.15 train to return with the Oxford-bound commuters, and only when he was alone in his room did he begin to study the results of his day's work. Though exhausted, he forced himself to sit at his desk until he had prepared the first neat draft of a dossier on Harvey Metcalfe.

Next day Stephen again caught the 8.17 to London, this time buying a second-class ticket. The ticket collector repeated his piece about leaving the restaurant car after he had finished his meal.

'Sure,' said Stephen, as he toyed with the remains of his coffee for the rest of the hour-long journey, never shifting from first-class. He was pleased with himself: he had saved £2, and that was exactly how Harvey Metcalfe would have behaved.

At Paddington he followed Terry Robard's advice and took a taxi to the American Embassy, a vast monolithic building which sprawls over 250,000 square feet and is nine storeys high, stretching the entire length of one side of Grosvenor Square. It was not, however, as elegant as the American Ambassador's magnificent official residence, Winfield House in Regents Park, where Stephen had been summoned to drinks last year, which was once the private home of Barbara Hutton before it was sold to the American government in 1946. Certainly, either of them was large enough for seven husbands, thought Stephen.

The entrance to the Embassy Reference Library on the ground floor was firmly shut. Stephen was reduced to a close study of the plaques on the wall in the corridor outside, honouring recent Ambassadors to the Court of St James. Reading backwards from Walter Annenberg, he had reached Joseph Kennedy when the doors of the library swung open, not unlike a bank. The prim girl behind a sign marked 'enquiries' was not immediately forthcoming on the subject of Harvey Metcalfe.

'Why do you require this information?' she asked sharply.

This threw Stephen for a moment, but he quickly recovered. 'I'm returning to Harvard in the fall as a professor and I feel I should know more about his involvement with the university. I'm at present a Visiting Fellow at Magdalen College, Oxford.'

Stephen's answer motivated the girl to immediate action and she produced a file within a few minutes. Though by no means as racy as the *New York Times*'s, it did put figures on the amounts Harvey Metcalfe had donated to charity and gave precise details of his gifts to the Democratic Party. Most people do not divulge the exact amount they give to political parties, but Harvey only knew about lights – no one seemed to have told him about bushels.

Having finished his research at the Embassy, Stephen took a taxi to the Cunard offices in St James's Square and spoke to a booking clerk and from there on to Claridge's in Brook Street, where he spent a few minutes with the duty manager. A telephone call to Monte Carlo completed his research. He travelled back to Oxford on the 5.15.

Stephen returned to his college rooms. He felt he now knew as much about Harvey Metcalfe as anyone, except perhaps for Arlene and Detective Inspector Clifford Smith of the Fraud Squad. Once again he stayed up into the early hours completing his dossier, which now ran to over forty typewritten pages.

When the dossier was finally completed he went to bed and fell into a deep sleep. He rose again early in the morning, strolled across the Cloisters to a Common Room breakfast and helped himself to eggs, bacon, coffee and toast. He then took his dossier to the Bursar's office where he made four copies of every document, ending up with five dossiers in all. He strolled back across Magdalen Bridge, admiring as always the trim flower beds of the University Botanic Gardens beneath him on his right, and called in at Maxwell's Bookshop on the other side of the bridge.

Stephen returned to his rooms with five smart files all of different colours. He then placed the five dossiers in the separate files and put them in a drawer of his desk which he kept locked. Stephen had a tidy and methodical mind, as a mathematician must: a mind the like of which Harvey Metcalfe had never yet come up against.

Stephen then referred to the notes he had written after his interview with Detective Inspector Smith and rang Directory Enquiries, asking for the London addresses and telephone numbers of Dr Robin Oakley, Jean-Pierre Lamanns and Lord Brigsley. Directory Enquiries refused to give him more than two numbers at any one time. Stephen wondered how the GPO expected to make a profit. In the States the Bell Telephone Company would happily have given him a dozen telephone numbers and still ended with the inevitable 'You're welcome'.

The two he managed to wheedle out of his reluctant informant were Dr Robin Oakley at 122 Harley Street, London W1, and Jean-Pierre Lamanns at the Lamanns Gallery, 40 New Bond Street, W1. Stephen then dialled Directory Enquiries a second time and requested the number and address of Lord Brigsley.

'No one under Brigsley in Central London,' said

the operator. 'Maybe he's ex-Directory. That is, if he really is a lord,' she sniffed.

Stephen left his study for the Senior Common Room, where he thumbed through the latest copy of *Who's Who* and found the noble lord:

> BRIGSLEY, Viscount; James Clarence Spencer; b. 11 Oct. 1942; Farmer; *s* and *heir* of 5th Earl of Louth, *cr* 1764, *qv. Educ*: Harrow; Christ Church, Oxford (BA). Pres. Oxford University Dramatic Society. Lt Grenadier Guards 1966–68. *Recreations*: polo (not water), shooting. *Address*: Tathwell Hall, Louth, Lincs. *Clubs*: Garrick, Guards.

Stephen then strolled over to Christ Church and asked the secretary in the Treasurer's office if she had in her records a London address for James Brigsley, matriculated 1963. It was duly supplied as 119 King's Road, London SW3.

Stephen was beginning to warm to the challenge of Harvey Metcalfe. He left Christ Church by Peckwater and the Canterbury Gate, out into the High and back to Magdalen, hands in pockets, composing a brief letter in his mind. Oxford's nocturnal slogan-writers had been at work on a college wall again: 'Deanz meanz feinz' said one neatly painted graffito. Stephen, the reluctant Junior Dean of Magdalen, responsible for undergraduate discipline, smiled. If they were funny enough he would allow them to remain for one term, if not, he would have the porter scrub them out immediately. Back at his desk, he wrote down what had been in his mind.

Magdalen College,
Oxford.
April 15th

Dear Dr Oakley,

I am holding a small dinner party in my rooms next Thursday evening for a few carefully selected people.

I would be delighted if you could spare the time to join me, and I think you would find it worth your while to be present.

Yours sincerely,
Stephen Bradley

PS: I am sorry David Kesler is unable to join us.
Black Tie: 7.30 for 8 pm.

Stephen changed the sheet of letter paper in his old Remington typewriter and addressed similar letters to Jean-Pierre Lamanns and Lord Brigsley. Then he sat thinking for a little while before picking up the internal telephone.

'Harry?' he said to the head porter. 'If anyone rings the lodge to ask if the college has a fellow called Stephen Bradley, I want you to say, "Yes, sir, a new Mathematics Fellow from Harvard, already famous for his dinner parties." Is that clear, Harry?'

'Yes, sir,' said Harry Woodley, the head porter.

He had never understood Americans – Dr Bradley was no exception.

All three men did ring and enquire, as Stephen had anticipated they might. He himself would have done the same in the circumstances. Harry remembered his message and repeated it carefully, although the callers still seemed a little baffled.

'No more than me, or is it I?' muttered the head porter.

Stephen received acceptances from all three during the next week, James Brigsley's arriving last, on the Friday. The crest on his letter paper announced a promising motto: *ex nihilo omnia.*

The butler to the Senior Common Room and the college chef were consulted, and a meal to loosen the tongues of the most taciturn was planned:

Coquilles St Jacques	Pouilly Fuissé 1969
Carrée d'agneau en croûte	Feux St Jean 1970
Casserôle d'artichauts et champignons	
Pommes de terre boulangère	
Griestorte with raspberries	Barsac Ch. d'Yquem 1927
Camembert frappé	Port Taylor 1947
Café	

Everything was ready; all Stephen could do now was wait for the appointed hour.

On the stroke of 7.30 pm on the appointed Thursday Jean-Pierre arrived. Stephen admired the elegant dinner-jacket and large floppy bow-tie that his guest wore, while he fingered his own little clip-on, surprised that Jean-Pierre Lamanns, who had such obvious savoir-faire, could also have fallen victim to Prospecta Oil. Stephen plunged into a monologue on the significance of the isosceles triangle in modern art while Jean-Pierre stroked his moustache. It was not a subject Stephen would normally have chosen to speak on without a break for five minutes, and he was only saved from the inevitability of more direct questions from Jean-Pierre by the arrival of Dr Robin Oakley. Robin had lost a few pounds in the past month, but Stephen could see why his practice in Harley Street was a success. He was, in the words of H. H. Munro, a man whose looks made it possible for women to forgive any other trifling inadequacies. Robin studied his shambling host, wondering whether he dared to ask immediately if they had ever met before. No, he decided; he would leave it a little and hope perhaps some clue as to why he had been invited would materialise during dinner. The David Kesler P.S. worried him.

Stephen introduced him to Jean-Pierre and they chatted while their host checked the dinner-table. Once again the door opened, and with a little more respect than previously displayed, the porter announced, 'Lord Brigsley'. Stephen walked forward to greet him, suddenly unsure whether he should bow or shake hands. Although James did not know anyone present at the strange gathering, he showed no signs of discomfort and entered easily into the conversation. Even Stephen was impressed by James's relaxed line of small talk, although he couldn't help recalling his academic results when at Christ Church and wondered whether the noble lord would in fact be an asset to his plans.

The culinary efforts of the chef worked their intended magic. No guest could possibly have asked his host why the dinner party was taking place while such delicately garlic-flavoured lamb, such tender almond pastry, such excellent wine, were still to hand.

Finally, when the servants had cleared the table and the port was on its way round for the second time, Robin could stand it no longer:

'If it's not a rude question, Dr Bradley.'

'Do call me Stephen.'

'Stephen, may I ask what is the purpose of this select little gathering?'

Six eyes bored into him demanding an answer to the same question.

Stephen rose and surveyed his guests. He walked around the table twice before speaking and then started his discourse by recalling the entire history of the past few weeks. He told them of his meeting in that very room with David Kesler, his investment in Prospecta Oil, followed soon afterwards by the visit of the Fraud Squad, and their disclosure about Harvey Metcalfe. He ended his carefully prepared speech with the words, 'Gentlemen, the truth is that the four of us are in the same bloody mess.' He felt that sounded suitably British.

Jean-Pierre reacted even before Stephen could finish what he was saying.

'Count me out. I couldn't be involved in anything quite so ridiculous as that. I am a humble art dealer, not a speculator.'

Robin Oakley also jumped in before Stephen was given the chance to reply:

'I've never heard anything so preposterous. You must have contacted the wrong man. I'm a Harley Street doctor – I don't know the first thing about oil.'

Stephen could see why the Fraud Squad had had trouble with these two and why they had been so thankful for his co-operation. They all looked at Lord Brigsley, who raised his eyes and said very quietly:

'Absolutely right on every detail, Dr Bradley, and I'm in more of a pickle than you. I borrowed £150,000 to buy the shares against the security of my small farm in Hampshire and I don't think it will be long before the bank insists that I dispose of it. When they do and my dear old pa, the fifth earl, finds out, it's curtains for me unless I become the sixth earl overnight.'

'Thank you,' said Stephen. As he sat down, he turned to Robin and raised his eyebrows interrogatively.

'What the hell,' said Robin. 'You're quite right – I was involved. David Kesler was a patient of mine and in a rash moment I invested £100,000 in Prospecta Oil as a temporary advance against my securities. God only knows what made me do it. As the shares are only worth 50 pence I'm stuck with them. I have a shortfall at my bank which they're beginning to fuss about. I also have a large mortgage on my country home in Berkshire and a heavy rent on my Harley Street consulting-room, a wife with expensive tastes and two boys at the best private prep school in England. I've hardly slept a wink since Detective Inspector Smith visited me two weeks ago.' He looked up. His face had drained of colour and the suave self-confidence of Harley Street had gone. Slowly, they all turned and stared at Jean-Pierre.

'All right, all right,' he admitted, 'me too. I was in Paris when the damned thing folded under me, so now, I'm stuck with the useless shares. £80,000 borrowed against my stock at the gallery. And what's worse, I advised some of my friends to invest in the bloody company too.'

Silence enveloped the room. It was Jean-Pierre who broke it again:

'So what do you suggest, Professor,' he said sarcastically. 'Do we hold an annual dinner to remind us what fools we've been?'

'No, that was not what I had in mind.' Stephen hesitated, realising that what he was about to suggest was bound to cause even more commotion. Once again he rose to his feet, and said quietly and deliberately:

'We have had our money stolen by a very clever man who has proved to be an expert in share fraud. None of us is knowledgeable about stocks and shares, but we are all experts in our own fields. Gentlemen, I therefore suggest we steal it back.

'– NOT A PENNY MORE AND NOT A PENNY LESS.'

A few seconds' silence was followed by uproar.

'Just walk up and take it I suppose?' said Robin.

'Kidnap him,' mused James.

'Why don't we just kill him and claim the life insurance?' said Jean-Pierre.

Several moments passed. Stephen waited until he had complete silence again, and then he handed round the four dossiers marked 'Harvey Metcalfe' with each of their names below. A green dossier for Robin, a blue one for James and a yellow for Jean-Pierre. The red master copy Stephen kept for himself. They were all impressed. While they had been wringing their hands in unproductive dismay, it was obvious that Stephen Bradley had been hard at work.

Stephen continued:

'Please read your dossier carefully. It will brief you on everything that is known about Harvey Metcalfe. Each of you must take the document away and study the information, and then return with a plan of how we are, between us, to extract $1,000,000 from him without his ever being aware of it. All four of us must come up with a separate plan. Each may involve the other three in his own operation. We will return here in fourteen days' time and present our conclusions. Each member of the team will put $10,000 into the kitty as a float and I, as the mathematician, will keep a running account. All expenses incurred in retrieving our money will be added to Mr Metcalfe's bill, starting with your journey down here this evening and the cost of the dinner tonight.'

Jean-Pierre and Robin began to protest again, but it was James who stopped the proceedings, by simply saying:

'I agree. What have we got to lose? On our own we've no chance at all: together we might just tweak the bastard.'

Robin and Jean-Pierre looked at each other, shrugged and nodded.

The four of them settled down to discuss in detail the material Stephen had acquired over the past few days. They left the college a little after midnight, each agreeing to have a plan ready for the Team's consideration in fourteen days' time. None of them was quite sure where it all might end, but each was relieved to know he was no longer on his own.

Stephen decided that the first part of the Team versus Harvey Metcalfe had gone as well as he could have wished. He only hoped his co-conspirators would now get down to work. He sat in his armchair, stared at the ceiling and continued thinking.

6

Robin retrieved his car from the High Street, not for the first time in his life being thankful for the 'Doctor on Call' sticker which always gave him an extra degree of freedom when parking. He headed back towards his home in Berkshire. There was no doubt about it, Stephen Bradley was a very impressive man; Robin was determined to come up with something that would ensure that he played his full part.

Robin let his mind linger a little on the delightful prospect of recovering the money he had so ill-advisedly entrusted to Prospecta Oil and Harvey Metcalfe. It must be worth a try: after all, he might as well be struck off the register of the General Medical Council for attempted robbery as for bankruptcy. He wound the window of the car down a little way to dispel the last delicious effects of the claret and considered Stephen's challenge more carefully.

The journey between Oxford and his country house passed very quickly. His mind was so preoccupied with Harvey Metcalfe that when he arrived home to his wife there were large sections of the journey that he could not even remember. Robin had only one talent to offer, apart from his natural charm, and he hoped that he was right in thinking that particular talent was the strength in his armour and a weakness in Harvey Metcalfe's. He began to repeat aloud something that was written on page 16 of Stephen's dossier, 'One of Harvey Metcalfe's recurrent worries is . . .'

'What was it all about, darling?'

His wife's voice brought Robin quickly to his senses and he locked the briefcase containing the green Metcalfe dossier.

'You still awake, Mary?'

'Well, I'm not talking in my sleep, love.'

Robin had to think quickly. He had not yet steeled himself to tell Mary the details of his foolish investment, but he had let her know about the dinner in Oxford, not at that time realising it was in any way connected with Prospecta Oil.

'It was a tease, sweetheart. An old friend of mine from Cambridge has been appointed a lecturer at Oxford, so he dragged a few of his contemporaries down for dinner and we had a damn good evening. Jim and Fred from my old college were there, but I don't expect you remember them.'

A bit weak, thought Robin, but the best he could do at 1.15 in the morning.

'Sure it wasn't some beautiful girl?' said Mary.

'I'm afraid Jim and Fred could hardly be described as beautiful, even by their loving wives.'

'Do lower your voice, Robin, or you'll wake the children.'

'I'm going down again in two weeks time to . . .'

'Oh, come to bed and tell me about it at breakfast.'

Robin was relieved to be let off the hook until the morning. He clambered in beside his fragrant silk-clad wife and ran his finger hopefully down her vertebral column to her coccyx.

'You'll be lucky, at this time of night,' she mumbled.

They both slept.

Jean-Pierre had booked himself in at the Eastgate Hotel in the High. There was to be an undergraduate exhibition the next day at the Christ Church Art Gallery. Jean-Pierre was always on the look-out for new young talent which he could contract to the Lamanns Gallery. It was the Marlborough Gallery, a few doors away from him in Bond Street, that had taught the London art world the astuteness of buying up young artists and being closely identified with their careers. But for the moment, the artistic future of his gallery was not uppermost in Jean-Pierre's mind: its very survival was threatened, and the quiet American don from Magdalen had offered him the chance of redress. He settled down in his comfortable hotel bedroom, oblivious of the late hour, reading his dossier and working out where he could fit into the jigsaw. He was not going to allow two Englishmen and a Yank to beat him. His father had been relieved at Rochefort by the British in 1918 and released from a prisoner-of-war camp near Frankfurt by the Americans in 1945. Nothing was going to stop him being a full participant in this operation. He read his yellow dossier late into the night: the germ of an idea was beginning to form in his mind.

James made the last train from Oxford and looked for an empty carriage where he could settle down to study the blue dossier. He was a worried man: he was sure the other three would each come up with a brilliant plan and, as had always seemed to be the case in the past, he would be found lacking. He had never been under any real pressure before – everything had come to him so easily; now it had all gone just as easily. A foolproof scheme for relieving Harvey Metcalfe of some of his excess profits was not James's idea of an amusing pastime. Still, the awful vision of his father discovering that the Hampshire farm was mortgaged up to the hilt was always there to keep his mind on the job. But fourteen days was such a short time: where on earth should he begin? He was not a professional man like the other three and had no particular skills to offer. He could only hope that his stage experience might come in useful at some point.

He bumped into the ticket collector, who was not surprised to find James was the holder of a first-class ticket. The quest for an empty compartment was in vain. James concluded that Richard Marsh must be trying to run the railways at a profit. Whatever next?

Still more aggravating, they would probably give him a knighthood for his pains.

The next best thing to an empty compartment, James always thought, was one containing a beautiful girl – and this time his luck was in. One of the compartments was occupied by a truly stunning creature who looked as if she was alone. The only other person in the carriage was a middle-aged lady reading *Vogue*, who showed no signs of knowing her travelling companion. James settled down in the corner with his back to the engine, realising he could not study the Metcalfe dossier on the train. They had all been sworn to total secrecy, and Stephen had cautioned them against reading the dossiers in anyone else's company. James feared that of the four of them he was going to find it the most difficult to remain silent: a companionable man, he found secrets rather burdensome. He touched his overcoat pocket, the one holding the dossier in the envelope supplied by Stephen Bradley. What an efficient man he was, thought James. Alarmingly brainy, too. He was bound to have a dozen clever plans ready for consideration by the next meeting. James frowned and stared out of the window hoping some serendipitous idea would strike him. Instead he found himself studying the reflection of the profile of the girl sitting opposite him . . .

She had a shiny bob of dark brown hair, a slim straight nose and her large hazel eyes seemed fixed on the book she held in her lap. James wondered if she was as entirely oblivious of his presence as she appeared to be, and reluctantly decided that she was. His eyes slipped down to the gentle curve of her breast, softly encased in angora. He craned his neck slightly to see what sort of legs the reflection had. Damn it, she was wearing boots. He looked back at the face again. It was now looking back at him, faintly amused. Embarrassed, he switched his attention to the third occupant of the carriage, the unofficial chaperone in front of whom James lacked the courage even to strike up a conversation with the beautiful profile.

In desperation he stared at the cover of the middle-aged lady's *Vogue*. Another beautiful girl. And then he looked more carefully. It wasn't another girl, it was the same girl. To begin with, he could hardly believe his eyes, but a quick check against the genuine article left him in no doubt. As soon as *Vogue* was relinquished in favour of *Queen*, James leant across and asked the chaperone if he might be allowed to read it.

'Station bookstalls are closing earlier and earlier,' he said idiotically. 'I couldn't get anything to read.'

The chaperone agreed reluctantly.

He turned to the second page. 'Cover: Picture yourself like this . . . black silk georgette dress with chiffon handkerchief points. Ostrich-feather boa. Turban with flower, matching dress. Made to measure by Zandra Rhodes. Anne's hair by Jason at Vidal Sassoon. Photograph by Lichfield. Camera: Hasselblad.'

James was quite unable to picture himself like that. But at least he now knew the girl's name, Anne. The next time the real-life version looked up, he showed her by sign language that he had spotted the photograph. She smiled briefly at James and then returned to her book.

At Reading station the middle-aged lady left, taking *Vogue* with her. Couldn't be better, mused James. Anne looked up, faintly embarrassed, and smiled hopefully at the few passers-by walking up and down the corridor looking for a seat. James glared at them as they passed. No one entered the carriage. James had won the first round. As the train gathered speed he tried his opening gambit, which was quite good by his normal standards:

'What a super picture on the front of *Vogue* taken by my old friend Patrick Lichfield.'

Anne Summerton looked up. She was even more beautiful than the picture James had referred to. Her dark hair, cut softly in the latest Vidal Sassoon style, her big hazel eyes and faultless skin gave her a gentle look that James found irresistible. She had that slim, graceful body that all leading models need to earn their living, but Anne also had a presence that most of them would never have. James was quite stunned and wished she would say something.

Anne was used to men trying to pick her up but she was rather taken aback by the remarks about Lord Lichfield. If he was a friend, it would be offhand not to be at least polite. On a second glance she found James's diffidence rather charming. He had used the self-deprecating approach many times with great success, but this time it was perfectly genuine. He tried again.

'It must be a hell of a job being a model.'

What a bloody silly line, he thought. Why couldn't he just say to her, I think you're absolutely fantastic? Can we talk a little and if I still think you're fantastic perhaps we can take it from there? But it never worked that way. He knew he would have to go through the usual routine.

'It's bearable if the contracts are good,' she replied, 'but today's been particularly tiring.' Her voice was gentle, and the faint transatlantic accent appealed to James. 'I've been smiling my head off all day, modelling an advertisement for Close-Up toothpaste: the photographer never seemed to be satisfied. The only good thing about it was that it ended a day earlier than expected. How do you know Patrick?'

'We were fags together at Harrow in our first year. He was rather better than me at getting out of work.'

Anne laughed – a gentle, warm laugh. It was obvious he knew Lord Lichfield.

'Do you see much of him now?'

'Occasionally at dinner parties, but not regularly. Does he photograph you a lot?'

'No,' said Anne, 'the cover picture for *Vogue* was the only time.'

As they chatted on, the thirty-five-minute journey between Reading and London seemed to pass in a flash. Walking down the platform of Paddington Station with Anne, James ventured:

'Can I give you a lift home? My car is parked round the corner in Craven Street.'

Anne accepted, relieved not to have to search for a taxi at that late hour.

James drove her home in his Alfa Romeo. He had already decided that he could not hold on to that particular luxury for much longer with petrol going up and cash flow going down. He chattered merrily all the way to her destination, which turned out to be a block of flats in Cheyne Row overlooking the Thames; much to Anne's surprise he just dropped her off at the front door and said goodnight. He did not even ask for her telephone number and he only knew her Christian name. In fact, she did not have any idea what his name was. Pity, she thought as she closed the front door; he had been a rather pleasant change from the men who worked on the fringe of the advertising media, who imagined they had an automatic right to a girl's compliance just because she posed in a bra.

James knew exactly what he was doing. He had always found a girl was more flattered if he called her when she least expected it. His tactics were to leave the impression that she had seen the last of him, especially when the first meeting had gone well. He returned to his home in the King's Road and considered the situation. Unlike Stephen, Robin and

Jean-Pierre, with thirteen days to go, he still had no ideas for defeating Harvey Metcalfe. But he was hatching plans for Anne.

On waking in the morning, Stephen began to do a little more research. He started with a close study of the way the university was administered. He visited the Vice-Chancellor's office in the Clarendon Building, where he spent some time asking strange questions of his personal secretary, Miss Smallwood. She was most intrigued. He then left for the office of the University Registrar, where he was equally inquisitive. He ended the day by visiting the Bodleian Library, and copying out some of the University Statutes. Among other outings during the next fourteen days was a trip to the Oxford tailors, Shepherd and Woodward, and a full day at the Sheldonian Theatre to watch the brief ceremony as a batch of students took their Bachelor of Arts degrees. Stephen also studied the layout of the Randolph, the largest hotel in Oxford. This he took some considerable time over, so much so that the manager became inquisitive and Stephen had to leave before he became suspicious. His final trip was a return journey to the Clarendon to meet the Secretary of the University Chest, and to be taken on a guided tour of the building by the porter. Stephen warned him that he anticipated showing an American around the building on the day of Encaenia, but remained vague.

'Well, that won't be easy . . .' began the porter. Stephen carefully and deliberately folded a pound note and passed it to the porter '. . . though I'm sure we'll be able to work something out, sir.'

In between his trips all over the university city, Stephen did a lot of thinking in the big leather chair and a lot more writing at his desk. By the fourteenth day his plan was perfected and ready for presentation to the other three. He had put the show on the road, as Harvey Metcalfe might have said, and he intended to see it had a long run.

Robin rose early on the morning after the Oxford dinner, and avoided awkward questions from his wife at breakfast about his experience the night before. He travelled up to London as soon as he could get away, and on arrival in Harley Street was greeted by his efficient secretary-cum-receptionist, Miss Meikle.

Elspeth Meikle was a dedicated, dour Scot who looked upon her work as nothing less than a vocation. Her devotion to Robin, not that she ever called him that even in her own mind, was obvious for all to see.

'I want as few appointments as possible over the next fourteen days, Miss Meikle.'

'I understand, Dr Oakley,' she said.

'I have some research to carry out and I don't want to be interrupted when I'm alone in my study.'

Miss Meikle was somewhat surprised. She had always thought of Dr Oakley as a good physician, but had never known him in the past to over-indulge in research work. She padded off noiselessly in her white-shod feet to admit the first of a bunch of admirably healthy ladies to Dr Oakley's clinic.

Robin disposed of his patients with less than dignified speed. He went without lunch and began the afternoon by making several telephone calls to the Boston Infirmary and several to a leading gastro-enterologist for whom he had been a houseman at Cambridge. Then he pressed the buzzer to summon Miss Meikle.

'Could you pop round to H. K. Lewis for me, Miss Meikle, and put two books on my account. I want the latest edition of Polson and Tattersall's *Clinical Toxicology* and Harding Rain's book on the bladder and abdomen.'

'Yes, sir,' she said, quite unperturbed at the thought of interrupting her lunchtime sandwich to fetch them.

They were on his desk before he had completed his calls, and he immediately started reading long sections of them carefully. The following day he cancelled his morning clinic and went to St Thomas's Hospital to watch two of his old colleagues at work. His confidence in the plan he had formulated was growing. He returned to Harley Street and wrote some notes on the techniques he had observed that morning, much as he had done in his student days. He paused to remember the words Stephen had used:

'Think as Harvey Metcalfe would. Think for the

first time in your life, not as a cautious professional man, but as a risk-taker, as an entrepreneur.'

Robin was tuning in to Harvey Metcalfe's wavelength, and when the time came he would be ready for the American, the Frenchman and the lord. But would they be willing to fall in with his plan? He looked forward to their meeting.

Jean-Pierre returned from Oxford the next day. None of the youthful artists had greatly impressed him, though he had felt that Brian Davis's still life showed considerable promise and had made a mental note to keep an eye on his future work. When he arrived back in London he started, like Robin and Stephen, on his research. A tentative idea that had come to him in the Eastgate Hotel was beginning to germinate. Through his numerous contacts in the art world he checked all the buying and selling of major Impressionist paintings over the previous twenty years and made a list of the pictures which were currently thought to be on the market. He then contacted the person who held it in his power to set his plan in motion. Fortunately the man whose help he most needed, David Stein, was in England and free to visit him: but would he fall in with the plan?

Stein arrived late the following afternoon and spent two hours with Jean-Pierre privately in his little room in the basement of the Lamanns Gallery. When he left Jean-Pierre was smiling to himself. A final afternoon spent at the German Embassy in Belgrave Square, followed by a call to Dr Wormit of the Preussischer Kulturbesitz in Berlin and a further one to Mme Tellegen at the Rijksbureau in The Hague, gave him all the information he required. Even Metcalfe would have praised him for the final touch. There would be no relieving the French this time. The American and the Englishman had better be up to scratch when he presented his plan.

On waking in the morning the last thing James had on his mind was an idea for outwitting Harvey Metcalfe. His thoughts were fully occupied with more important things. He telephoned Patrick Lichfield at home.

'Patrick?'

'Yes,' mumbled a voice.

'James Brigsley.'

'Oh, hello James. Haven't seen you for some time. What are you doing waking a fellow up at this filthy hour?'

'It's 10 am Patrick.'

'Is it? It was the Berkeley Square Ball last night and I didn't get to bed until four. What can I do for you?'

'You took a picture for *Vogue* of a girl whose first name was Anne.'

'Summerton,' said Patrick without hesitation. 'Got her from the Stacpoole Agency.'

'What's she like?'

'No idea,' said Patrick. 'I thought she was awfully nice. She just thought I wasn't her type.'

'Obviously a woman of taste, Patrick. Now go back to sleep.' James put the phone down.

Anne Summerton was not listed in the telephone directory – so that ploy had failed. James remained in bed, scratching the stubble on his chin, when a triumphant look came into his eye. A quick flip through the S–Z directory revealed the number he required. He dialled it.

'The Stacpoole Agency.'

'Can I speak to the manager?'

'Who's calling?'

'Lord Brigsley.'

'I'll put you through, my lord.'

James heard the phone click and the voice of the manager.

'Good morning, my lord. Michael Stacpoole speaking. Can I help you?'

'I hope so, Mr Stacpoole. I have been let down at the last moment and I'm looking for a model for the opening of an antique shop and I'll need a classy sort of bird. You know the kind of girl.'

James then described Anne as if he had never met her.

'We have two models on our books who I think would suit you, my lord,' offered Stacpoole. 'Pauline Stone and Anne Summerton. Unfortunately, Pauline is in Birmingham today for the launching of the new

Allegro car and Anne is completing a toothpaste session in Oxford.'

'I need a girl today,' James said. How he would have liked to have informed Stacpoole that Anne was back in town. 'If you find either of them are free for any reason, perhaps you would ring me at 735–7227.'

James rang off, a little disappointed. At least, he thought, if nothing comes of it today he could start planning his part in the Team versus Harvey Metcalfe. He was just resigning himself to that when the phone rang. A shrill, high-pitched voice announced:

'This is the Stacpoole Agency. Mr Stacpoole would like to speak to Lord Brigsley.'

'Speaking,' said James.

'I'll put you through, my lord.'

'Lord Brigsley?'

'Yes.'

'Stacpoole here, my lord. It seems Anne Summerton is free today. When would you like her to come to your shop?'

'Oh,' said James, taken aback for a second. 'The shop is in Berkeley Street, next to the Empress Restaurant. It's called Albemarle Antiques. Perhaps we could meet outside at 12.45?'

'I'm sure that will be acceptable, my lord. If I don't ring you back in the next ten minutes, you can assume the meeting is on. Perhaps you'd be kind enough to let us know if she's suitable. We normally prefer you to come to the office, but I'm sure we can make an exception in your case.'

'Thank you,' said James and put the phone down, pleased with himself.

James stood on the west side of Berkeley Street in the doorway of the Mayfair Hotel so that he could catch Anne arriving. When it came to work, Anne was always on time, and at 12.40 pm she appeared from the Piccadilly end of the street. Her skirt was of the latest elegant length, but this time James could see that her legs were as slim and shapely as the rest of her. She stopped outside the Empress Restaurant and looked in bewilderment at the Brazilian Trade Centre on her right and the Rolls Royce showrooms of H. R. Owen on her left.

James strode across the road, a large grin on his face.

'Good morning,' he said casually.

'Oh hello,' said Anne, 'what a coincidence.'

'What are you doing here all alone and looking lost?' said James.

'I'm trying to find a shop called Albemarle Antiques. You don't know it by any chance? I must have the wrong street. As you go in for knowing lords, you might know the owner, Lord Brigsley?'

James smiled:

'I am Lord Brigsley.'

Anne looked surprised and then burst out laughing. She realised what James had done and was flattered by the compliment.

They lunched together at the Empress, James's favourite eating place in town. He explained to Anne why it had been Lord Clarendon's favourite restaurant as well – 'Ah,' he had once declared, 'the millionaires are just a little fatter, and the mistresses are just a little thinner, than in any other restaurant in town.'

The meal was a triumph and James had to admit that Anne was the best thing that had happened to him for a long time. After lunch she asked where the agency should send their account.

'With what I have in mind for the future,' replied James, 'they'd better be prepared for a large bad debt.'

7

Stephen wrung James warmly by the hand the way the Americans will and presented him with a large whisky on the rocks. Impressive memory, thought James, as he took a gulp to give himself a little Dutch courage, and then joined Robin and Jean-Pierre. By unspoken mutual consent, the name of Harvey Metcalfe was not mentioned. They chattered inconsequentially of nothing in particular, each clutching his own dossier, until Stephen summoned them to the table. Stephen had not, on this occasion, exercised the talents of the college chef and the butler to the Senior Common Room. Instead, sandwiches, beer and coffee were stacked neatly on the table, and the college servants were not in evidence.

'This is a working supper,' said Stephen firmly, 'and as Harvey Metcalfe will eventually be footing the bill, I've cut down considerably on the hospitality. We don't want to make our task unnecessarily harder by eating our way through hundreds of dollars per meeting.'

The other three sat down quietly as Stephen took out some closely-typed sheets of paper.

'I'll begin,' he said, 'with a general comment. I've been doing some further research into Harvey Metcalfe's movements over the next few months. He seems to spend every summer doing the same round of social and sporting events. Most of the details are already well documented in your files. My latest findings are summarised on this separate sheet which should be added as page 38A of your dossiers. It reads:

> Harvey Metcalfe will arrive in England on the morning of June 21st on board the QE2, docking at Southampton. He has already reserved the Trafalgar Suite for his crossing and booked a Rolls Royce from Guy Salmon to take him to Claridge's. He will stay there for two weeks in the Royal Suite and he has his own debenture tickets for every day of the Wimbledon Championships. When they are over he flies to Monte Carlo to stay on his yacht *Messenger Boy* for another two weeks. He then returns to London and Claridge's to see his filly, Rosalie, run in the King George VI and Queen Elizabeth Stakes. He has a private box at Ascot for all five days of Ascot Week. He returns to America on a Pan American jumbo jet from London Heathrow on July 29th, flight No. 009 at 11.15 to Logan International Airport, Boston.'

The others attached page 38A to their dossiers, aware once again how much detailed research Stephen had undertaken. James was beginning to feel ill, and it certainly was not the excellent salmon sandwiches that were causing his discomfort.

'The next decision to be taken,' said Stephen, 'is to allocate the times during Metcalfe's trip to Europe when each plan will be put into operation. Robin, which section would you prefer?'

'Monte Carlo,' said Robin without hesitation. 'I need to catch the bastard off his home ground.'

'Anyone else want Monte Carlo?'

Nobody spoke.

'Which would you prefer, Jean-Pierre?'

'I'd like Wimbledon fortnight.'

'Any other takers?'

Again, nobody spoke. Stephen continued:

'I'm keen to have the Ascot slot myself and the short time before he returns to America. What about you, James?'

'It won't make any difference what period I have,' said James rather sheepishly.

'Right,' said Stephen.

Everybody, except James, seemed to be warming to the exercise.

'Now expenses. Have all of you brought your cheques for $10,000? I think it's wise to think in dollars as that was the currency Harvey Metcalfe worked in.'

Each member of the Team passed over a cheque to Stephen. At least, thought James, this is something I can do as well as the others.

'Expenses to date?'

Each passed a chit to Stephen again and he began to work out figures on his stylish little HP 65 calculator, the digits glowing red in the dimly-lit room.

'The shares cost us $1 million. Expenses to date $142, so Mr Metcalfe is in debt to us to the tune of $1,000,142. Not a penny more and not a penny less,' he repeated. 'Now to our individual plans. We will take them in the order of execution.' Stephen was pleased with that word. 'Jean-Pierre, Robin, myself and finally James. The floor is yours, Jean-Pierre.'

Jean-Pierre opened a large envelope and took out four sets of documents. He was determined to show that he had the measure of Stephen as well as of Harvey Metcalfe. He handed round photographs and road maps of the West End and Mayfair. Each street was marked with a number, indicating how many minutes it took to walk. Jean-Pierre explained his plan in great detail, starting with the crucial meeting he had had with David Stein, and ending with the roles the others would have to carry out.

'All of you will be needed on the day. Robin will be the journalist, James the representative from Sotheby's, and Stephen, you will act as the purchaser. You must practise speaking English with a German accent. I shall also require two tickets for the whole of Wimbledon fortnight on the Centre Court opposite Harvey Metcalfe's debenture box.'

Jean-Pierre consulted his notes.

'That is to say, opposite box No. 17. Can you arrange that, James?'

'No problem. I'll have a word with Mike Gibson, the Club referee, in the morning.'

'Good. Finally, then, you must all learn to operate

these little boxes of tricks. They are called Pye Pocketfones and don't forget that the use and ownership of them are illegal.'

Jean-Pierre produced four miniature sets and handed three to Stephen.

'Any questions?'

There was a general murmur of approval. There were going to be no loose ends in Jean-Pierre's plan.

'My congratulations,' said Stephen. 'That should get us off to a good start. Now, how about you, Robin?'

Robin relayed the story of his fourteen days. He reported on his meeting with the specialist, and explained the toxic effects of anticholinesterase drugs.

'This one will be hard to pull off; we'll have to be patient and wait for the right opportunity. But, we must stay prepared every moment Metcalfe is in Monte Carlo.'

'Where will we be staying in Monte Carlo?' asked James. 'I usually go to the Metropole. Better not make it there.'

'No, it's all right, James, I have provisional reservations at the Hôtel de Paris from June 29th to July 4th. However, before that you are all to attend several working sessions at St Thomas's Hospital.'

Diaries were consulted, and a series of meetings agreed upon.

'Here is a copy of Houston's *Short Textbook of Medicine* for each of you. You must all read the chapter on severe cuts and bruises. I don't want any of you to stick out like sore thumbs when we're all dressed in white. You, Stephen, will come to Harley Street the week after next for an intensive medical course, as you must be totally convincing as a doctor.'

Robin had chosen Stephen because he felt that with his academic mind he would pick up the most in the short time available.

'Jean-Pierre, you must attend a gaming club every evening for the next month and learn exactly how baccarat and blackjack are played, and how to continue playing for several hours at a time without losing money. It'll help if you get hold of Peter Arnold's *The Encyclopedia of Gambling* from Hatchards. James, you will learn to drive a small van through the rush hour traffic, and you are also to report to Harley Street next week so that we can try a dry run together.'

All eyes were wide open. If they pulled that one off they could do anything. Robin could see the anxiety in their faces.

'Don't worry,' he said, 'my profession has been carried on by witch-doctors for a thousand years. People never argue when they're confronted with a trained man, and you, Stephen, are going to be a trained man.'

Stephen nodded. Academics could be equally naïve. Hadn't that been exactly what had happened to all of them with Prospecta Oil?

'Remember,' said Robin, 'Stephen's comment at the bottom of page 33 of the dossier . . . "At all times we must think like Harvey Metcalfe".'

Robin gave a few more details of how certain rocedures were to be carried out. He then answered demanding questions for twenty-eight minutes. Finally, Jean-Pierre softened:

'I thought none of you would beat me, but Robin's plan is brilliant. If we get the timing right we'll only need an ounce of luck.'

James was beginning to feel distinctly uneasy as his time drew nearer. He rather wished he had never accepted the invitation to dinner in the first place and regretted being the one to urge the others to take up Stephen's challenge. At least the duties he had been given in the first two operations were well within his scope.

'Well, gentlemen,' said Stephen, 'you've both risen admirably to the occasion, but my proposals will make more demands on you.'

Stephen began to reveal the fruits of his research during the past two weeks and the substance of his plan. They all felt rather like students in the presence of a professor. Stephen's lecturing tone was not intentional; it was a manner he had developed, and like so many academics, he was unable to switch it off in private company. He produced a calendar for Trinity Term and outlined how the university weeks worked, the role of its Chancellor, Vice-Chancellor, the Registrar and the Secretary of the University Chest. Like Jean-Pierre, he supplied maps to each member of the Team, this time of Oxford. He had carefully marked a route from the Sheldonian Theatre to Lincoln

College, and from Lincoln to the Randolph Hotel, and had drawn up a contingency plan if Harvey Metcalfe insisted on using his car, despite the one-way system.

'Robin, you must study what the Vice-Chancellor does at Encaenia. It won't be like Cambridge; the two universities do everything similarly but not identically. You must know the route he's likely to take on that day and his habits backwards. I've arranged for a room at Lincoln to be at your disposal on the final day. Jean-Pierre, you will study and master the duties of the Registrar at Oxford and know the alternative route marked on your map so that you never come face to face with Robin. James, you must know how the Secretary of the University Chest goes about his work – the location of his office, which banks he deals with and how the cheques are cashed. You must also know the routes he's likely to take on the day of Encaenia as if they were part of your father's estate. I have the easiest role on the day, because I will be myself in everything but name. You must all learn how to address each other correctly and we'll have a dress rehearsal in the ninth week of term, on a Tuesday when the university is fairly quiet. Any questions?'

Silence reigned, but it was a silence of respect. All could see that Stephen's operation would demand split-second timing and that they would have to run through it several times to cover all contingencies. But if they were convincing they could hardly fail.

'Now, the Ascot part of my plan is simple. I will

only want Jean-Pierre and James inside the Members' Enclosure. I shall need two Enclosure tickets which I'm hoping you can acquire, James.'

'You mean badges, Stephen,' corrected James.

'Oh, do I?' said Stephen. 'I also require someone in London to send the necessary telegram. That'll have to be you, Robin.'

'Agreed,' said Robin.

For nearly an hour the others asked several questions of detail in order to be as familiar with the plan as Stephen was.

James asked no questions and his mind began to drift, hoping the earth would swallow him up. He even began to wish that he had never met Anne, although she was hardly to blame. In fact, he could not wait to see her again. What was he going to say when they . . .

'James, wake up,' said Stephen sharply. 'We're all waiting.'

Six eyes were now fixed on him. They had produced the ace of hearts, diamonds and spades. But had he the ace of trumps? James was flustered and poured himself another drink.

'You bloody upper-class twit,' said Jean-Pierre, 'you haven't got an idea, have you?'

'Well, actually, I've given the problem a lot of thought, but nothing seemed to come.'

'Useless – worse than useless,' said Robin.

James was stammering helplessly. Stephen cut him short.

'Now listen, James, and listen carefully. We meet here again in twenty-one days' time. By then we must know each other's plans backwards. One error could blow the whole thing. Do you understand?'

James nodded – he was determined not to let them down in that.

'And what's more,' said Stephen firmly, 'you must have your own plan ready for scrutiny. Is that also clear?'

'Yes,' mumbled James unhappily.

'Any other questions?' said Stephen.

There were none.

'Right. We go through the three individual operations again in full.'

Stephen ignored the muttered protests.

'Remember, we're up against a man who isn't used to being beaten. We won't get a second chance.'

For an hour and a half they went through the details of each operation in the order of action. First, Jean-Pierre during Wimbledon fortnight: second, Robin in Monte Carlo: third, Stephen during and after Ascot.

It was late and they were all weary when they finally rose from the table. They departed sleepily, each with several tasks to carry out before their next meeting. Each went his separate way, but all were due to meet again the following Friday in the Jericho Theatre of St Thomas's Hospital.

8

The next twenty days turned out to be an exacting time for all four of them. Each had to master the other plans as well as organising his own. Friday brought them all together for the first of many sessions at St Thomas's Hospital, which would have been entirely successful if James had managed to stay on his feet. It was not the sight of blood that daunted him – the sight of the knife was enough. The only virtue from James's standpoint was that he once again avoided having to explain why he had not come up with any ideas of his own.

The next week was almost full time, with Stephen in Harley Street taking a potted course in one particular field of medicine at a fairly high level.

James spent several hours driving an old van through the heavy traffic from St Thomas's to Harley Street, preparing for his final test in Monte Carlo, which he felt could only be considerably easier. He also returned to Oxford for a week, learning how the Secretary of the University Chest's office operated, and also studying the movements of the Secretary himself, Mr Caston.

Jean-Pierre, at a cost to Mr Metcalfe of $25 and a 48-hour wait, became an overseas member of The Claremont, London's most distinguished gaming club, and passed his evenings watching the wealthy and lazy play baccarat and blackjack, their stakes often reaching $1,000. After three weeks of watching he ventured to join the Golden Nugget casino in Soho, where the stakes rarely exceeded £5. By the end of the month he had played for 56 hours, but so conservatively that he was only showing a small loss.

James's overriding worry was still his personal contribution. The more he grappled with the problem, the less he came to grips with it. He turned it over and over in his mind, even when he was travelling through London at high speed. One night after returning the van to Carnie's in Lots Road, Chelsea, he drove his Alfa Romeo over to Anne's flat by the river, wondering if he dared confide in her.

Anne was preparing a special meal for James. She was aware that he not only appreciated good food, but had taken it for granted all his life. The home-made gazpacho was smelling good and the *Coq au vin* was all but ready. Lately she had found herself avoiding modelling assignments out of London as she did not care to be away from James for any length of time. She was also conscious that he was the first man for some time that she would have been willing to go to bed with – and to date he had made no efforts to leave the dining-room.

James arrived carrying a bottle of Beaune Montée

Rouge 1971 – even his wine cellar was fast diminishing. He only hoped it would last long enough for the plans to come to fruition. Not that he felt an automatic right to a part of the bounty while he failed to contribute his own plan.

Anne looked stunning. She was wearing a long black dress of some soft material that tantalised James with the reticence with which it outlined her shape. She wore no makeup or jewellery, and her heavy hair gleamed in the candlelight. The meal was a triumph for Anne, and James started wanting her badly. She seemed nervous, spilling a little ground coffee as she filtered two strong tiny cups. What was in her mind? He did not want to blunder with unwanted attentions. James had had much more practice at being loved than at being in love. He was used to adulation, to ending up in bed with girls who made him shudder in the cold clear light of morning. Anne affected him in an entirely different way. He wanted to be close to her, to hold her and to love her. Above all, he wanted her to be there in the morning.

Anne cleared away the supper, avoiding James's eye, and they settled down to brandy and Lena Horne singing 'I Get Along Without You Very Well'. She sat, hands clasped round her knees on the floor at James's feet, staring into the fire. Tentatively, he put out a hand and stroked her hair. She sat unresponsive for a moment and then bent her head back and stretched out her arm to bring his face down to hers. He responded, leaning forward and stroking her cheek and nose with his mouth, holding her head in his hands, his fingers gently exploring her ears and neck. Her skin smelled faintly of jasmine and her open mouth glinted in the firelight as she smiled up at him. He kissed her and slid his hands down on to her body. She felt soft and slight under his hands. He caressed her breasts gently, and moved down beside her, his body pressing against hers. Wordlessly, he reached behind her and unzipped her dress and watched it fall to the ground. He stood up, his eyes never leaving hers, and undressed quickly. She glanced at his body and smiled shyly.

'Darling James,' she said softly.

After they had made love, like two people in love and not as lovers, Anne settled her head on James's shoulder and stroked the hair on his chest with a fingertip.

'What's the matter, James? I know I'm rather shy. But it will . . .'

'You were beautiful. God knows, you were perfect. That's not the problem . . . Anne, I have to tell you something, so just lie back and listen.'

'You're married.'

'No, it's far worse than that.' James lay silent for a moment, lit a cigarette and inhaled deeply. There are occasions in life when revelation is made easier by circumstance; it all came out in an unco-ordinated jumble. 'Anne darling, I've made a bloody fool of myself by investing a vast sum of money with a bunch of crooks who've stolen it. I haven't even told my family – they'd be terribly distressed if they ever found out. To make matters better or worse, I've got myself involved with three other chaps who found themselves in the same predicament, and now we're all trying to get our money back. They're nice fellows, full of bright ideas, but I haven't a clue how to begin to keep my part of the bargain. What with the worry of being £150,000 down the drain and having to keep racking my brain for a good idea, I'm half frantic. You're the only thing that's kept me sane the last month.'

'James, start again, but slower this time,' said Anne.

Thus James revealed the entire history of Prospecta Oil from his meeting with David Kesler at Annabel's to his invitation to dine with Stephen Bradley at Magdalen, finally explaining why he had been driving a hired van like a maniac through the rush hour. The only detail James left out was the name of their intended victim, as he felt that by withholding that he was not completely violating his bond of secrecy with the rest of the Team.

Anne inhaled very deeply.

'I hardly know what to say. It's incredible. It's so unbelievable that I believe every word.'

'I feel better just for telling someone, but it would be terrible if the others ever found out.'

'James, you know I won't say a word to anyone. I'm just so very sorry you're in such a mess. You must let me see if I can come up with an idea. Why don't we work together without letting the others know?'

James felt better already.

She began stroking the inside of his leg. Twenty minutes later, they sank into a blissful sleep, dreaming up plans to defeat Harvey Metcalfe.

9

In Lincoln, Massachusetts, Harvey Metcalfe began to prepare for his annual trip to England. He intended to enjoy himself thoroughly and expensively. He had plans for transferring some more money from his numbered accounts in Zürich to Barclays Bank, Lombard Street, ready to buy yet another stallion from one of the Irish stables to join his stud in Kentucky. Arlene had decided not to accompany him on this trip: she did not care too much for Ascot and even less for Monte Carlo. In any case, it gave her the chance to spend some time with her ailing mother in Vermont, who still had little respect for her prosperous son-in-law.

Harvey checked with his secretary that all the arrangements for the holiday had been completed. There was never any need to check up on Miss Fish, it was simply a habit on Harvey's part. Miss Fish had been with him for twenty-five years, from the days when he had first taken over the Lincoln Trust. Most of the respectable staff had walked out on Harvey's arrival, or shortly afterwards, but Miss Fish had remained, nursing in her unalluring bosom ever fainter hopes of eventual marriage to Harvey. By the time Arlene appeared on the scene, Miss Fish was an able and completely discreet accomplice without whom Harvey could hardly have operated. He paid her accordingly, so she swallowed her chagrin at the thought of another Mrs Metcalfe, and stayed put.

Miss Fish had already booked the short flight to New York and the Trafalgar Suite on the *QE2*. The trip across the Atlantic was almost the only total break Harvey ever had from the telephone or telex. The bank staff were instructed to contact the great liner only in dire emergency. On arrival at Southampton it would be the usual Rolls Royce to London and the private suite at Claridge's, which Harvey judged to be one of the last English hotels, along with the Connaught and Browns, where his money allowed him to mix with what he called 'class'.

Harvey flew to New York in high good humour, relaxing and drinking a couple of Manhattans on the way. The arrangements on board ship were as impeccable as ever. The Captain, Peter Jackson, always invited the occupant of the Trafalgar Suite or the Queen Anne Suite to join him on the first night out at the Captain's table. At $1,250 a day for the suites it could hardly be described as an extravagant gesture on Cunard's part. On such occasions, Harvey was always on his best behaviour, although even that struck most onlookers as somewhat brash.

One of the Italian stewards was detailed to arrange a little diversion for Harvey, preferably in the shape

of a tall blonde with a large bosom. The going rate for the night was $200, but the Italian could charge Harvey $250 and still get away with it. At 5 ft 7 in and 227 lb, Harvey's chances of picking up a young thing in the discothèque were slender, and by the time he had lashed out on drinks and dinner, he could have spent almost as much money and achieved absolutely nothing. Men in Harvey's position do not have time for that sort of failure and expect everything in life to have its price. As the voyage was only five nights, the steward was able to keep Harvey fully occupied, although he felt it was just as well that Harvey had not booked a three-week Mediterranean cruise.

Harvey spent his days catching up with the latest novels he had been told he must read and also taking a little exercise, a swim in the morning and a painful session in the gymnasium during the afternoon. He reckoned to lose 10 lb during the crossing, which was pleasing, but somehow Claridge's always managed to put it back on again before he returned to the States. Fortunately, his suits were tailored by Bernard Weatherill of Dover Street, Mayfair, who by dint of near-genius and impeccable skill made him look well-built rather than distinctly fat. At £300 per suit it was the least he could expect.

When the five days were drawing to a close, Harvey was more than ready for land again. The women, the exercise and the fresh air had quite revived him and he had lost all of 11 lb on the crossing.

He felt a good deal of this must have come off the night before, which he had spent with a young Indian girl who had made the *Kama Sutra* look like a Boy Scout's handbook.

One of the advantages of real wealth is that menial tasks can always be left to someone else. Harvey could no longer remember when he last packed or unpacked a suitcase, and when the ship docked at the Ocean Terminal it came as no surprise to him to discover everything packed and ready for Customs – a $100 bill for the head steward seemed to bring men in little white coats from every direction.

Harvey always enjoyed disembarking at Southampton. The English were a race he liked, though he feared he would never understand them. He found them always so willing to be trodden on by the rest of the world. Since the Second World War, they had relinquished their colonial power in a way no American business man would have ever considered for an exit from his own boardroom. Harvey had finally given up trying to understand the British way of business during the 1967 devaluation of the pound. Every jumped-up speculator on the face of the globe had taken advantage of the inside knowledge. Harvey knew on the Tuesday morning that Harold Wilson was going to devalue any time after Friday, 5 pm Greenwich Mean Time, when the Bank of England closed for the weekend. On the Thursday even the junior clerk at the Lincoln Trust knew. It was no wonder that the Old Lady of Threadneedle

Street was raped and despoiled of an estimated £1½ billion over the next few days. Harvey had often thought that if only the British could liven up their boardrooms and get their tax structure right, they might end up being the richest nation in the world, instead of a nation which, as *The Economist* had stated, could now be taken over by the Arabs with ninety days of oil revenue. While the British flirted with socialism and still retained a *folie de grandeur*, they seemed doomed to sink into insignificance. But still Harvey adored them.

He strode down the gangplank like a man with a purpose. Harvey had never learnt to relax completely, even when he was on vacation. He could spend just about four days away from the world, but if he had been left on the *QE2* any longer he would have been negotiating to buy the Cunard Steamship Company. Harvey had once met the Chairman of Cunard, Vic Matthews, at Ascot and had been baffled to hear him harking on the prestige and reputation of the company. Harvey had expected him to brag about the balance sheet. Prestige interested Harvey, of course, but he always let people know how much he was worth first.

Customs clearance was given with the usual speed. Harvey never had anything of consequence to declare on his European trips, and after they had checked two of his Gucci suitcases, the other seven were allowed through without inspection. The chauffeur opened the door of the white Rolls Royce Corniche. The vehicle sped through Hampshire and into London in a little over two hours, which gave Harvey time for a rest before dinner.

Albert, the head doorman at Claridge's, stood smartly to attention and saluted as the car drew up. He knew Harvey of old and was aware that he had come, as usual, for Wimbledon and Ascot. Albert would undoubtedly receive a 50 pence tip every time he opened the white Rolls door. Harvey didn't know the difference between a 50 pence and 10 pence piece – a difference which Albert had welcomed since the introduction of decimalisation in Britain. Moreover, Harvey always gave Albert £5 at the end of Wimbledon fortnight if an American won the singles title. An American invariably reached the finals, so Albert always placed a bet with Ladbrokes on the other finalist and won either way. Gambling appealed to both Harvey and Albert; only the sums involved were different.

Albert arranged for the luggage to be sent up to the Royal Suite, which during the year had already been occupied by King Constantine of Greece, Princess Grace of Monaco and Emperor Hailé Selassie of Ethiopia, all with considerably more conviction than Harvey. But Harvey still considered that his annual holiday at Claridge's was more assured than theirs.

The Royal Suite is on the first floor at Claridge's and can be reached by an elegant sweeping staircase from the ground floor, or by a commodious lift with its own seat. Harvey always took the lift up and walked down. At least that way he convinced himself he was taking some exercise. The suite itself consists of four rooms: a small dressing-room, a bedroom, a bathroom, and an elegant drawing-room overlooking Brook Street. The furniture and pictures make it possible for you to believe that you are still in Victorian England. Only the telephone and television dispel the illusion. The room is large enough to be used for cocktail parties or by visiting heads of state to entertain large parties. Henry Kissinger had received Harold Wilson there only the week before. Harvey enjoyed the thought of that. It was about as close as he was going to get to either man.

After a shower and change of clothes, Harvey glanced through his waiting mail and telexes from the bank, which were all routine. He took a short nap before going down to dine in the main restaurant.

There in the large foyer was the usual string quartet, looking like out-of-work refugees from Hungary. Harvey even recognised the four musicians. He had reached that time in life when he did not like change; the management of Claridge's, aware that the average age of their customers was over fifty, catered accordingly. François, the head waiter, showed Harvey to his usual table.

Harvey managed a little shrimp cocktail and a medium fillet steak with a bottle of Mouton Cadet. As he leaned forward to study the sweets trolley, he did not notice the four young men eating in the alcove on the far side of the room.

Stephen, Robin, Jean-Pierre and James all had an excellent view of Harvey Metcalfe. He would have had to bend double and move slightly backwards to have any sight of them.

'Not exactly what I expected,' commented Stephen.

'Put on a bit of weight since those photographs you supplied,' said Jean-Pierre.

'Hard to believe he's real after all this preparation,' remarked Robin.

'The bastard's real enough,' said Jean-Pierre, 'and a million dollars richer because of our stupidity.'

James said nothing. He was still in disgrace after his futile efforts and excuses at the last full briefing, although the other three had to admit that they did receive good service wherever they went with him. Claridge's was proving to be no exception.

'Wimbledon tomorrow,' said Jean-Pierre. 'I wonder who'll win the first round?'

'You will of course,' chipped in James, hoping to soften Jean-Pierre's acid comments about his own feeble efforts.

'We can only win your round, James, if we ever fill in an entry form.'

James sank back into silence.

'I must say, looking at the size of Metcalfe we ought to get away with your plan, Robin,' said Stephen.

'If he doesn't die of cirrhosis of the liver before we're given the chance,' replied Robin. 'How do you feel about Oxford now you've seen him, Stephen?'

'I don't know yet. I'll feel better when I've belled the cat at Ascot. I want to hear him speak, watch him in his normal environment, get the feel of the man. You can't do all that from the other side of the dining-room.'

'You may not have to wait too long. This time tomorrow we may know everything we need to know – or all be in West End Central Police Station,' said Robin. 'Maybe we won't even pass Go, let alone collect £200.'

'We have to – I can't afford bail,' said Jean-Pierre.

When Harvey had downed a large snifter of Rémy Martin VSOP he left his table, slipping the head waiter a crisp new pound note.

'The bastard,' said Jean-Pierre with great feeling. 'It's bad enough knowing he's stolen our money, but it's humiliating having to watch him spend it.'

The four of them prepared to leave, the object of their outing achieved. Stephen paid the bill and carefully added the sum to the list of expenses against Harvey Metcalfe. Then they left the hotel separately and as inconspicuously as possible. Only James found this difficult as all the waiters and porters insisted on saying 'Good night, my lord.'

Harvey took a stroll round Berkeley Square and did not even notice the tall young man slip into the doorway of Moyses Stevens, the florists, for fear of being spotted by him. Harvey could never resist asking a policeman the way to Buckingham Palace, just to compare his reaction with that of a New York cop, leaning on a lamp post, chewing gum, holster on hip. As Lenny Bruce had said on being deported from England, 'Your pigs is so much better than our pigs'. Yes, Harvey liked England.

He arrived back at Claridge's at about 11.15 pm, showered and went to bed – a large double bed with that glorious feel of clean sheets. There would be no women for him at Claridge's or, if there were, it would be the last time he would find the Royal Suite available to him during Wimbledon or Ascot. The room moved just a little, but then after five days on an ocean liner it was unlikely to be still for a couple of nights. He slept well in spite of it, without a worry on his mind.

10

HARVEY ROSE AT at 7.30 am, a habit he could not break, but he did allow himself the holiday luxury of breakfast in bed. Ten minutes after he had called room service, the waiter arrived with a trolley laden with half a grapefruit, bacon and eggs, toast, steaming black coffee, a copy of the previous day's *Wall Street Journal*, and the morning edition of *The Times*, *Financial Times* and *International Herald Tribune*.

Harvey was not sure how he would have survived on a European trip without the *International Herald Tribune*, known in the trade as the 'Trib'. This unique paper, published in Paris, is jointly owned by the *New York Times* and the *Washington Post*. Although only one edition of 120,000 copies is printed, it does not go to press until the New York Stock Exchange is closed. Therefore, no American need wake up in Europe out of touch. When the *New York Herald Tribune* folded in 1966, Harvey had been among those who advised John H. Whitney to keep the *International Herald Tribune* going in Europe. Once again, Harvey's judgment had been proved sound. The *International Herald Tribune* went on to absorb its faltering rival, the *New York*

Times, which had never been a success in Europe. From then on the paper went from strength to strength.

Harvey ran an experienced eye down the Stock Exchange lists in the *Wall Street Journal* and the *Financial Times*. His bank now held very few shares as he, like Jim Slater in England, had suspected that the Dow-Jones Index would collapse and had therefore gone almost entirely liquid, holding only some South African gold shares and a few well-chosen stocks about which he had inside information. The only monetary transaction he cared to undertake with the market so shaky was to sell the dollar short and buy gold, so that he caught the dollar on the way down and gold on the way up. There were already rumours in Washington that the President of the United States had been advised by his Secretary of the Treasury, George Schultz, to allow the American people to buy gold on the open market later that year or early the following year. Harvey had been buying gold for the past fifteen years: all the President was going to do was to stop him from breaking the law. Harvey was of the opinion that the moment the Americans were able to buy gold, the bubble would burst and the price of gold would recede – the real money would be made while the speculators anticipated the rise, and Harvey intended to be out of gold well before it came on to the American market. Once the President made it legal, Harvey couldn't see a profit in it.

Harvey checked the commodity market in Chicago. He had made a killing in copper a year before. Inside information from an African ambassador had made this possible – information the ambassador had imparted to too many people. Harvey had not been surprised to read that he had later been recalled to his homeland and shot.

He could never resist checking the price of Prospecta Oil, now at an all-time low of $\$^1/_8$: there could be no trading in the stock, simply because there would only be sellers and no buyers. The shares were virtually worthless. He smiled sardonically and turned to the sports page of *The Times*.

Rex Bellamy's article on the forthcoming Wimbledon Championships tipped John Newcombe as favourite and Jimmy Connors, the new American star who had just won the Italian Open, as the best outside bet. The British press wanted the 39-year-old Ken Rosewall to win. Harvey could well remember the epic final between Rosewall and Drobny in 1954, which had run to 58 games. Like most of the crowd, he had supported the 33-year-old Drobny, who had finally won after three hours of play, 13–11, 4–6, 6–2, 9–7. This time, Harvey wanted history to repeat itself and Rosewall to win, though he felt the popular Australian's chance had slipped by during the ten years when the professionals were barred from Wimbledon. Still, he saw no reason why the fortnight should not be a pleasant break, and perhaps there might be an American victor even if Rosewall couldn't manage it.

Harvey had time for a quick glance at the art reviews before finishing his breakfast, leaving the papers strewn over the floor. The quiet Regency furniture, the elegant service and the Royal Suite did nothing for Harvey's habits. He padded into the bathroom for a shave and a shower. Arlene told him that most people did it the other way round – showered and then ate breakfast. But, as Harvey pointed out to her, most people did things the other way round from him, and look where it got them.

Harvey habitually spent the first morning of Wimbledon fortnight visiting the Summer Exhibition at the Royal Academy in Piccadilly. He would then follow this with visits to most of the West End's major galleries – Agnew's, Tooths, the Marlborough, Wildenstein – all within easy walking distance of Claridge's. This morning would be no exception. If Harvey was anything, he was a creature of habit, which was something the Team were quickly learning.

After he had dressed and bawled out room service for not leaving enough whisky in his cabinet, he headed down the staircase, emerged through the swing door on to Davies Street and strode off towards Berkeley Square. Harvey did not observe a studious young man with a two-way radio on the other side of the road.

'He's left the hotel by the Davies Street entrance,' said Stephen quietly to his little Pye Pocketfone, 'and he's heading towards you, James.'

'I'll pick him up as he comes into Berkeley Square, Stephen. Robin, can you hear me?'

'Yes.'

'I'll let you know as soon as I spot him. You stay put at the Royal Academy.'

'Right you are,' said Robin.

Harvey strolled round Berkeley Square, down into Piccadilly and through the Palladian arches of Burlington House. With a bad grace, he stood and queued with the assorted humanity in the forecourt, shuffling past the Astronomical Society and the Society of Antiquaries. He did not see another young man opposite standing in the entrance of the Chemical Society, deep in a copy of *Chemistry in Britain.* Finally, Harvey made it up the red-carpeted ramp into the Royal Academy itself. He handed the cashier £5.00 for a season ticket, realising that he would probably want to return at least three or four times. He spent the rest of the morning studying the 1,182 pictures, none of which had been exhibited anywhere else in the world before the opening day, in accordance with the stringent rules of the Academy. Despite that ruling, the Hanging Committee had still had over 5,000 pictures to choose from.

On the opening day of the exhibition the month before, Harvey had acquired, through his agent, a watercolour by Alfred Daniels of the House of

Commons for £350 and two oils by Bernard Dunstan of English provincial scenes for £125 each. The Summer Exhibition was still, in Harvey's estimation, the best value in the world. Even if he did not want to keep all the pictures himself, they made wonderful presents when he returned to the States. The Daniels reminded him of a Lowry he had bought some twenty years before at the Academy for £80: that had turned out to be another shrewd investment.

Harvey made a special point of looking at the Bernard Dunstans in the Exhibition. Of course, they were all sold. Dunstan was one of the artists whose pictures always sold in the first minutes of the opening day. Although Harvey had not been in London on that day, he had had no difficulty in buying what he wanted. He had planted a man at the front of the queue, who had obtained a catalogue and marked those artists he knew Harvey could resell easily if he made a mistake and keep if his judgment were right. When the exhibition opened on the dot of 10 am, the agent had gone straight to the purchasing desk and acquired the five or six pictures he had marked in the catalogue before he or anyone other than the Academicians had seen them. Harvey studied his vicarious purchases with care. On this occasion he was happy to keep them all. If there had been one that did not quite fit in with his collection, he would have returned the picture for resale, undertaking to purchase it if nobody else showed any interest. In twenty years he had acquired over a hundred pictures by this method and returned a mere dozen, never once failing to secure a resale. Harvey had a system for everything.

At 1 pm, after a thoroughly satisfactory morning, he left the Royal Academy. The white Rolls Royce was waiting for him in the forecourt.

'Wimbledon.'

'Shit.'

'What did you say?' queried Stephen.

'S.H.I.T. He's gone to Wimbledon, so today's down the drain,' said Robin.

That meant Harvey would not return to Claridge's until at least seven or eight that evening. A rota had been fixed for watching him, and Robin accordingly picked up his Rover 3500 V8 from a parking meter in St James's Square and headed off to Wimbledon. James had obtained two tickets for every day of the Championships opposite Harvey Metcalfe's debenture box.

Robin arrived at Wimbledon a few minutes after Harvey and took his seat in the Centre Court, far enough back in the sea of faces to remain inconspicuous. The atmosphere was already building up for the opening match. Wimbledon seemed to be getting more popular every year and the Centre Court was packed to capacity. Princess Alexandra and the Prime Minister were in the Royal Box awaiting the entrance of the gladiators. The little green scoreboards at the southern end of the court were flashing up the names of Kodeš and Stewart as the umpire took his seat on the high chair in the middle of the court directly overlooking the net. The crowd began to applaud as the two athletes, both dressed in white, entered the court carrying four rackets each. Wimbledon does not allow its competitors to dress in any colour other than white, although they had relaxed a little by permitting the trimming of the ladies' dresses to be coloured.

Robin enjoyed the opening match between Kodeš and an unseeded player from the United States, who gave the champion a hard time before losing to the Czech 6–3, 6–4, 9–7. Robin was sorry when Harvey decided to leave in the middle of an exciting doubles match. Back to duty, he told himself, and followed the white Rolls at a safe distance to Claridge's. On arriving, he telephoned James's flat, which was being used as the Team's headquarters in London, and briefed Stephen.

'May as well call it a day,' said Stephen. 'We'll try again tomorrow. Poor old Jean-Pierre's heart-beat reached 150 this morning. He may not last many days of false alarms.'

When Harvey left Claridge's the following morning he went through Berkeley Square into Bruton Street and then on into Bond Street, stopping only 50 yards from Jean-Pierre's gallery. But he turned east instead of west and slipped into Agnew's, where he had an appointment with Sir Geoffrey Agnew, the head of the family firm, for news of Impressionist pictures on the market. Sir Geoffrey was anxious to get away to another meeting and could only spend a few minutes with Harvey. He had nothing worthwhile to offer him.

Harvey left Agnew's soon afterwards clutching a small consolation prize of a maquette by Rodin, a mere bagatelle at £800.

'He's coming out,' said Robin, 'and heading in the right direction.' Jean-Pierre held his breath, but Harvey stopped once again, this time at the Marlborough Gallery to study their latest exhibition of Barbara Hepworth. He spent over an hour appreciating her beautiful work, but decided the prices were now outrageous. He had bought two Hepworths only ten years before for £800. The Marlborough was now asking between £7,000 and £10,000 for her work. So he left and continued up Bond Street.

'Jean-Pierre?'

'Yes,' replied a nervous voice.

'He's reached the corner of Conduit Street and he's about 50 yards away from your front door.'

Jean-Pierre prepared his window, removing the Graham Sutherland watercolour of the Thames and the Boatman.

'He's turned left, the bastard,' said James, who was stationed opposite the gallery. 'He's walking down Bruton Street on the right-hand side.'

Jean-Pierre put the Sutherland back on the easel in the window and retired to the lavatory, muttering to himself:

'I can't cope with two shits at once.'

Harvey meanwhile stepped into an inconspicuous entrance on Bruton Street and climbed the stairs to Tooths, more hopeful of finding something in a gallery which had become famous for its Impressionists. A Klee, a Picasso and two Salvador Dalis – not what Harvey was looking for. Though very well executed, the Klee was not as good as the one in his dining-room in Lincoln, Massachusetts. Besides, it might not fit in with any of Arlene's decorative schemes. Nicholas Tooth, the managing director, promised to keep his eyes open and ring Harvey at Claridge's should anything of interest turn up.

'He's on the move again, but I think he's heading back to Claridge's.'

James willed him to turn round and return in the direction of Jean-Pierre's gallery, but Harvey strode purposefully towards Berkeley Square, only making a detour to the O'Hana Gallery. Albert, the head doorman, had told him there was a Renoir in the window, and indeed there was. But it was only a half-finished canvas which Renoir had obviously used for a practice run or had disliked enough to leave unfinished. Harvey was curious as to the price and entered the gallery.

'£30,000,' said the assistant, as if it was $10 and a snip at that.

Harvey whistled through the gap between his front teeth. It never ceased to amaze him that an inferior picture by a first-rank name could fetch £30,000 and an outstanding picture by an artist with no established reputation could only bring a few hundred dollars. He thanked the assistant and left.

'A pleasure, Mr Metcalfe.'

Harvey was always flattered by people who remembered his name. But hell, they ought to remember – he had purchased a Monet from them last year for £62,000.

'He's definitely on his way back to the hotel,' said James.

Harvey spent only a few minutes in Claridge's, picking up one of their famous specially prepared luncheon hampers of caviar, beef, ham and cheese sandwiches and chocolate cake for later consumption at Wimbledon.

James was next on the rota for the Championships and decided to take Anne with him. Why not – she knew the truth. It was Ladies' Day and the turn of Billie Jean King, the vivacious American champion, to take the court. She was up against the unseeded American, Kathy May, who looked as if she was in for a rough time. The applause Billie Jean received was unworthy of her abilities, but for some reason she had never become a Wimbledon favourite. Harvey was accompanied by a guest who James thought had a faintly mid-European look.

'Which one is your victim?' asked Anne.

'He's almost exactly opposite us talking to the man in a light grey suit who looks like a government official from the EEC.'

'The short fat one?' asked Anne.

'Yes,' said James.

Whatever comments Anne made were interrupted by the umpire's call of 'Play' and everyone's attention focused on Billie Jean. It was exactly 2 pm.

'Kind of you to invite me to Wimbledon, Harvey,' said Jörg Birrer. 'I never seem to get the chance for much relaxation nowadays. You can't leave the market for more than a few hours without some panic breaking out somewhere in the world.'

'If you feel that way it's time for you to retire,' said Harvey.

'No one to take my place,' said Birrer. 'I've been chairman of the bank for ten years now and finding a successor is turning out to be my hardest task.'

'First game to Mrs King. Mrs King leads by one game to love in the first set.'

'Now, Harvey, I know you too well to expect this invitation to have been just for pleasure.'

'What an evil mind you have, Jörg.'

'In my profession I need it.'

'I just wanted to check how my three accounts stand and brief you on my plans for the next few months.'

'Game to Mrs King. Mrs King leads by two games to love in the first set.'

'Your No. 1 official account is a few thousand dollars in credit. Your numbered commodity account'

– at this point Birrer unfolded a small piece of unidentifiable paper with a set of neat figures printed on it – 'is short by $3,726,000, but you are holding 37,000 ounces of gold at today's selling price of $135 an ounce.'

'What's your advice on that?'

'Hold on, Harvey. I still think your President is either going to announce a new gold standard or allow your fellow-countrymen to buy gold on the open market some time next year.'

'That's my view too, but I'm still convinced we want to sell a few weeks before the masses come in. I have a theory about that.'

'I expect you're right, as usual, Harvey.'

'Game to Mrs King. Mrs King leads by three games to love in the first set.'

'What are your charges on my overdraft?'

'One-and-a-half per cent above inter-bank rate, which at present is 13.25, and therefore we're charging you 14.75 per cent per annum, while gold is rising in price at nearly 70 per cent per annum. It can't go on that way; but there are still a few months left in it.'

'OK,' said Harvey, 'hold on until November 1st and we'll review the position again then. Coded telex as usual. I don't know what the world would do without the Swiss.'

'Just take care, Harvey. Do you know there are more specialists in our police force on fraud than there are for homicide?'

'You worry about your end, Jörg, and I'll worry

about mine. The day I get uptight about a few underpaid bureaucrats from Zürich who haven't got any balls, I'll let you know. Now, enjoy your lunch and watch the game. We'll have a talk about the other account later.'

'Game to Mrs King. Mrs King leads by four games to love in the first set.'

'They're very deep in conversation,' said Anne. 'I can't believe they're enjoying the match.'

'He's probably trying to buy Wimbledon at cost price,' laughed James. 'The trouble with seeing the man every day is that one begins to have a certain respect for him. He's the most organised man I've ever come across. If he's like this on holiday, what the hell is he like at work?'

'I can't imagine,' said Anne.

'Game to Miss May. Mrs King leads by four games to one in the first set.'

'No wonder he's so overweight. Just look at him stuffing that cake down.' James lifted his Zeiss binoculars. 'Which reminds me to ask, darling, what have you brought for lunch?'

Anne dug into her hamper and unpacked a crisp salad in French bread for James. She contented herself with nibbling a stick of celery.

'Getting far too fat,' she explained. 'I'll never get into those winter clothes I'm supposed to be modelling next week.' She touched James's knee and smiled. 'It must be because I'm so happy.'

'Well, don't get too happy. I prefer you thin.'

'Game to Mrs King. Mrs King leads by five games to one in the first set.'

'This is going to be a walkover,' said James. 'It so often is in the opening match. People only come to see if the champion's in good form, and I think she'll be very hard to beat this year now she's after Helen Moody's record of eight Wimbledon championships.'

'Game and first set to Mrs King by six games to one. Mrs King leads one set to love. New balls, please. Miss May to serve.'

'Do we have to watch him all day?' asked Anne.

'Yes, we must make sure he returns to the hotel and doesn't change his plans suddenly or anything silly like that. If we miss our chance when he walks past Jean-Pierre's gallery, we may not get another one.'

'What do you do if he does decide to change his plans?'

'God knows, or to be more accurate, Stephen knows – he's the mastermind.'

'Game to Mrs King. Mrs King leads by one game to love in the second set.'

'Poor Miss May, she's about as successful as you are, James. How is the Jean-Pierre operation looking?'

'Awful. Metcalfe hasn't been anywhere near the gallery. He was within 30 yards of the window today and marched off in the opposite direction. Poor Jean-Pierre nearly had heart failure. But we're more hopeful of tomorrow. So far he seems to have covered Piccadilly and the top end of Bond Street, and the one thing we can be sure of with Harvey Metcalfe is that he's thorough. So he's almost bound to cover our bit of territory at one time or another.'

'You should all have taken out life insurance for $1 million, naming the other three as beneficiaries,' said Anne, 'and then if one of you had a heart attack, the others would all get their money back.'

'It's no laughing matter, Anne. It's bloody nerve-racking while you're hanging around, especially when you have to wait for him to make all the moves.'

'Game to Mrs King. Mrs King leads by two games to love in the second set and by one set to love.'

'How about your own plan?'

'Nothing. Useless. And now we've started on the others I seem to have less time to concentrate on my own.'

'Why don't I seduce him?'

'Not a bad idea, but you'd have to be pretty special to get £100,000 out of him, when he can hang around outside the Hilton or in Shepherd Market and get it for £30. If there's one thing we've learnt about that gentleman it's that he expects value for money. At £30 a night it would take you just under fifteen years to repay my share, and I'm not sure the other three would be willing to wait that long. In fact, I'm not sure they'll wait another fifteen days.'

'We'll think of something, don't worry,' said Anne.

'Game to Miss May. Mrs King leads by two games to one and by one set to love.'

'Well, well. Miss May has managed another game. Excellent lunch, Harvey.'

'A Claridge's special,' said Harvey, 'so much better than getting caught up with the crowds in the restaurant where you can't even watch the tennis.'

'Billie Jean is making mincemeat of the poor girl.'

'No more than I expected,' said Harvey. 'Now, Jörg, to my second numbered account.'

Once again the unidentifiable piece of paper that bore a few numbers appeared. It is this discretion of the Swiss that leads half the world, from heads of state to Arab sheiks, to trust them with their money. In return the Swiss maintain one of the healthiest economies in the world. The system works, so why go elsewhere? Birrer spent a few seconds studying the figures.

'On April 1st – only you could have chosen that day, Harvey – you transferred $7,486,000 to your No. 2 account which was already in credit $2,791,428. On April 2nd, on your instructions, we placed $1 million in the Banco do Minas Gerais in the names of Mr Silverman and Mr Elliott. We covered the bill with Reading & Bates for the hire of the rig for $420,000 and several other bills amounting to $104,112, leaving your present No. 2 account standing at $8,753,316.'

'Game to Mrs King. Mrs King leads three games to one in the second set and by one set to love.'

'Very good,' said Harvey.

'The tennis or the money?' said Birrer.

'Both. Now, Jörg, I anticipated needing about $2

million over the next six weeks. I want to purchase one or two pictures in London. I have seen a Klee that I quite like and there are still a few galleries I want to visit. If I'd known the Prospecta Oil venture was going to be such a success, I'd have outbid Armand Hammer at the Sotheby-Parke Bernet for that Van Gogh last year. I shall also need some ready cash for some new horses at the Ascot Blood Stock Auctions. My stud's running down and it's still one of my greatest ambitions to win the King George and Elizabeth Stakes.' (James would have winced if he could have heard Harvey describe the race so inaccurately.) 'My best result so far, as you know, was third place, and that's not good enough. This year I've entered Rosalie, my best filly for years. If I lose I'll have to build up the stud again, but I'm damn well going to win this year.'

'Game to Mrs King. Mrs King leads four games to one and by one set to love.'

'So is Mrs King, it seems,' said Birrer. 'I'll brief my senior cashier that you're likely to be drawing large amounts over the next few weeks.'

'Now I don't wish the remainder to lie idle, so I want you to purchase more gold carefully over the next few months, with a view to off-loading it in the New Year. If the market does take a downward turn, I'll phone you in Zürich. At the close of business each day you are to loan the outstanding balance on an overnight basis to first-class banks and triple "A" commercial names.'

'What are you going to do with it all, Harvey, if those cigars don't get you first?'

'Oh, lay off, Jörg. You sound like my doctor. I've told you a hundred times, next year I retire, I quit, finito.'

'I can't see you dropping out of the rat race voluntarily, Harvey. It pains me to think how much you're worth now.'

Harvey laughed.

'I can't tell you that, Jörg. It's like Aristotle Onassis said – if you can count it, you haven't got any.'

'Game to Mrs King. Mrs King leads by five games to one and by one set to love.'

'How's Rosalie? We still have your instructions to pass the accounts on to her in Boston if anything should happen to you.'

'She's well. Phoned me this morning to tell me she won't be able to join me at Wimbledon because she's tied up with her work. I expect she'll end up marrying some rich American and won't need it. Enough of them have asked her. Can't be easy for her to decide if they like her or my money. I'm afraid we had a row about that a couple of years back and she still hasn't forgiven me.'

'Game, set and match to Mrs King: 6–1, 6–1.'

Harvey, Jörg, James and Anne joined in the applause while the two women left the court, curtseying in front of the Royal Box to the President of the All England Club, His Royal Highness, The Duke of Kent. Harvey and Jörg Birrer stayed for the next match, a doubles, and then returned to Claridge's together for dinner.

James and Anne had enjoyed their afternoon at Wimbledon and when they had seen Harvey safely back to Claridge's, accompanied by his mid-European friend, they returned to James's flat.

'Stephen, I'm back. Metcalfe is settled in for the night. On parade at 8.30 tomorrow morning.'

'Well done, James. Maybe he'll bite then.'

'Let's hope so.'

The sound of running water led James to the kitchen in search of Anne. She was elbow-deep in suds, attacking a soufflé dish with a scourer. She turned and brandished it at him.

'Darling, I don't want to be offensive about your daily, but this is the only kitchen I've ever been in where you have to do the washing up before you make the dinner!'

'I know. She only ever cleans the clean bits of the flat. Her work load's getting lighter by the week.'

He sat on the kitchen table, admiring her slim body.

'Will you scrub my back like that if I go and have a bath before dinner?'

'Yes, with a scourer.'

*

The water was deep and comfortably hot. James lay back in it luxuriously, letting Anne wash him. Then he stepped dripping out of the bath.

'You're a bit overdressed for a bathroom attendant, darling,' he said. 'Why don't we do something about it?'

Anne slipped out of her clothes while James dried himself. When he went into the bedroom, Anne was already huddled under the sheets.

'I'm cold,' she said.

'Fear not,' said James. 'You're about to be presented with your very own six-foot hot water bottle.'

She took him in her arms.

'Liar, you're freezing.'

'And you're lovely,' said James, trying to hold on to every part of her at once.

'How's your plan going, James?'

'I don't know yet, I'll tell you in about twenty minutes.'

She didn't speak again for nearly half an hour, when she said:

'Out you get. The baked cheese will be ready by now and in any case I want to remake the bed.'

'No need to bother about that, you silly woman.'

'Yes, there is. Last night I didn't sleep at all. You pulled all the blankets over to your side and I just watched you huddled up like a self-satisfied cat while I froze to death. Making love to you isn't at all what Harold Robbins promised it would be.'

'When you've finished chattering, woman, set the alarm for 7 am.'

'Seven am? You don't have to be at Claridge's until 8.30.'

'I know, but I want to go to work on an egg.'

'James, you really must give up your undergraduate sense of humour.'

'Oh, I thought it was rather funny.'

'Yes, darling. Why don't you get dressed before the dinner is burnt to a cinder?'

James arrived at Claridge's at 8.29 am. Whatever his own inadequacies, he was determined not to fail the others in their plans. He tuned in to check that Stephen was in Berkeley Square and Robin in Bond Street.

'Morning,' said Stephen. 'Had a good night?'

'Bloody good,' said James.

'Sleep well, did you?' asked Stephen.

'Hardly a wink.'

'Stop making us jealous,' said Robin, 'and concentrate on Harvey Metcalfe.'

James stood in the doorway of Slater's, the furriers, watching the early morning cleaners leave for home and the first of the office staff arriving.

Harvey Metcalfe was going through his normal routine of breakfast and the papers. Just before he had gone to bed he had a telephone call from his wife in Boston and another from his daughter during breakfast the next morning, which started his day well. He decided to continue his pursuit of an Impressionist picture in some of the other galleries in Cork Street and Bond Street. Perhaps Sotheby's would be able to help him.

He left the hotel at 9.47 am at his usual brisk pace.

'Action stations.'

Stephen and Robin snapped out of their day-dreaming.

'He's just entered Bruton Street. Now he's heading for Bond Street.'

Harvey walked briskly down Bond Street, past the territory he had already covered.

'Only 50 yards off now, Jean-Pierre,' said James. 'Forty yards, 30 yards, 20 yards . . . Oh no, damn it, he's gone into Sotheby's. There's only a sale of medieval painted panels on there today. Hell, I didn't know he was interested in them.'

He glanced up the road at Stephen, padded out and aged to the condition of a wealthy, middle-class business man for the third day in a row. The cut of the collar and the rimless glasses proclaimed him as West German. Stephen's voice came over the speaker:

'I am going into Jean-Pierre's gallery. James, you stay north of Sotheby's on the far side of the street and report in every fifteen minutes. Robin, you go inside and dangle the bait under Harvey's nose.'

'But that's not in the plan, Stephen,' stammered Robin.

'Use your initiative and get on with it, otherwise

all you'll be doing is taking care of Jean-Pierre's heart condition and receiving no fees. Right?'

'Right,' said Robin nervously.

Robin walked into Sotheby's and made a surreptitious bee-line for the nearest mirror. Yes, he was still unrecognisable. Upstairs, he spotted Harvey near the back of the sale room, and planted himself on a nearby seat in the row behind him.

The sale of medieval painted panels was well under way. Harvey knew he ought to like them, but could not bring himself to condone the Gothic partiality for jewellery and bright, gilded colours. Behind him, Robin hesitated but then struck up a quiet-voiced conversation with his neighbour.

'Looks all very fine to me, but I've no knowledge of the period. I'm so much happier with the modern era. Still, I must think of something appropriate to say for my readers.'

Robin's neighbour smiled politely.

'Do you have to cover all the auctions?'

'Almost all – especially when there may be surprises. In any case, at Sotheby's you can always find out what's going on everywhere else. Only this morning one of the assistants gave me a tip that the Lamanns Gallery may have something special in the Impressionist field.'

Robin beamed the whispered information carefully at Harvey's right ear and then sat back and waited to see if it had created any effect. Shortly afterwards, he was rewarded by the sight of Harvey squeezing out of his row to leave. Robin waited for three more lots to be auctioned, then followed him, fingers crossed.

Outside, James had been keeping a patient vigil.

'10.30 – no sign of him.'

'Roger.'

'10.45 – still no sign of him.'

'Roger.'

'11.00 – he's still inside.'

'Roger.'

'11.12 action stations, action stations.'

James slipped quickly into the Lamanns Gallery as Jean-Pierre once again removed from his window the Sutherland watercolour of the Thames and the Boatman, and replaced it with an oil by Van Gogh, as magnificent an example of the master's work as a London gallery had ever seen. Now came the acid test: the litmus paper was walking purposefully down Bond Street towards it.

The picture had been painted by David Stein, who had achieved notoriety in the art world for faking 300 paintings and drawings by well-known Impressionists, for which he had received a total of $864,000 and, later, four years. He was only exposed when he put on a Chagall exhibition at the Niveaie Gallery in Madison Avenue in 1969. Unknown to Stein, Chagall himself was in New York at the time for an exhibition at the museum in Lincoln Center where two of his most famous works were on display. On being informed of the Niveaie exhibition, Chagall furiously reported the pictures to the District Attorney's office as fakes. Stein had already sold one of the imitation Chagalls to Louis D. Cohen at a price of nearly $100,000, and to this day there is a Stein Chagall and a Stein Picasso at the Galleria d'Arte Moderna in Milan. Jean-Pierre was confident that what Stein had achieved in the past in New York and Milan he could now repeat in London.

Stein had continued to paint Impressionist pictures, but now signed them with his own name; thanks to his indubitable talent he was still making a handsome living. He had known and admired Jean-Pierre for several years and when he heard the story of Metcalfe and Prospecta Oil, he agreed to produce a Van Gogh for $10,000 and to sign the painting with the master's famous 'Vincent'.

Jean-Pierre had gone to considerable lengths to identify a Van Gogh that had vanished in mysterious circumstances, so that Stein could resurrect it to tempt Harvey. He had started with de la Faille's comprehensive *oeuvres* catalogue, *The Works of Vincent Van Gogh*, and selected from it three pictures that had hung in the National Gallery in Berlin prior to the Second World War. In de la Faille, they were entered under Nos. 485, *Les Amoureux* (*The Lovers*), 628, *La Moisson* (*The Harvest*), and 766, *Le Jardin de Daubigny* (*The Garden of Daubigny*). The last two were known to have been bought in 1929 by the Berlin Gallery, and *Les Amoureux* probably bought around the same time. At the start of the war, all three had disappeared.

Jean-Pierre then contacted Professor Wormit of

the Preussischer Kulturbesitz. The Professor, a world authority on missing works of art, was able to rule out one of the possibilities, *Le Jardin de Daubigny*; soon after the war it apparently had reappeared in the collection of Siegfried Kramarsky in New York, though how it got there remains a mystery. Kramarsky had subsequently sold the painting to the Nichido Gallery in Tokyo, where it now hangs. The Professor confirmed that the fate of the other two Van Goghs remained unknown.

Next Jean-Pierre turned to Madame Tellegen-Hoogendoorm of the Dutch Rijksbureau voor Kunsthistorische Documentatie. Madame Tellegen was the acknowledged authority on Van Gogh and gradually, with her expert help, Jean-Pierre pieced together the story of the missing paintings. They had been removed, along with many others, from the Berlin National Gallery in 1937 by the Nazis, despite vigorous protests from the Director, Dr Hanfstaengl, and the Keeper of Paintings, Dr Hentzen. The paintings, stigmatised by the philistinism of the National Socialists as degenerate art, were stored in a depot in the Kopenickerstrasse in Berlin. Hitler himself visited the depot in January 1938, and legalised the proceedings as an official confiscation.

What happened to the two Van Goghs after that, nobody knows. Many of the Nazi-confiscated works were quietly sold abroad by Joseph Angerer, an agent of Hermann Goering, to obtain much-needed foreign currency for the Führer. Some were disposed of in a sale organised by the Fischer Art Gallery in Lucerne on June 30th, 1939. But many of the works in the depot in the Kopenickerstrasse were simply burned, stolen, or are still missing.

Jean-Pierre managed to obtain black-and-white reproductions of *Les Amoureux* and *La Moisson*: no colour positives survive, if they were ever made. It seemed to Jean-Pierre unlikely that any colour reproductions of two paintings last seen in 1938 would exist anywhere. He therefore settled down to choose between the two.

Les Amoureux was the larger of the two, at 76 × 91 cm. However, Van Gogh did not seem to have been satisfied with it. In October 1889 (letter No. 556) he referred to 'a very poor sketch of my last canvas'. Moreover, it was impossible to guess the colour of the background. *La Moisson*, in contrast, had pleased Van Gogh. He had painted the oil in September 1889 and written of it, 'I feel very much inclined to do the reaper once more for my mother' (letter No. 604). He had in fact already painted three other very similar pictures of a reaper at harvest time. Jean-Pierre was able to obtain colour transparencies of two of them, one from the Louvre and the other from the Rijksmuseum, where they now hang. He studied the sequence. The position of the sun, and the play of light on the scene, were practically the only points of difference. Jean-Pierre was therefore able to see in his mind's eye what *La Moisson* must have looked like in colour.

Stein agreed with Jean-Pierre's final choice and he studied the black-and-white reproduction of *La Moisson* and the colour transparencies of its sister paintings long and minutely before he set to work. He then found an insignificant late-nineteenth-century French work, and skilfully removed the paint from it, leaving a clean canvas except for a vital stamp on the back which even Stein could not have reproduced. He marked on the canvas the exact size of the picture, 48.5 × 53 cm and selected a palette knife and brush of the type that Van Gogh had favoured. Six weeks later *La Moisson* was finished. Stein varnished it, and baked it for four days in an oven at a gentle 85°F to age it. Jean-Pierre provided a heavy gilt Impressionist frame and it was well ready for Harvey Metcalfe's scrutiny.

Harvey, acting on his overheard tip, could see no harm in dropping into the Lamanns Gallery. He was about five paces away when he first caught sight of the picture being taken out of the window. He could not believe his eyes. A Van Gogh, without a doubt, and a superlative one at that. *La Moisson* had actually been on display for only two minutes.

Harvey almost ran into the gallery, only to discover Jean-Pierre deep in conversation with Stephen and James. None of them took any notice of him. Stephen was addressing Jean-Pierre in a guttural accent.

'170,000 guineas seems high, but it is a fine example. Can you be sure it is the picture that disappeared from Berlin in 1937?'

'You can never be sure of anything, but you can see on the back of the canvas the stamp of the Berlin National Gallery, and the Bernheim Jeune have confirmed they sold it to the Germans in 1927. The rest of its history is well chronicled back to 1890. It seems certain that it was looted from the museum in the upheaval of the war.'

'How did you come into possession of the painting?'

'From the private collection of a member of the British aristocracy who wishes to remain anonymous.'

'Excellent,' said Stephen. 'I would like to reserve it until 4 pm when I will bring round a cheque for 170,000 guineas from the Dresdner Bank AG. Will that be acceptable?'

'Of course, sir,' replied Jean-Pierre. 'I will place a red dot on it.'

James, in the sharpest of suits and a dashing trilby, hovered knowledgeably behind Stephen.

'It certainly is a marvellous example of the master's work,' he remarked ingratiatingly.

'Yes. I took it round to Julian Barron at Sotheby's and he seemed to like it.'

James retreated mincingly to the end of the gallery, relishing his role as a connoisseur. At that moment Robin walked in, a copy of the *Guardian* sticking out of his pocket.

'Good morning, Mr Lamanns. I heard a rumour at Sotheby's about a Van Gogh which I'd always thought must be in Russia. I'd like to write a few paragraphs about the history of the painting and how you came into possession of it for tomorrow's paper. Is that OK by you?'

'I should be delighted,' said Jean-Pierre, 'although actually I have just reserved the picture for Herr Drosser, the distinguished German dealer, at 170,000 guineas.'

'Very reasonable,' said James knowingly from the end of the gallery. 'I think it's the best Van Gogh I have seen in London since *Mademoiselle Ravoux* and I'm only sorry my house won't be auctioning it. You're a lucky man, Mr Drosser. If you ever decide to sell it, don't hesitate to contact me.' James handed Stephen a card and smiled at Jean-Pierre.

Jean-Pierre watched James. It was a fine performance. Robin began to take notes in what he hoped looked like shorthand and again addressed Jean-Pierre.

'Do you have a photograph of the picture?'

'Of course.'

Jean-Pierre opened a drawer and took out a colour photograph of the picture with a typewritten description attached. He handed it to Robin.

'Do watch the spelling of Lamanns, won't you? I get so bored with being confused with a French motor car race.'

He turned to Stephen.

'So sorry to keep you waiting, Herr Drosser. How would you like us to despatch the picture?'

'You can send it to me at the Dorchester tomorrow morning, room 120.'

'Certainly, sir.'

Stephen started to leave.

'Excuse me, sir,' said Robin, 'can I take the spelling of your name?'

'D.R.O.S.S.E.R.'

'And may I have permission to quote you in my article?'

'You may. I am with my purchase very pleased. Good day, gentlemen.'

Stephen bowed his head smartly, and departed. He stepped out into Bond Street and to the horror of Jean-Pierre, Robin and James, Harvey, without a moment's hesitation, also walked out.

Jean-Pierre collapsed heavily on his Georgian mahogany desk and looked despairingly at Robin and James.

'God Almighty, the whole thing's a fiasco. Six weeks of preparation, three days of agony, and then he walked out on us.' Jean-Pierre looked at *La Moisson* angrily.

'I thought Stephen assured us that Harvey would stay and bargain with Jean-Pierre. It's in his character,' mimicked James plaintively. 'He'd never let the picture out of his sight.'

'Who the hell thought up this bloody silly enterprise?' muttered Robin.

'Stephen,' they all cried together, and rushed to the window.

'What an interesting maquette by Henry Moore,' said an impeccably corseted middle-aged lady, her hand firmly placed on the bronze loin of a naked acrobat. She had slipped unnoticed into the gallery while the three had been grumbling. 'How much are you asking for it?'

'I will be with you in a minute, madam,' said Jean-Pierre. 'Oh hell, I think Metcalfe's following Stephen. Get him on the pocket radio, Robin.'

'Stephen, can you hear me? Whatever you do, don't look back. We think Harvey's only a few yards behind you.'

'What the hell do you mean he's only a few yards behind me? He's meant to be in the gallery with you buying the Van Gogh. What are you playing at?'

'Harvey didn't give us a chance. He walked straight out after you before any of us could continue as planned.'

'Very clever. Now what am I meant to do?'

Jean-Pierre took over:

'You'd better go to the Dorchester just in case he is actually following you.'

'I don't even know where the Dorchester is,' yelped Stephen.

Robin came to his rescue:

'Take the first right, Stephen, and that'll bring you into Bruton Street, keep walking as straight as you can until you reach Berkeley Square. Stay on the line, but don't look back or you may turn into a pillar of salt.'

'James,' said Jean-Pierre, thinking on his feet for the first time in his life. 'You take a taxi immediately to the Dorchester and book room 120 in the name of Drosser. Have the key ready for Stephen the moment he walks through the door, then make yourself scarce. Stephen, are you, still there?'

'Yes.'

'Did you hear all that?'

'Yes. Tell James to book 119 or 121 if 120 is not available.'

'Roger,' replied Jean-Pierre. 'Get going, James.'

James bolted out of the gallery and barged in front of a woman who had just hailed a taxi, a thing he had never done before.

'The Dorchester,' he hollered, 'as fast as you can go.'

The taxi shot off.

'Stephen, James has gone and I'm sending Robin to follow Harvey so he can keep you briefed and guide you to the Dorchester. I'm staying put. Everything else OK?'

'No,' said Stephen, 'start praying. I've reached Berkeley Square. Where now?'

'Across the garden then continue down Hill Street.'

Robin left the gallery and ran all the way to Bruton Street until he was only 50 yards behind Harvey.

'Now about the Henry Moore,' said the well-corseted lady.

'Screw Henry Moore,' said Jean-Pierre, not even looking around.

The steel-reinforced bosom heaved.

'Young man, I have never been spoken to in . . .'

But Jean-Pierre had already reached the lavatory, and closed the door.

'You're crossing South Audley Street now, then continue into Deanery Street. Keep going, don't turn right or left and don't whatever you do look back. Harvey is still about 50 yards behind you. I'm a little more than 50 yards behind him,' said Robin. Passers-by stared at the man talking into his little instrument.

'Is Room 120 free?'

'Yes, sir, they checked out this morning, but I'm not sure if it's ready for occupancy yet. I think the maid may still be clearing the room. I'll have to check, sir,' said the tall receptionist in the morning suit, which indicated that he was a senior member of the floor staff.

'Oh, don't worry about that,' said James, his German accent far better than Stephen's. 'I always have that room. Can you book me in for one night? Name's Drosser, Herr – um – Helmut Drosser.'

He slipped a pound over the counter.

'Certainly, sir.'

'That's Park Lane, Stephen. Look right – the big hotel on the corner straight in front of you is the Dorchester. The semi-circle facing you is the main entrance. Go up the steps, past the big man in the green overcoat, and through the revolving door and you'll find reception on your right. James ought to be there waiting for you.'

Robin was grateful that the annual dinner of the Royal Society for Medicine had been held at the Dorchester last year.

'Where's Harvey?' bleated Stephen.

'Only 40 yards behind you.'

Stephen quickened his pace, ran up the steps of the Dorchester and pushed through the revolving door so hard that the other residents coming out found themselves on the street faster than they had planned. Thank God, James was standing there holding a key.

'The lift's over there,' said James, pointing. 'You've only chosen one of the most expensive suites in the hotel.'

Stephen glanced in the direction James had indicated and turned back to thank him. But James was already heading off to the American Bar to be sure he was well out of sight when Harvey arrived.

Stephen left the lift at the first floor and found that the Dorchester, which he had never entered before, was as traditional as Claridge's, its thick royal blue and golden carpets leading to a magnificently appointed corner suite which overlooked Hyde Park. He collapsed into an easy chair, not quite sure what to expect next. Nothing had gone as planned.

Jean-Pierre waited at the gallery, James sat in the American Bar and Robin loitered by the side of Barclays Bank, Park Lane, a mock-tudor building 50 yards from the entrance of the Dorchester.

'Have you a Mr Drosser staying at this hotel? I think it's room 120,' barked Harvey.

The receptionist looked through the card index.

'Yes, sir. Is he expecting you?'

'No, but I'll have a word with him on the house phone.'

'Of course, sir. If you'd be kind enough to go through the small archway on your left you will find five telephones. One of them is a house phone.'

Harvey marched through the archway as directed.

'Room 120,' he instructed the operator, who sat in his own little section, wearing the green Dorchester uniform with golden castles on the lapels.

'Cubicle No. 1, please, sir.'

'Mr Drosser?'

'Speaking,' said Stephen, summoning up his German accent for a sustained effort.

'My name is Harvey Metcalfe. I wonder if I could come up and have a word with you? It's about the Van Gogh you bought this morning.'

'Well, it's a little inconvenient at the moment. I am about to take a shower and I do have a lunch appointment.'

'I won't keep you more than a few minutes.'

Before Stephen could reply, the telephone clicked. A few moments later there was a knock on the door. Stephen's legs wobbled. He answered it nervously. He had changed into a white Dorchester dressing-gown and his brown hair was somewhat dishevelled and darker than normal. It was the only disguise he could think of at such short notice as the original plan had not allowed for a face-to-face meeting with Harvey.

'Sorry to intrude, Mr Drosser, but I had to see you immediately. I know you have just purchased a Van Gogh from the Lamanns Gallery and I was hoping that, as you are a dealer, you might be willing to sell it on for a quick profit.'

'No, thank you,' said Stephen, relaxing for the first time. 'I've wanted a Van Gogh for my gallery in Munich for many years. I'm sorry, Mr Metcalfe, it's not for sale.'

'Listen, you paid 170,000 guineas for it. What's that in dollars?'

Stephen paused.

'Oh, about $435,000.'

'I'll give you $15,000 if you release the picture to me. All you have to do is ring the gallery and tell them that the picture is now mine and that I will cover the bill.'

Stephen sat silent, not sure how to handle the situation without blowing it. Think like Harvey Metcalfe, he told himself.

'$20,000 in cash and you've got a deal.'

Harvey hesitated. Stephen's legs wobbled again.

'Done,' said Harvey. 'Ring the gallery immediately.'

Stephen picked up the telephone.

'Can you get me the Lamanns Gallery in Bond Street as quickly as possible, please – I have a lunch appointment.'

A few seconds later the call came through.

'Lamanns Gallery.'

'I would like to speak to Mr Lamanns.'

'At last, Stephen. What the hell is happening your end?'

'Ah, Mr Lamanns, this is Herr Drosser. You remember, I was in your gallery earlier this morning.'

'Of course I remember, you fool. What are you going on about, Stephen? It's me – Jean-Pierre.'

'I have a Mr Metcalfe with me.'

'Christ, I'm sorry, Stephen. I didn't . . .'

'And you can expect him in the next few minutes.'

Stephen looked towards Harvey who nodded his assent.

'You are to release the Van Gogh I purchased this morning to Mr Metcalfe and he will give you a cheque for the full amount, 170,000 guineas.'

'Out of disaster, triumph,' said Jean-Pierre quietly.

'I'm very sorry I shall not be the owner of the picture myself, but I have, as the Americans would say, had an offer I can't refuse. Thank you for the part you played,' said Stephen and put the telephone down.

Harvey was writing out a cheque to cash for $20,000.

'Thank you, Mr Drosser. You have made me a happy man.'

'I am not complaining myself,' said Stephen honestly. He escorted Harvey to the door and they shook hands.

'Goodbye, sir.'

'Good day, Mr Metcalfe.'

Stephen closed the door and tottered to the chair, almost too weak to move.

Robin and James saw Harvey leave the Dorchester. Robin followed him in the direction of the gallery, his hopes rising with each stride. James took the lift to the first floor and nearly ran to Room 120. He banged on the door. Stephen jumped at the noise. He didn't feel he could face Harvey again. He opened the door.

'James, it's you. Cancel the room, pay for one night and then join me in the cocktail bar.'

'Why? What for?'

'A bottle of Krug 1964 Privée Cuvée.'

One down and three to go.

11

JEAN-PIERRE was the last to arrive at Lord Brigsley's King's Road flat. He felt he had earned the right to make an entrance. Harvey's cheque had been cleared and the Lamanns Gallery account was for the moment $447,560 in credit. The painting was in Harvey's possession and the heavens had not yet fallen in. Jean-Pierre had cleared more money in two months of crime than he had in ten years of legitimate trading.

The other three greeted him with the acclaim normally reserved for a sporting hero, and a glass of James's last bottle of Veuve Clicquot 1959.

'We were lucky to pull it off,' said Robin.

'We weren't lucky,' said Stephen. 'We kept our nerve under pressure, and the one thing we've learned from the exercise is that Harvey can change the rules in the middle of the game.'

'He almost changed the game, Stephen.'

'Agreed. So we must always remember that we shall fail unless we can be as successful, not once, but four times. We must not underestimate our opponent just because we've won the first round.'

'Relax, Professor,' said James. 'We can get down

to business again after dinner. Anne came in this afternoon especially to make the salmon mousse, and it won't go down well with Harvey Metcalfe.'

'When am I going to meet this fabulous creature?' asked Jean-Pierre.

'When this is all over and behind us.'

'Don't marry her, James. She's only after our money.'

They all laughed. James hoped the day would come when he could tell them she had known all along. He produced the *boeuf en croûte* and two bottles of Echezeaux 1970. Jean-Pierre sniffed the sauce appreciatively.

'On second thoughts she ought to be seriously considered if her touch in bed is half as deft as it is in the kitchen.'

'You're not going to get the chance to be the judge of that, Jean-Pierre. Content yourself with admiring her French dressing.'

'You were quite outstanding this morning, James,' said Stephen, steering the conversation away from Jean-Pierre's pet subject. 'You should go on the stage. As a member of the British aristocracy, your talent's simply wasted.'

'I've always wanted to, but my old pa is against it. Those who live in expectation of a large inheritance must expect to have to toe the filial line.'

'Why don't we let him play all four parts in Monte Carlo?' suggested Robin.

The mention of Monte Carlo sobered them up.

'Back to work,' said Stephen. 'We have so far received $447,560. Expenses with the picture and an unexpected night at the Dorchester were $11,142 so Metcalfe still owes us $563,582. Think of what we've still lost, not of what we've gained. Now for the Monte Carlo operation, which depends upon split-second timing and our ability to sustain our roles for several hours. Robin will bring us up to date.'

Robin retrieved the green dossier from the brief-case by his side and studied his notes for a few moments.

'Jean-Pierre, you must grow a beard, starting today, so that in three weeks' time you'll be unrecognisable. You must also cut your hair very short.' Robin grinned unsympathetically at Jean-Pierre's grimace. 'Yes, you'll look absolutely revolting.'

'That,' said Jean-Pierre; 'will not be possible.'

'How are the baccarat and blackjack coming on?' continued Robin.

'I have lost $37 in five weeks, which includes my member's fee at the Claremont and the Golden Nugget.'

'It all goes on expenses,' said Stephen. 'That puts the bill up to $563,619.'

The others laughed. Only Stephen's lips did not move. He was in sober earnest.

'James, how is your handling of the van going?'

'I can reach Harley Street from St Thomas's in 14 minutes. I should be able to do the actual run in Monte Carlo in about 11 minutes, though naturally

I shall want to do some practice runs the day before. To start with I'll have to master driving on the wrong side of the road.'

'Strange how everybody except the British drives on the wrong side of the road,' observed Jean-Pierre.

James ignored him.

'I'm not sure of all the continental road signs either.'

'They are detailed in the Michelin guide that I gave you as part of my dossier.'

'I know, but I'll still feel easier when I've experienced the actual run and not just studied maps. There are quite a few one-way streets in Monaco and I don't want to be stopped going down the wrong one with Harvey Metcalfe unconscious in the back.'

'Don't worry. You'll have ample time when we're there. So, that only leaves Stephen, who's about the most competent medical student I've ever had. You're confident of your newly acquired knowledge, I hope?'

'About as confident as I am with your American accent, Robin. Anyway, I trust that Harvey Metcalfe will be in no state of mind to worry about such trivialities by the time we meet up.'

'Don't worry, Stephen. Believe me, he wouldn't even register who you were if you introduced yourself as Herr Drosser with a Van Gogh under both arms.'

Robin handed round the final schedule of rehearsals for Harley Street and St Thomas's, and once again consulted the green file.

'I've booked four single rooms on different floors

at the Hôtel de Paris and confirmed all the arrangements with the Centre Hospitalier Princesse Grace. The hotel is reputed to be one of the best in the world – it's certainly expensive enough – but it's convenient for the Casino. We fly to Nice on Monday, the day Harvey is due to arrive on his yacht.'

'What do we do for the rest of the week?' enquired James innocently.

Stephen resumed control:

'We master the green dossier backwards, frontwards and sideways for a full dress rehearsal on Friday. The most important thing for you, James, is to get a grip of yourself and let us know what you intend to do.'

James sank back into gloom.

Stephen closed his file briskly.

'That seems to be all we can cover tonight.'

'Hang on, Stephen,' said Robin. 'Let's strip you off once more. I'd like to see if we can do it in 90 seconds.'

Stephen lay down slightly reluctantly in the middle of the room, and James and Jean-Pierre swiftly and carefully removed all his clothes.

'Eighty-seven seconds. Excellent,' said Robin, looking down at Stephen, naked except for his watch. 'Hell, look at the time. I must get back to Newbury. My wife will think I have a mistress and I don't fancy any of you.'

Stephen dressed himself quickly while the others prepared to leave. A few minutes later, James stood by the front door, watching them depart one by one. As soon as Stephen was out of sight, he bounded downstairs into the kitchen.

'Did you listen?'

'Yes, darling. They're all rather nice and I don't blame them for being cross with you. They're being very professional about the whole venture, while you sounded like the only amateur. We'll have to think up something good for you to match them. We've over a week before Mr Metcalfe goes to Monte Carlo and we must use the time constructively.'

James sighed: 'Well, let's enjoy tonight. At least this morning was a triumph.'

'Yes, but not yours. Tomorrow we work.'

12

'PASSENGERS FOR flight 017 to Nice are now requested to board the aircraft at gate No. 7,' boomed the loudspeaker at Heathrow's No. 1 terminal.

'That's us,' said Stephen.

The four of them took the escalator to the first floor, and walked down the long corridor. After being searched for guns, bombs, and whatever else terrorists are searched for, they proceeded down the ramp.

They sat separately, never speaking or even looking at each other. Stephen had warned them that the flight could well be sprinkled with Harvey's friends, and each imagined himself to be sitting next to the closest of them.

James gazed moodily at the cloudless sky and brooded. He and Anne had read every book they could lay their hands on that even hinted at stolen money or successful duplicity, but they had found nothing they could plagiarise. Even Stephen, in between being undressed and practised upon at St Thomas's, was becoming daunted by the task of finding a winning plan for James.

The Trident touched down at Nice at 13.40, and

the train journey from Nice to Monte Carlo took them a further twenty minutes. Each member of the team made his own way to the elegant Hôtel de Paris in the Place du Casino. At 7 pm they were all present in room 217.

'All settled into your rooms?'

The other three nodded. 'So far, so good,' said Robin. 'Right, let's go over the timing. Jean-Pierre, you will go to the Casino tonight and play a few hands of baccarat and blackjack. Try to acclimatise to the place and learn your way around. In particular, master any variations in the rules there might be from the Claremont, and be sure you never speak in English. Do you foresee any problems?'

'No, can't say I do, Robin. In fact I may as well go now and start rehearsing.'

'Don't lose too much of our money,' said Stephen.

Jean-Pierre, resplendent in beard and dinner-jacket, grinned and slipped out of room 217 and down the staircase, avoiding the lift. He walked the short distance from the hotel to the famous Casino.

Robin continued:

'James, you take a taxi from the Casino to the hospital. On arrival you will leave the meter running for a few minutes and then return to the Casino. You can normally rely on a taxi to take the shortest route, but to be sure, tell the driver it's an emergency. That'll give you the opportunity of seeing which traffic lanes he uses under pressure. When he's returned you to the Casino, walk the route from there to the hospital and back. Then you can assimilate it in your own time. After you've mastered that, repeat the same procedure for the route between the hospital and Harvey's yacht. Never enter the Casino or even get close enough to the boat to be seen. Being seen now means being recognised later.'

'What about my knowledge of the Casino on the night of the operation?'

'Jean-Pierre will take care of that. He'll meet you at the door because Stephen won't be able to leave Harvey. I don't think they will charge you the 12 franc entrance fee if you're wearing a white coat and carrying a stretcher, but have it ready to be sure. When you've completed the walk, go to your room and stay there until our meeting at 11 am tomorrow. Stephen and I will also be going to the hospital to check that all the arrangements have been carried out as cabled from London. If at any time you see us, ignore us.'

As James left room 217, Jean-Pierre arrived at the Casino.

The Casino stands in the heart of Monte Carlo overlooking the sea, surrounded by the most beautiful gardens. The present building has several wings, the oldest of which was designed by Charles Garnier, the architect of the Paris Opera House. The gambling rooms, which were added in 1910, are linked by an atrium to the Salle Garnier in which operas and ballets are performed.

Jean-Pierre marched up the marble staircase to the

entrance and paid his 12 francs. The gambling rooms are vast, full of the decadence and grandeur of Europe at the turn of the century. Massive red carpets, statues, paintings and tapestries give the building an almost regal appearance and the portraits lend an air of a country home still lived in. Jean-Pierre found the clientèle were of all nationalities: Arabs and Jews played next to each other at the roulette wheel and chatted away with an ease that would have been unthinkable at the United Nations. Jean-Pierre felt totally relaxed in the unreal world of the wealthy. Robin had assessed his character accurately and given him a role he could master with aplomb.

Jean-Pierre spent over three hours studying the layout of the Casino – its gambling rooms, bars and restaurants, the telephones, the entrances and exits. Then he turned his attention to the gambling itself. He discovered that two shoes of baccarat were played in the Salons Privés at 3 pm and 11 pm, and learned from Pierre Cattalano, the head of the public relations department of the Casino, which of the private rooms Harvey Metcalfe preferred to play in.

Blackjack is played in the Salon des Amériques from 11 am daily. There are three tables, and Jean-Pierre's informant told him that Harvey always played on table No. 2, seat No. 3. Jean-Pierre played a little blackjack and baccarat, to discover any slight variations in rules there might be from the Claremont. In fact there were none, as the Claremont still adheres to French rules.

Harvey Metcalfe arrived noisily at the Casino just after 11 pm, leaving a trail of cigar ash leading to his baccarat table. Jean-Pierre, inconspicuous at the bar, watched as the head croupier first showed Harvey politely to a reserved seat, and then walked through to the Salon des Amériques to the No. 2 blackjack table and placed a discreet white card marked '*Réservé*' on one of the chairs. Harvey was clearly a favoured client. The management knew as well as Jean-Pierre which games Harvey Metcalfe played. At 11.27 pm Jean-Pierre left quietly and returned to the solitude of his hotel room where he remained until 11 am the next day. He phoned no one and did not use room service.

James's evening also went well. The taxi-driver was superb. The word 'emergency' brought out the Walter Mitty in him: he travelled through Monte Carlo as if it were nothing less than the Rally itself. When James arrived at the hospital in 8 minutes 44 seconds, he genuinely felt a little sick and had to rest for a few minutes in the Entrée des Patients before returning to the taxi.

'Back to the Casino, but much slower, please.'

The journey back along the Rue Grimaldi took just over eleven minutes and James decided he would settle for trying to cover it in about ten. He paid off the taxi-driver and carried out the second part of his instructions.

Walking to the hospital and back took just over an hour. The night air was gentle on his face, and the streets crowded with lively chattering people. Tourism is the chief source of income for the Principality, and the Monégasques take the welfare of their visitors very seriously. James passed innumerable little pavement restaurants and souvenir shops stocked with expensive trinkets of no significance that once bought would be forgotten or lost within a week. Noisy groups of holiday-makers strolled along the pavements, their multilingual babel forming a meaningless chorus to James's thoughts of Anne. On arrival back at the Casino. James then took a taxi to the harbour to locate *Messenger Boy*, Harvey's yacht, and from there once more to the hospital. He then walked the same route and, like Jean-Pierre, he was safely in his room before midnight, having completed his first task.

Robin and Stephen found the walk to the hospital from their hotel took a little over 40 minutes. On arrival Robin asked the receptionist if he could see the superintendent.

'The night superintendent is now on duty,' said a freshly starched French nurse. 'Who shall I say is asking him for?'

Her English pronunciation was excellent and they both avoided a smile at her slight mistake.

'Doctor Wiley Barker of the University of California.'

Robin began to pray that the French superintendent would not happen to know that Wiley Barker, President Nixon's physician and one of the most respected surgeons in the world, was actually touring

Australia at the time lecturing to the major universities.

'*Bonsoir, Docteur Barker. Monsieur Bartise à votre service. Votre visite fait grand honneur à notre hôpital humble.*'

Robin's newly acquired American accent stopped any further conversation in French.

'I would like to check the layout of the theatre,' said Robin, 'and confirm that we have it provisionally booked for tomorrow from 11 pm to 4 am for the next five days.'

'That is quite correct, *Docteur Barker*,' said the superintendent, looking down at a clip-board. 'The theatre is off the next corridor. Will you follow me, please?'

The theatre was not dissimilar to the one the four of them had been practising in at St Thomas's – two rooms with a rubber swing door dividing them. The main theatre was well equipped and a nod from Robin showed Stephen that it had all the instruments he required. Robin was impressed. Although the hospital had only some 200 beds, the theatre itself was of the highest standard. Rich men had obviously been ill there before.

'Will you be requiring an anaesthetist or any nurses to assist you, *Docteur Barker*?'

'No,' said Robin. 'I have my own anaesthetist and staff but I will require a tray of laparotomy instruments to be laid out every night. However, I will be able to give you at least an hour's warning before you need make any final preparations.'

'That's plenty of time. Will there be anything else, sir?'

'Yes, the special vehicle I ordered. Can it be ready for my driver at 12 pm tomorrow?'

'Yes, *Docteur Barker*. It will be in the small car park behind the hospital and your driver can pick up the keys from the reception.'

'Can you recommend an agency from which I can hire an experienced nurse for post-operative care?'

'*Bien sûr*, the Auxiliaire Médical of Nice will be only too happy to oblige – at a certain price, of course.'

'Of course,' said Robin. 'And that reminds me to ask, have all your expenses been dealt with?'

'Yes, *Docteur*. We received a cheque from California last Thursday for $7,000.'

Robin had been very pleased with that touch. It had been so simple. Stephen had contacted his bank at Harvard and asked them to send a draft from the First National City Bank in San Francisco to the hospital secretary at Monte Carlo.

'Thank you all for your help, Monsieur Bartise. You have been most obliging. Now you do understand that I am not quite sure which night I shall be bringing my patient in. He's a sick man, although he doesn't know it, and I have to prepare him for the operation.'

'Of course, *mon cher Docteur*.'

'Finally, I would appreciate it if you would tell as few people as possible that I am in Monte Carlo. I am trying to snatch a holiday at the same time as working.'

'I understand, Docteur Barker. You can be assured of my discretion.'

Robin and Stephen bade farewell to Monsieur Bartise and took a taxi back to the hotel.

'I'm always slightly humiliated by how well the French speak our language compared with our grasp of theirs,' said Stephen.

'It's all the fault of you bloody Americans,' said Robin.

'No, it isn't. If France had conquered America, your French would be excellent. Blame it on the Pilgrim Fathers.'

Robin laughed. Neither of them spoke again until they reached room 217 for fear of being overheard. Stephen had no doubts about the responsibility and risk they were taking with Robin's plan.

Harvey Metcalfe was on the deck of his yacht, sunbathing and reading the morning papers. *Nice-Matin*, irritatingly enough, was in French. He read it laboriously, with the aid of a dictionary, to see if there were any social events to which he ought to get himself invited. He had gambled late into the night, and was enjoying the sun's rays on his fleshy back. If money could have obtained it, he would have been 6 ft and 170 lb with a handsome head of hair, but no amount of suntan oil would stop his balding dome from burning, so he covered it with a cap inscribed with the words 'I'm sexy'. If Miss Fish could see him now . . .

At 11 am, as Harvey turned over and allowed the sun to see his massive stomach, James strolled into room 217 where the rest of the Team were waiting for him.

Jean-Pierre reported on the layout of the Casino and Harvey Metcalfe's habits. James brought them up to date on the result of his race through the city the night before and confirmed that he thought he could cover the distance in just under eleven minutes.

'Perfect,' said Robin. 'Stephen and I took 15 minutes by taxi from the hospital to the hotel so if Jean-Pierre warns me immediately the balloon goes up in the Casino, I should have enough time to see that everything is ready before you all arrive.'

'I do hope the balloon will be going down, not up, in the Casino,' remarked Jean-Pierre.

'I have booked an agency nurse to be on call from tomorrow night. The hospital has all the facilities I require. It'll take about two minutes to walk a stretcher from the front door to the theatre, so from the moment James leaves the car park I should have at least 16 minutes to prepare myself. James, you'll be able to pick up the vehicle from the hospital car park at 12 pm. The keys have been left in reception in the name of Dr Barker. Do a couple of practice runs and no more. I don't want you causing interest by looking conspicuous. And could you leave this parcel in the back, please.'

'What is it?'

'Three long white laboratory coats and a stethoscope for Stephen. While you're at it, better check that you can unfold the stretcher easily. When you've finished the two runs, put the vehicle back in the car park and return to your room until 11 pm. From then through to 4 am you'll have to wait in the car park until you get the "action stations" or "all clear" signal from Jean-Pierre. Everybody buy new batteries for your transmitters. I don't want the whole plan to collapse for the sake of a ten-penny battery. I'm afraid there's nothing much for you to do, Jean-Pierre until this evening, except relax. I hope you have some good books in your room.'

'Can't I go to the Princess Cinema and see François Truffaut's *La Nuit Américaine*? I just adore Jacqueline Bisset. *Vive la France*.'

'My dear Jean-Pierre, Miss Bisset's from Reading,' said James.

'I don't care. I still want to see her.'

'A frog he would a-wooing go,' said James mockingly.

'But why not?' said Robin. 'The last thing Harvey will do is take in an intellectual French film with no sub-titles. Hope you enjoy it – and good luck tonight, Jean-Pierre.'

Jean-Pierre left for his room as quietly as he had come, leaving the rest of them together in room 217.

'Right, James. You can do your practice runs any time that suits you. Just make sure you're wide awake tonight.'

'Fine. I'll go and pick up the keys from the hospital reception. Let's just hope nobody stops me for a real emergency.'

'Now, Stephen, let's go over the details again. There's more than money to lose if we get this wrong. We'll start from the top. What do you do if the nitrous oxide falls below five litres . . .'

'Station check – station check – operation Metcalfe. This is Jean-Pierre. I am on the steps of the Casino. Can you hear me, James?'

'Yes. I am in the car park of the hospital. Out.'

'Robin here. I am on the balcony of room 217. Is Stephen with you, Jean-Pierre?'

'Yes. He's drinking on his own at the bar.'

'Good luck and out.'

Jean-Pierre carried out a station check every hour on the hour from 7 pm until 11 pm, merely to inform Robin and James that Harvey had not arrived.

Eventually, at 11.16, he did show up, and took his reserved place at the baccarat table. Stephen stopped sipping his tomato juice and Jean-Pierre moved over and waited patiently by the table for one of the men seated on the left or right of Harvey to leave. An hour passed by. Harvey was losing a little, but continued to play. So did the tall thin American on his right and the Frenchman on his left. Another hour and still no movement. Then suddenly the Frenchman on the left of Metcalfe had a particularly bad run, gathered his few remaining chips and left the table. Jean-Pierre moved forward.

'I am afraid, Monsieur, that that seat is reserved for another gentleman,' said the banker. 'We do have an unreserved place on the other side of the table.'

'It's not important,' said Jean-Pierre, who backed away, not wanting to be remembered, cursing the deference with which the Monégasques treat the wealthy. Stephen could see from the bar what had happened and made furtive signs to leave. They were all back in room 217 just after 2 am.

'What a bloody silly mistake. *Merde, merde, merde.* I should have thought of reservations the moment I knew Harvey had one.'

'No, it was my fault. I don't know anything about how casinos work and I should have queried it during rehearsals,' said Robin, stroking his newly acquired moustache.

'No one is to blame,' chipped in Stephen. 'We still have three more nights, so no need to panic. We'll just have to work out how to overcome the seating problem, but for now we'll all get some sleep and meet again in this room at 10 am.'

They left, a little depressed. Robin had sat waiting in the hotel on edge for four hours. James was cold and bored in the hospital car park, Stephen was sick of tomato juice and Jean-Pierre had been on his feet by the baccarat table waiting for a seat that wasn't even available.

Once again Harvey lounged in the sun. He was now a light pink and was hoping to be a better colour towards the end of the week. According to his copy of the *New York Times*, gold was still climbing and the Deutschmark and the Swiss franc remained firm, while the dollar was on the retreat against every currency except sterling. Sterling stood at $2.42. Harvey thought a more realistic price was $1.80 and the sooner it reached that the better.

Nothing new, he thought, when the sharp ring of a French telephone roused him. He never could get used to the sound of foreign telephones. The attentive steward bustled out on deck with the instrument on an extension lead.

'Hi, Lloyd. Didn't know you were in Monte . . . why don't we get together? . . . 8 pm? . . . Me too . . . I'm even getting brown . . . Must be getting old . . . What? . . . Great, I'll see you then.'

Harvey replaced the receiver and asked the steward for a large whisky on the rocks. He once again settled down happily to the morning's financial bad news.

'That seems to be the obvious solution,' said Stephen.

They all nodded their approval.

'Jean-Pierre will give up the baccarat table and book a place next to Harvey Metcalfe on his black-jack table in the Salon des Amériques and wait for him to change games. We know both the seat numbers Harvey plays at and we'll alter our own plans accordingly.'

Jean-Pierre dialled the number of the Casino and asked to speak to Pierre Cattalano:

'*Réservez-moi la deuxième place à la table 2 pour le vingt-et-un ce soir et demain soir, s'il vous plaît.*'

'*Je pense que cette place est déjà réservée, Monsieur. Un instant, s'il vous plaît, je vais vérifier.*'

'*Peut-être que 100 francs la rendra libre,*' replied Jean-Pierre.

'*Mais certainement, Monsieur. Présentez-vous à moi dès votre arrivée, et le nécessaire sera fait.*'

'*Merci,*' said Jean-Pierre and replaced the receiver. 'That's under control.'

Jean-Pierre was visibly sweating, though had his call had no other outcome than to secure him a reserved seat, not a drop of perspiration would have appeared. They all returned to their rooms.

When the clock in the town square struck twelve, Robin was waiting quietly in room 217, James stood in the car park humming 'I Get Along Without You Very Well', Stephen was at the bar of the Salon des Amériques toying with yet another tomato juice and Jean-Pierre was at seat No. 2 on table No. 2, playing blackjack. Both Stephen and Jean-Pierre saw Harvey come through the door, chatting to a man in a loud-checked jacket which only a Texan could have worn outside his own back yard. Harvey and his friend sat down together at the baccarat table. Jean-Pierre beat a hasty retreat to the bar.

'Oh, no. I give up.'

'No, you don't,' whispered Stephen. 'Back to the hotel.'

Spirits were very low when they were all assembled in room 217, but it was agreed that Stephen had made the right decision. They could not risk the entire exercise being carefully observed by a friend of Harvey's.

'The first operation is beginning to look a bit too good to be true,' said Robin.

'Don't be silly,' said Stephen. 'We had two false alarms then, and the entire plan had to be changed at the last minute. We can't expect him just to walk in and hand over his money. Now snap out of it, all of you, and go and get some sleep.'

They returned to their separate rooms, but not to much sleep. The strain was beginning to tell.

'That's enough I think, Lloyd. A goodish evening.'

'For you, you mean, Harvey, not for me. You are one of nature's winners.'

Harvey patted the checked shoulder expansively. If anything pleased him more than his own success, it was other people's failure.

'Do you want to spend the night on my yacht, Lloyd?'

'No thanks. I must get back to Nice. I have a meeting in Paris, France, tomorrow lunch. See you soon, Harvey – take care of yourself.' He dug Harvey in the ribs jocularly. 'That's a fair-sized job.'

'Goodnight, Lloyd,' said Harvey, a little stiffly.

The next evening Jean-Pierre did not arrive at the Casino until 11 pm. Harvey Metcalfe was already at the baccarat table minus Lloyd. Stephen was at the bar looking angry, and Jean-Pierre glanced at him apologetically as he took his seat at the blackjack table. He played a few hands to get the feel, trying to keep his losses fairly limited without drawing attention to the modesty of his stakes. Suddenly Harvey left the baccarat table and stalked into the Salon des Amériques, glancing at the roulette tables as he passed more out of curiosity than interest. He detested games of pure chance, and considered baccarat and blackjack games of skill. He headed to table No. 2 seat No. 3, on Jean-Pierre's left. Jean-Pierre felt his adrenalin start pumping round and his heart-beat rise up to 120 again. Stephen left the Casino for a few minutes to warn James and Robin that Harvey had moved to the blackjack table and was now sitting next to Jean-Pierre. He then returned to the bar and waited.

There were seven punters at the blackjack table. On box No. 1, a middle-aged lady smothered in diamonds, who looked as if she might be passing time while her husband played roulette or perhaps baccarat. On box No. 2, Jean-Pierre. On Box No. 3, Harvey. On Box No. 4, a dissipated young man with the world-weariness that usually goes with a large unearned income. On box No. 5, an Arab in full robes. On box No. 6, a not-unattractive actress who was clearly resting, Jean-Pierre suspected, with the occupant of box No. 5; and on box No. 7, an elderly straight-backed aristocratic Frenchman in evening dress.

'A large black coffee,' Harvey drawled to the slim waiter in his smart brown jacket.

Monte Carlo does not allow hard liquor to be sold at the tables or girls to serve the customers. In direct contrast to Las Vegas, the Casino's business is gambling, not booze or women. Harvey had enjoyed Vegas when he was younger, but the older he became the more he appreciated the sophistication of the French. He had grown to prefer the formal atmosphere and decorum of this particular Casino. Although at the No. 3 table only he, the aristocratic Frenchman and Jean-Pierre wore dinner-jackets, it was frowned upon by the management to be dressed in any way that might be described as casual.

A moment later, piping hot coffee in a large golden cup arrived at Harvey's side. Jean-Pierre eyed it nervously while Harvey placed 100 francs on the table next to Jean-Pierre's 3-franc chip, the minimum and maximum stake allowed. The dealer, a tall young man of not more than thirty, who was proud of the fact that he could deal a hundred hands in an hour, slipped the cards deftly out of the shoe. A king for Jean-Pierre, a four for Harvey, a five for the young man on Harvey's left and a six for the dealer. Jean-Pierre's second card was a seven. He stuck. Harvey drew a ten and also stuck. The young man on Harvey's left also drew ten and asked the dealer to twist again. It was an eight – bust.

Harvey despised amateurs in any field and even fools know you don't twist if you have twelve or more when the dealer's card face up is a three, four, five or six. He grimaced slightly. The dealer dealt himself a ten and a six. Harvey and Jean-Pierre were winners. Jean-Pierre ignored the fate of the other players.

The next round was unwinnable. Jean-Pierre stuck at eighteen, two nines which he chose not to split as the dealer had an ace. Harvey stuck on eighteen, an eight and a jack, and the young man on the left bust again. The bank drew a queen – 'Black Jack' – and took the table.

The next hand gave Jean-Pierre a three, Harvey a seven and the young man a ten. The dealer drew himself a seven. Jean-Pierre drew an eight and doubled his stake to 6 francs and then drew a ten – vingt-et-un. Jean-Pierre did not blink. He realised he was playing well and that he must not draw attention to himself, but let Harvey take it for granted. In fact Harvey hadn't even noticed him: his attention was riveted on the young man on his left, who seemed anxious to make a gift to the management on every hand. The dealer continued, giving Harvey a ten and the young man an eight, leaving them both no choice but to stick. The dealer drew a ten, giving himself seventeen. He paid Jean-Pierre, left Harvey's stake and paid the young man. The management was happy to pay the young man occasionally, if only to keep him sitting there all night.

There were no more cards left in the shoe. The dealer made a great show of re-shuffling the four packs and invited Harvey to cut the cards before replacing them in the shoe. They slipped out again: a ten for Jean-Pierre, a five for Harvey, a six for the young man and a four for the dealer. Jean-Pierre drew an eight. The cards were running well. Harvey drew a ten and stuck at fifteen. The young man drew a ten and asked for another card. Harvey could not believe his eyes and whistled through the gap in his front teeth. Sure enough, the next card was a king. The young man was bust. The dealer dealt himself a jack and then an eight, making twenty-two, but the young man had learned nothing from it. Harvey stared at him. When would he discover that, of the fifty-two cards in the pack, no less than sixteen have a face value of ten?

Harvey's distraction gave Jean-Pierre the opportunity he had been waiting for. He slipped his hand into his pocket and took the prostigmin tablet Robin had given him into the palm of his left hand. He sneezed, pulling his handkerchief from his breast pocket in a well-rehearsed gesture with his right hand. At the same time, he quickly and unobtrusively dropped the tablet into Harvey's coffee. It would, Robin had assured him, be an hour before it took effect. To begin with Harvey would only feel a little sick; then he would get rapidly worse until the pain was too much to bear, before finally collapsing in absolute agony.

Jean-Pierre turned to the bar, gripped his right-hand fist three times and then placed it in his pocket. Stephen left immediately and warned Robin and James from the steps of the Casino that the prostigmin tablet was in Metcalfe's drink. It was now Robin's turn to be tested under pressure. First he rang the hospital and asked the sister on duty to have the theatre in full preparation. Then he rang the nursing agency and asked for the nurse he had booked to be waiting in the hospital reception in exactly ninety minutes' time. He sat alone, nervously waiting for another call from the Casino.

Stephen returned to the bar. Harvey had started to feel a little sick, but was loath to leave. Despite the growing pain, his greed was forcing him to play on. He drank the rest of this coffee and ordered another one, hoping it would clear his head. The coffee did not help and Harvey began to feel steadily worse. An ace and a king followed by a seven, a four and a ten, and then two queens helped him to stay at the table. Jean-Pierre forced himself not to look at his watch. The dealer gave Jean-Pierre a seven, Harvey another ace and the young man a two. Quite suddenly, almost exactly on the hour, Harvey could bear the pain no longer. He tried to stand up to leave the table.

'*Le jeu a commencé, Monsieur*,' the dealer said formally.

'Go stuff yourself,' said Harvey and collapsed to the ground, gripping his stomach in agony. Jean-Pierre sat motionless while the croupiers and gamblers milled around helplessly. Stephen fought his way through the circle which had gathered round Harvey.

'Stand back, please. I am a doctor.'

The crowd moved back quickly, relieved to have a professional man on the scene.

'What is it, Doctor?' gasped Harvey, who felt the end of the world was about to come.

'I don't know yet,' replied Stephen. Robin had warned him that from collapse to passing out might be as short a time as ten minutes, so he set to work fast. He loosened Harvey's tie and took his pulse. He then undid his shirt and started feeling his abdomen.

'Have you a pain in the stomach?'

'Yes,' groaned Harvey.

'Did it come on suddenly?'

'Yes.'

'Can you try and describe the quality of the pain? Is it stabbing, burning or gripping?'

'Gripping.'

'Where is it most painful?'

Harvey touched the right side of his stomach. Stephen pressed down the tip of the ninth rib, making Harvey bellow with pain.

'Ah,' said Stephen, 'a positive Murphy's sign. You probably have an acutely inflamed gall-bladder. I'm afraid that may mean gallstones.' He continued to palpate the massive abdomen, gently. 'It looks as if a stone has come out of your gall-bladder and is passing down the tube to your intestine – it's the squeezing of that tube that's giving you such a dreadful pain. I'm afraid your gall-bladder and the stone must be removed at once. I can only hope there is someone at the hospital who can perform an emergency operation.'

Jean-Pierre came in bang on cue:

'Doctor Wiley Barker is staying at my hotel.'

'Wiley Barker, the American surgeon?'

'Yes, yes,' said Jean-Pierre. 'The chap who's been taking care of Nixon.'

'My God, what a piece of luck. We couldn't have

anyone better, but he might turn out to be very expensive.'

'I don't give a damn about expense,' wailed Harvey.

'Well, it might be as high as $50,000.'

'I don't care if it's $100,000,' screamed Harvey. At that moment he would have been willing to part with his entire fortune.

'Right,' said Stephen. 'You, sir,' looking at Jean-Pierre, 'ring for an ambulance and then contact Doctor Barker and ask if he can get to the hospital immediately. Tell him it's an emergency. This gentleman requires a surgeon of the highest qualifications.'

'You're damn right I do,' said Harvey, and passed out.

Jean-Pierre left the Casino and called over his transmitter:

'Action stations. Action stations.'

Robin left the Hôtel de Paris and took a taxi. He would have given $100,000 to change places with the driver, but the car was already moving relentlessly towards the hospital. It was too late to turn back now.

James smashed the ambulance into first gear and rushed to the Casino, siren blaring. He was luckier than Robin. With so much to concentrate on he didn't have time to consider the consequences of what he was doing.

Eleven minutes and forty-one seconds later he arrived, leapt out of the driver's seat, opened the back door, gathered the stretcher and rushed up the Casino steps in his long white coat. Jean-Pierre was standing expectantly on the top step waiting for him. No words passed between them as he guided James quickly through the Salon des Amériques where Stephen was bending over Harvey. The stretcher was placed on the floor. It took all three of them to lift Harvey Metcalfe's 227 lb on to the canvas. Stephen and James picked up the stretcher and took him quickly through to the waiting ambulance, followed by Jean-Pierre.

'Where are you going with my boss?' demanded a voice.

Startled, the three of them turned round. It was Harvey Metcalfe's chauffeur, standing by the white Rolls Royce. After a moment's hesitation, Jean-Pierre took over.

'Mr Metcalfe has collapsed and has to go to hospital for an emergency operation. You must return to the yacht immediately, tell the staff to have his cabin ready and await further instructions.'

The chauffeur touched his cap and ran to the Rolls Royce. James leapt behind the wheel, while Stephen and Jean-Pierre joined Harvey in the back of the vehicle.

'Hell, that was close. Well done, Jean-Pierre. I was speechless,' admitted Stephen.

'It was nothing,' said Jean-Pierre, sweat pouring down his face.

The ambulance shot off like a scalded cat. Stephen and Jean-Pierre both replaced their jackets with the long white laboratory coats left on the seat and Stephen put the stethoscope round his neck.

'It looks to me as if he's dead,' said Jean-Pierre.

'Robin says he isn't,' said Stephen.

'How can he tell from four miles away?'

'I don't know. We'll just have to take his word for it.'

James screeched to a halt outside the entrance to the hospital. Stephen and Jean-Pierre hurried their patient through to the operating theatre. James returned the ambulance to the car park and quickly joined the others in the theatre.

Robin, scrubbed up and gowned, was there to meet them at the door and while they were strapping Harvey Metcalfe to the operating table in the small room next to the theatre, he spoke for the first time:

'All of you, change your clothes. And Jean-Pierre, you scrub up as instructed.'

All three of them changed and Jean-Pierre started to wash immediately – a long, laborious process which Robin had firmly taught him must never be cut short. Post-operative septicaemia formed no part of his plan. Jean-Pierre appeared from the scrubbing-up room ready for action.

'Now, relax. We've done this nine times already. Just carry on exactly as if we were still in St Thomas's.'

Stephen moved behind the mobile Boyles machine. For four weeks he had been training as an anaesthetist: he had rendered James and a faintly protesting Jean-Pierre unconscious twice each in practice runs at St Thomas's. Now was his chance to exercise his new powers over Harvey Metcalfe.

Robin removed a syringe from a plastic packet and injected 250 mg of thiopentone into Harvey's arm. The patient sank back into a deep sleep. Quickly and efficiently Jean-Pierre and James undressed Harvey and then covered him in a sheet. Stephen placed the mask from the Boyles machine over Metcalfe's nose. The two flow-meters on the back of the machine showed 5 litres of nitrous oxide and 3 litres of oxygen.

'Take his pulse,' said Robin.

Stephen placed a finger in front of the ear just above the lobe to check the pre-auricular pulse. It was 70.

'Wheel him through into the theatre,' instructed Robin.

James pushed the trolley into the next room until it was just under the operating lights. Stephen trundled the Boyles machine along behind them.

The operating theatre was windowless and coldly sterile. Gleaming white tiles covered every wall from floor to ceiling, and it contained only the equipment needed for one operation. Jean-Pierre had covered Harvey with a sterile green sheet, leaving only his head and left arm exposed. One trolley of sterile instruments, drapes and towels had been carefully laid out by the theatre nurse, and stood covered with a sterile sheet. Robin hung the bottle of intravenous fluid from a standard near the head of the table and taped the end of the tubing to Harvey's left arm to complete the preparation. Stephen sat at the head of the table with the Boyles machine and adjusted the face-mask over Harvey's mouth and nose. Only one of the three massive operating lights hanging directly over Harvey had been turned on, causing a spotlight effect on the protruding bulge of his abdomen.

Eight eyes stared down on their victim. Robin continued:

'I shall give exactly the same instructions as I did in all our rehearsals, so just concentrate. First, I shall clean the abdomen with a skin preparation of iodine.'

Robin had all the instruments ready on the side of the table next to Harvey's feet. James lifted the sheet and folded it back over Harvey's legs, then he carefully removed the sterile sheet covering the trolley of instruments and poured iodine into one of the small basins. Robin picked up a swab in a pair of forceps and dipped it in the iodine solution. With a swift action up, down, and over the abdomen, he cleaned about 1 square foot of Harvey's massive body, throwing the swab into a bin and repeating the action with a fresh one. Next he placed a sterile towel below Harvey's chin, covering his chest, and another over his hips and thighs. A third one he placed lengthways along the left-hand side of his body and a final one along the right-hand side, leaving a 9 inch square of flabby belly exposed. He put a towel clip on each corner to secure them safely and then placed the laparotomy drapes over the prepared site. Robin was now ready.

'Scalpel.'

Jean-Pierre placed what he would have called a knife firmly in Robin's outstretched palm, as a runner might when passing a baton. James's apprehensive eyes met Jean-Pierre's across the operating table, while Stephen concentrated on Harvey's breathing. Robin hesitated only for a second and then made a 10 cm paramedian incision, reaching about 3 cm into the fat. Robin had rarely seen a larger stomach: he could probably have gone as far as 8 cm deep without reaching the muscle. Blood started flowing everywhere, which Robin stopped with diathermy. No sooner had he finished the incision and stanched the flow of blood than he began to stitch up the patient's wound with a 3/0 interrupted plain catgut for ten stitches.

'That will dissolve within a week,' he explained.

He then closed the skin with a 2/0 interrupted plain silk, using an atraumatic needle. Then he cleaned the wound, removing the patches of blood that still remained. Finally, he placed a medium self-adhesive wound dressing over his handiwork.

James took off the drapes and sterile towels and placed them in the bin while Robin and Jean-Pierre put Metcalfe into a hospital gown and carefully packed his clothes in a grey plastic bag.

'He's coming round,' said Stephen.

Robin took another syringe and injected 10 mg of diazepam.

'That will keep him asleep for at least 30 minutes,' he said, 'and in any case, he'll be ga-ga for about three hours and won't remember much of what has happened. James, fetch the ambulance immediately and bring it round to the front of the hospital.'

James left the theatre and changed back into his clothes, a procedure which he could now perform in 90 seconds. He disappeared to the car park.

'Now, you two, get changed and then place Harvey very carefully in the ambulance and Jean-Pierre, wait in the back with him. Stephen, you carry out your next assignment.'

Stephen and Jean-Pierre changed quickly, back into their long white coats and wheeled the slumbering Harvey Metcalfe gently towards the ambulance. Once safely in, Stephen ran to the public telephone by the hospital entrance, checked a piece of paper in his wallet and dialled.

'Hello, *Nice-Matin*? My name's Terry Robards of the *New York Times*. I'm here on holiday, and I have a great little story for you . . .'

Robin returned to the operating theatre and wheeled the trolley of instruments he had used to the sterilising room, and left them there to be dealt with by the hospital theatre staff in the morning. He picked up the plastic bag containing Harvey's clothes and, going through to the changing room, quickly removed his operating gown, cap and mask and put on his own clothes. He went in search of the theatre sister, and smiled charmingly at her.

'All finished, *ma soeur*. I have left the instruments by the steriliser. Please thank Monsieur Bartise for me once again.'

'*Oui, Monsieur. Notre plaisir. Je suis heureuse d'être à même de vous aider. Votre infirmière de l'Auxiliaire Médicale est arrivée.*'

A few moments later, Robin walked to the ambulance, accompanied by the agency nurse. He helped her into the back.

'Drive very slowly and carefully to the harbour.'

James nodded and set off at funeral pace.

'Nurse Faubert.'

'Yes, Docteur Barker.' Her hands were tucked primly under her blue cape, and her French accent was enchanting. Robin thought Harvey would not find her ministrations unwelcome.

'My patient has just had an operation for the removal of a gall stone and will need plenty of rest.'

With that Robin took out of his pocket a gall stone the size of an orange with a hospital tag on it which read 'Harvey Metcalfe'. Robin had in fact acquired the huge stone from St Thomas's Hospital, the original owner being a 6 ft 6 in West Indian bus conductor on the No. 14 route. Stephen and Jean-Pierre stared at it in disbelief. The nurse checked her new charge's pulse and respiration.

'If I were your patient, Nurse Faubert,' said Jean-Pierre, 'I should take good care never to recover.'

By the time they arrived at the yacht, Robin had briefed the nurse on diet and rest, and told her that he would be round to see his patient at 11 am the next day. They left Harvey sleeping soundly in his large cabin, stewards and staff clucking attentively.

James drove the other three back to the hospital, deposited the ambulance in the car park and left the keys with reception. The four of them then headed back to the hotel by separate routes. Robin was the last to arrive at room 217, just after 3.30 am. He collapsed into an armchair.

'Will you allow me a whisky, Stephen?'

'Yes, of course.'

'Good God, he meant it,' said Robin, and downed a large Johnny Walker before handing the bottle over to Jean-Pierre.

'He will be all right, won't he?' said James.

'You sound quite concerned for him. Yes, he can have his ten stitches out in a week's time and all he'll have is a nasty scar to brag about to his friends. I must get some sleep. I have to see our victim at 11 tomorrow morning and the confrontation may well be harder than the operation. You were all great tonight. My God, am I glad we had all those sessions at St Thomas's. If you're ever out of work and I need a croupier, a driver and an anaesthetist, I'll know who to ring.'

The others left and Robin collapsed on to his bed, exhausted. He fell into a deep sleep and woke just after 8 the next morning, to discover he was still fully dressed. That had not happened to him since his days as a young houseman, when he had been on night duty after a fourteen-hour day without a break. Robin had a long soothing bath in very hot water. He dressed and put on a clean shirt and suit, ready for his face-to-face meeting with Harvey Metcalfe. His newly acquired moustache and rimless glasses and the success of the operation made him feel a little like the famous surgeon he was impersonating. The other three all appeared during the next hour to wish him luck and elected to wait in room 217 for his return. Stephen had checked them all out of the hotel and booked a flight to London for late that afternoon. Robin left, again taking the staircase rather than the lift. Once outside the hotel, he walked a little way before hailing a taxi to drive him to the harbour.

It was not hard to find the *Messenger Boy*. She was a gleaming, newly painted 100-footer lying at the east end of the harbour. She sported a massive Panamanian flag on her stern mast, which Robin assumed must be for tax purposes. He ascended the gangplank and was met by Nurse Faubert.

'*Bonjour, Docteur Barker.*'

'Good morning, Nurse. How is Mr Metcalfe?'

'He has had a very peaceful night and is having a light breakfast and making a few telephone calls. Would you like to see him now?'

'Yes, please.'

Robin entered the magnificent cabin and faced the

man he had spent eight weeks plotting and planning against. He was talking into the telephone:

'Yes, I'm fine, dear. But it was an A-1 emergency at the time. Don't worry, I'll live,' and he put the telephone down. 'Doctor Barker, I have just spoken to my wife in Massachusetts and told her that I owe you my life. Even at 5 am she seemed pleased. I understand that I had private surgery, a private ambulance and that you saved my life. Or that's what it says in *Nice-Matin*.'

There was the old picture of Harvey in Bermuda shorts on the deck of the *Messenger Boy*, familiar to Robin from his dossier. The headline read '*Millionaire s'évanouit au Casino*' over '*La Vie d'un Millionnaire Américain a été sauvée par une Opération Urgente Dramatique*!' Stephen would be pleased.

'Tell me, Doctor,' said Harvey with relish, 'was I really in danger?'

'Well, you were on the critical list, and the consequences might have been fairly serious if we hadn't removed this from your stomach.' Robin took out the inscribed gall stone from his pocket with a flourish.

Harvey's eye grew large as saucers.

'Gee, have I really been walking round with that inside me all this time? Isn't that something? I can't thank you enough. If ever I can do anything for you, Doctor, don't hesitate to call on me.' He offered Robin a grape. 'Look, you're going to see me through this thing, aren't you? I don't think the nurse fully appreciates the gravity of my case.'

Robin thought fast.

'I'm afraid I'm not free to do that, Mr Metcalfe. My holiday finishes today and I have to return to California. Nothing urgent: just a few elective surgeries and a rather heavy lecture schedule.' He shrugged deprecatingly. 'Not exactly earth-shattering but it helps me keep up a way of life I have grown accustomed to.'

Harvey sat bolt upright, tenderly holding his stomach.

'Now you listen to me, Doctor Barker. I don't give a damn about a few students. I'm a sick man and I need you here until I've fully recovered. I'll make it worth your while to stay, don't you worry. I never grudge the money where my health is concerned, and what's more if it will persuade you, I'll make the cheque out to cash. The last thing I want Uncle Sam to know is how much I'm worth.'

Robin coughed delicately, wondering how American doctors approached the ticklish subject of fees with their patients.

'The cost could be rather high if I'm not to be out of pocket by staying. It might be as much as $80,000.' Robin drew a deep breath.

Harvey didn't blink.

'Sure. You're the best. That's not a lot of money to stay alive.'

'Very well. I'll get back to my hotel and see if it's possible to rearrange my schedule for you.'

Robin retreated from the sick-room and the white

Rolls Royce took him back to the hotel. In room 217 they all sat staring at Robin in disbelief as he completed his story.

'Stephen, for Christ's sake, the man's a raving hypochondriac. He wants me to stay on here while he convalesces. None of us planned for that.'

Stephen looked up coolly:

'You'll stay here and play ball. Why not give him value for money – at his own expense, of course. Go on, get on the blower and tell him you'll be round to hold his hand every day at 11 am. We'll just have to go back without you. And keep the hotel bill down, won't you?'

Robin picked up the telephone . . .

Three young men left the Hôtel de Paris after a long lunch in room 217, allowing themselves another bottle of Krug '64, and then returned to Nice Airport in a taxi, catching BA flight 012 at 16.10 to London Heathrow. They were once again in separate seats. One sentence remained on Stephen's mind from Robin's reported conversation with Harvey Metcalfe.

'If ever I can do anything for you, don't hesitate to call me at any time.'

Robin visited his patient once a day, borne in the white Corniche with white-walled tyres and a chauffeur in a white uniform. Only Harvey could be quite so brash, he thought. On the third, Nurse Faubert asked for a private word with him.

'My patient,' she said plaintively, 'is making improper advances when I change his dressing.'

Robin allowed Dr Wiley Barker the liberty of an unprofessional remark.

'Can't say I altogether blame him. Still, be firm, Nurse. I'm sure you must have encountered that sort of thing before.'

'*Naturellement*, but never from a patient only three days after major surgery. His constitution, it must be *formidable*.'

'I tell you what, let's catheterise him for a couple of days. That'll cramp his style.' She smiled. 'It must be pretty boring for you cooped up here all day,' Robin continued. 'Why don't you come and have a spot of supper with me after Mr Metcalfe has gone to sleep tonight?'

'I should love to, *Docteur*. Where shall I meet you?'

'Room 217, Hôtel de Paris,' said Robin unblushingly. 'Say 9 pm.'

'I'll look forward to it, *Docteur*.'

'A little more Chablis, Angeline?'

'No more, thank you, Wiley. That was a meal to remember. I think, maybe, you have not yet had everything you want?'

She got up, lit two cigarettes and put one in his

mouth. Then she moved away, her long skirt swinging slightly from the hips. She wore no bra under her pink shirt. She exhaled smokily and watched him.

Robin thought of the blameless Doctor Barker in Australia, of his wife and children in Newbury, and the rest of the Team in London. Then he put them all out of his mind.

'Will you complain to Mr Metcalfe if I make improper advances to you?'

'From you, Wiley,' she smiled, 'they will not be improper.'

Harvey made a talkative recovery, and Robin removed the stitches gravely on the sixth day.

'That seems to have healed very cleanly, Mr Metcalfe. Take it easy, and you should be back to normal by the middle of next week.'

'Great. I have to get over to England right away for Ascot week. You know, my horse Rosalie is favourite this year. I suppose you can't join me as my guest? What if I have a relapse.'

Robin suppressed a smile.

'Don't worry. You're getting along fine. Sorry I can't stay to see how Rosalie performs at Ascot.'

'So am I, Doc. Thanks again, anyway. I've never met a surgeon like you before.'

And you're not likely to again, thought Robin, his American accent beginning to fray at the edges. He bid his adieus to Harvey with relief and to Angeline with regret, and sent the chauffeur back from the hotel with a copper-plate bill:

Dr Wiley Franklin Barker
presents his Compliments to
Mr Harvey Metcalfe
and begs to inform him that the Bill for
Professional Services rendered is
$80,000
in respect of surgery and post-operative treatment.

The chauffeur was back within the hour with a cash cheque for $80,000. Robin bore it back to London in triumph.

Two down and two to go.

13

THE FOLLOWING DAY, Friday, Stephen sat on Robin's examination couch in Harley Street and addressed the troops.

'The Monte Carlo operation was a total success in every way, thanks to Robin keeping his cool. The expenses were fairly high, though. The hospital and hotel bills totalled $11,351, while we received $80,000. Therefore, we've had $527,560 returned to us, and expenses so far have come to $22,530, which leaves Mr Metcalfe still in debt to the tune of $494,970. Does everyone agree with that?'

There was a general murmur of approval. Their confidence in Stephen's arithmetic was unbounded, although in fact, like all algebraists, he found working with figures somewhat tedious.

'Incidentally, Robin, however did you manage to spend $73.50 on dinner last Wednesday night? What did you have, caviar and champagne?'

'Something a little out of the ordinary,' admitted Robin. 'It seemed to be called for at the time.'

'I'd bet more than I laid out in Monte Carlo that I know who joined you for dinner, and I bet she shared more than a table with you too,' said Jean-Pierre, taking his wallet out of his pocket. 'Here you are Stephen, 219 francs – my winnings from the Casino on Wednesday night. If you'd left me alone in peace, we needn't have bothered with Robin's butchery. I could have won the whole amount back on my own. I think the least I deserve is Nurse Faubert's telephone number.'

Jean-Pierre's remarks went straight over Stephen's head.

'Well done, Jean-Pierre, it'll all come off expenses. At today's exchange rate, your 219 francs,' he paused for a moment and tapped out on his calculator, 'is worth $46.76. That brings the expenses down to $22,483.24.

'Now, my plans for Ascot are simple. James has acquired two badges for the Members' Enclosure at a cost of $10. We know that Harvey Metcalfe also has a badge, as all owners do, so as long as we get our timing right and make it look natural, he should once again fall into our trap. James will keep us briefed on the walkie-talkie and will follow the movements of Metcalfe from his arrival to his leaving. Jean-Pierre will wait by the entrance of the Members' Enclosure and follow him in. Robin will send the telegram from Heathrow Airport at 1 pm, so Harvey ought to receive it during lunch in his private box. That part of the plan is easy. It's if we manage to lure him to Oxford that we all have to be on our toes. I must confess, it'd make a pleasant change if Ascot were to work first time.'

Stephen grinned widely.

'That would give us much needed extra time to go over the Oxford plan again. Any questions?'

'You don't need us for part (*a*) of the Oxford plan, only (*b*)?' asked Robin, checking Stephen's notes.

'That's right. I can manage part (*a*) on my own. In fact, it will be better if you all remain in London on that night, well out of the way. Our next priority must be to think up some ideas for James or he might, heaven preserve us, even think up something for himself. I'm becoming very concerned about this,' continued Stephen, 'because once Harvey returns to America we'll have to deal with him on his own ground. To date he's always been at the venue of our choosing. James would stick out like a sore thumb in Boston, even though he's the best actor of the four of us. In Harvey's words, "It would be a whole different ball game".'

James sighed lugubriously and studied the Axminster carpet.

'Poor old James – don't worry, you drove that ambulance like a trooper,' said Robin.

'Perhaps you could learn to fly a plane and then we could hijack him,' suggested Jean-Pierre.

Miss Meikle did not approve of the laughter coming from Doctor Oakley's room and she was glad to see the oddly assorted trio leave. When she had closed the door finally on James she returned to Robin's room.

'Will you see your patients now, Doctor Oakley?'

'Yes, if I must, Miss Meikle.'

Miss Meikle pursed her lips. Whatever had come over him? It must be those dreadful types he had started mixing with lately. He had become so unreliable.

'Mrs Wentworth-Brewster – Doctor Oakley will see you now, and I'll have the pills for your trip to Italy ready for you when you come out.'

Stephen returned for a few days' recuperation to Magdalen College. He had started the entire exercise eight weeks before and two of the Team had succeeded far beyond his expectations. He was conscious that he must crown their efforts with something that would live on in the legends of Oxford long after his departure.

Jean-Pierre returned to work in his gallery in Bond Street. Since he only had to deliver one sentence at Ascot he was not going to be overtaxed, although part (*b*) of Stephen's Oxford plan kept him nightly in front of a mirror rehearsing his role.

James took Anne down to Stratford-upon-Avon for the weekend. The Royal Shakespeare Company obliged with a sparkling performance of *Much Ado about Nothing* and afterwards, walking along the banks of the Avon, James proposed. Only the royal swans could have heard her reply. The diamond ring James had noticed in the window of Cartier while he had been waiting for Harvey Metcalfe to join Jean-Pierre in the gallery, looked even more beautiful on her slender finger. James's happiness seemed complete. If only he could come up with a plan and shock them all, he would want for nothing. He discussed it with Anne again that night, considering new ideas and old ones, still getting nowhere.

But an idea was beginning to formulate in her mind.

14

On Monday morning James drove Anne back to London and changed into the most debonair of his suits. Anne had to return to work, despite James's suggestion that she should accompany him to Ascot. She felt the others would not approve of her presence and would suspect that James had confided in her.

Although James had not told her the details of the Monte Carlo exercise, Anne knew every step of the planned proceedings at Ascot and she could tell that James was nervous. Still, she would be seeing him that night and would know the worst by then. James looked lost. Anne was only thankful that Stephen, Robin and Jean-Pierre held the baton most of the time in this relay team – but the idea that was taking shape in her mind just might surprise them all.

Stephen rose early and admired his grey hair in the mirror. The result had been expensively achieved the previous day in the hairdressing salon of Debenhams. He dressed carefully, putting on his one respectable grey suit and blue checked tie. These were brought out for all special occasions, ranging from a talk to students at Sussex University to a dinner with the American Ambassador. No one had told him the colours clashed and the suit sagged unfashionably at the elbow and knees, because by Stephen's standards it was elegance itself. He travelled from Oxford to Ascot by train, while Jean-Pierre came from London by car. They met up with James at the Belvedere Arms at 11 am, almost a mile from the course.

Stephen immediately telephoned Robin to confirm that all three of them had arrived and asked for the telegram to be read over to him.

'That's perfect, Robin. Now travel to Heathrow and send it at exactly 1 pm.'

'Good luck, Stephen. Grind the bastard into the dust.'

Stephen returned to the others and confirmed that Robin had the London end under control.

'Off you go, James, and let us know the minute Harvey arrives.'

James downed a bottle of Carlsberg and departed. The problem was that he kept bumping into friends and he could hardly explain why he was prevented from joining them.

Harvey arrived at the members' car park just after midday, his white Rolls Royce shining like a Persil advertisement. The car was being stared at by all the racegoers with an English disdain which Harvey mistook for admiration. He led his party to the private box. His newly tailored suit had taxed the ingenuity of Bernard Weatherill to the utmost. A red carnation in his buttonhole and a hat to cover his bald head left him nearly unrecognisable, and James might have missed him had it not been for the white Rolls Royce. James followed the little group at a careful distance until he saw Harvey enter a door marked 'Mr Harvey Metcalfe and Guests'.

'He's in his private box,' said James.

'Where are you?' asked Jean-Pierre.

'Directly below him on the ground level by a course bookmaker called Sam O'Flaherty.'

'No need to be rude about the Irish, James,' said Jean-Pierre. 'We'll be with you in a few minutes.'

James stared up at the vast white stand, which accommodated 10,000 spectators in comfort and gave an excellent view of the racecourse. He was finding it hard to concentrate on the job in hand as once again he had to avoid relations and friends. First was the Earl of Halifax, and then that frightful girl he had so unwisely agreed to take to Queen Charlotte's Ball last spring. What was the creature's name? Ah yes. The Hon. Selina Wallop. How appropriate. She was wearing a mini-skirt that was a good four years out of fashion and a hat which looked as if it could never come into fashion. James jammed his trilby over his ears, looked the other way and passed the time by chatting to Sam O'Flaherty about the 3.20, the King George VI and Queen Elizabeth Stakes. O'Flaherty quoted the latest odds on the favourite at the top of his voice:

'Rosalie at 6:4, owned by that American, Harvey Metcalfe, and ridden by Pat Eddery.'

Eddery was on the way to becoming the youngest-ever champion jockey – and Harvey always backed winners.

Stephen and Jean-Pierre joined James at the side of Sam O'Flaherty's bag. His tick-tack man was standing on an upturned orange box beside him and swinging his arms like a semaphore sailor aboard a sinking ship.

'What's your fancy, gentlemen?' Sam asked the three of them.

James ignored Stephen's slight frown of disapproval.

'£5 each way on Rosalie,' he said, and handed over a crisp £10 note, receiving in return a little green card with the series number and 'Sam O'Flaherty' stamped right across the middle.

'I must presume, James, this is an integral part of your as yet undisclosed plan,' said Jean-Pierre. 'What I should like to know is, if it works, how much do we stand to make?'

'£9.10 after tax if Rosalie wins,' chipped in Sam O'Flaherty, his stub cigar bobbing up and down in his mouth as he spoke.

'Hardly a great contribution towards $1 million, James. Well, we're off to the Members' Enclosure. Let us know the moment Harvey leaves his box. My guess is that around 1.45 he'll come and look at the runners and riders for the two o'clock, so that gives us a clear hour.'

The waiter opened another bottle of Krug 1964 and began pouring it for Harvey's guests; three bankers, two economists, a couple of ship-owners and a distinguished City journalist.

Preferring his guests to be famous and influential, Harvey always invited people who would find it almost impossible to refuse because of the business he might put their way. He was delighted with the company he had assembled for his big day. Senior among them was Sir Howard Dodd, the ageing chairman of the merchant bank that bore his name, but which actually referred to his great-grandfather. Sir Howard was 6 ft 2 in, as straight as a ramrod, and looked more like a Grenadier Guard than a respectable banker. The only thing he had in common with Harvey was the hair, or lack of hair, on his balding head. His young assistant, Jamie Clark, accompanied him. Just over thirty and extremely bright, he was there to be sure his chairman did not commit the bank to anything he might later regret. Although he had a sneaking admiration for Harvey, Clark did not think him the sort of customer the bank should do business with. Nevertheless, he was far from averse to a day at the races.

The two economists, Mr Colin Emson and Dr Michael Hogan from the Hudson Institute, were there to brief Harvey on the parlous state of the British economy. They could not have been more different. Emson was a totally self-made man who had left school at fifteen and educated himself. Using his social contacts, he had built up a company specialising in taxation, which had been remarkably successful thanks to the British Government's habit of putting through a new Finance Act every few weeks. Emson was 6 ft tall, solid and genial, game to help the party along whether Harvey lost or won. Hogan, in contrast, had been to all the right places – Winchester, Trinity College, Oxford, and the Wharton Business School in Pennsylvania. A spell with McKinsey, the management consultants, in London had made him one of the best-informed economists in Europe. Those who observed his slim, sinewy body would not have been surprised to learn that he had been an international squash player. Dark-haired, with brown eyes that rarely left Harvey, he found it hard not to show his contempt; this was his fifth invitation to Ascot – Harvey, it seemed, was never going to take no for an answer.

The Kundas brothers, second-generation Greeks who loved racing almost as much as ships, could hardly be told apart, with their black hair, swarthy skins and heavy dark eyebrows. It was difficult to guess how old they were, and nobody knew how much they were worth. They probably did not know themselves. Harvey's final guest, Nick Lloyd of the *News of the World*, had come along to pick up any dirt he could about his host. He had come near to exposing Metcalfe in the mid-sixties, but another scandal had kept less juicy stories off the front page for several weeks, and by then Harvey had escaped. Lloyd, hunched over the inevitable triple gin with a faint suggestion of tonic, watched the motley bunch with interest.

'Telegram for you, sir.'

Harvey ripped it open. He was never neat about anything.

'It's from my daughter Rosalie. It's cute of her to remember, but damn it all, I named the horse after her. Come on everybody, let's eat.'

They all took their seats for lunch – cold vichyssoise, pheasant and strawberries. Harvey was even more loquacious than usual, but his guests took no notice, aware he was nervous before the race and knowing that he would rather be a winner of this trophy than any he could be offered in America. Harvey himself could never understand why he felt that way. Perhaps it was the special atmosphere of Ascot which appealed to him so strongly – the combination of lush green grass and gracious surroundings, of elegant crowds and an efficiency of organisation which made Ascot the envy of the racing world.

'You must have a better chance this year than ever before, Harvey,' said the senior banker.

'Well, you know, Sir Howard, Lester Piggott is riding the Duke of Devonshire's horse, Crown Princess, and the Queen's Horse, Highclere, is the joint favourite, so I can't afford to over-estimate my chances. When you've been third twice before, and then favourite and not placed, you begin to wonder if one of your horses is going to make it.'

'Another telegram, sir.'

Once again Harvey's fat little finger ripped it open.

'"All the best wishes and good luck for the King George VI and Queen Elizabeth Stakes". It's from the staff of your bank, Sir Howard. Jolly good show.'

Harvey's Polish-American accent made the English expression slightly ridiculous.

'More champagne, everybody.'

Another telegram arrived.

'At this rate, Harvey, you'll need a special room at the Post Office.' There was laughter all round at Sir Howard's feeble joke. Once again Harvey read it out aloud:

'"Regret unable to join you Ascot. Heading soonest California. Grateful look out for old friend Professor Rodney Porter, Oxford Nobel Prize Winner. Don't let English bookies stitch you up. Wiley B., Heathrow Airport". It's from Wiley Barker. He's the guy who did stitch me up in Monte Carlo. He saved my life. He took out a gall stone the size of that bread roll you're eating, Dr Hogan. Now how the hell am I supposed to find this Professor Porter?' Harvey turned to the head waiter. 'Find my chauffeur.'

A few seconds later the smartly-clad Guy Salmon flunkey appeared.

'There's a Professor Rodney Porter of Oxford here today. Go find him.'

'What does he look like, sir?'

'How the hell do I know,' said Harvey. 'Like a professor.'

The chauffeur regretfully abandoned his plans for an afternoon at the railings and departed, leaving Harvey and his guests to enjoy the strawberries, the champagne and the string of telegrams that were still arriving.

'You know if you win, the cup will be presented by the Queen,' said Nick Lloyd.

'You bet. It'll be the crowning moment of my life to win the King George and Elizabeth Stakes and meet Her Majesty The Queen. If Rosalie wins, I'll suggest my daughter marries Prince Charles – they're about the same age.'

'I don't think even you will be able to fix that, Harvey.'

'What'll you do with the odd £81,000 prize money, Mr Metcalfe?' asked Jamie Clark.

'Give it to some charity,' said Harvey, pleased with the impression the remark made on his guests.

'Very generous, Harvey. Typical of your reputation.' Nick Lloyd gave Michael Hogan a knowing look. Even if the others didn't, they both knew what was typical of his reputation.

The chauffeur returned to report that there was no trace of a solitary professor anywhere in the champagne bar, balcony luncheon room or the paddock buffet, and that he'd been unable to gain access to the Members' Enclosure.

'Naturally not,' said Harvey rather pompously. 'I shall have to find him myself. Drink up and enjoy yourselves.'

Harvey rose and walked to the door with the chauffeur. Once he was out of earshot of his guests, he said, 'Get your ass out of here and don't give me any crap about not being able to find him or you can find something for yourself – another job.'

The chauffeur bolted. Harvey turned to his guests and smiled.

'I'm going to look at the runners and riders for the 2 o'clock.'

'He's leaving the box now,' said James.

'What's that you're saying?' asked an authoritative voice he recognised. 'Talking to yourself, James?'

James stared at the noble Lord Somerset, 6 ft 1 in and still able to stand his full height, an MC and a DSO in the First World War. He still exuded enthusiastic energy although the lines on his face suggested that he had passed the age at which the Maker had fulfilled his contract.

'Oh hell. No, sir, I was just . . . em . . . coughing.'

'What do you fancy in the King George VI and Queen Elizabeth Stakes?' asked the peer of the realm.

'Well, I have put £5 each way on Rosalie, sir.'

*

'He seems to have cut himself off,' said Stephen.

'Well, buzz him again,' said Jean-Pierre.

'What's that noise, James? Have you taken to a hearing-aid or something?'

'No, sir. It's . . . it's . . . it's a transistor radio.'

'Those things ought to be banned. Bloody invasion of privacy.'

'Absolutely right, sir.'

'What's he playing at, Stephen?'

'I don't know – I think something must have happened.'

'Oh my God, it's Harvey heading straight for us. You go into the Members' Enclosure, Stephen, and I'll follow you. Take a deep breath and relax. He hasn't seen us.'

Harvey marched up to the official blocking the entrance to the Members' Enclosure.

'I'm Harvey Metcalfe, the owner of Rosalie, and this is my badge.'

The official let Harvey through. Thirty years ago, he thought, they would not have let him into the Members' Enclosure if he'd owned every horse in the race. Then racing at Ascot was only held on four days a year, jolly social occasions. Now it was twenty-four days a year and big business. Times had changed.

Jean-Pierre followed closely, showing his pass without speaking to the official.

A photographer broke away from stalking the outrageous hats for which Ascot has such a reputation, and took a picture of Harvey just in case Rosalie won the King George VI Stakes. As soon as his bulb flashed he rushed over to the other entrance, where Linda Lovelace, the star of *Deep Throat*, the film running to packed houses in New York but banned in England, was trying to enter the Members' Enclosure. In spite of being introduced to a well-known London banker, Richard Szpiro, just as he was entering the Enclosure, she was not succeeding. She was wearing a top hat and morning suit with nothing under the top coat, and no one was going to bother with Harvey while she was around. When Miss Lovelace was quite certain that every photographer had taken a picture of her attempting to enter the Enclosure she left, swearing at the top of her voice, her publicity stunt completed.

Harvey returned to studying the horses as Stephen moved up to within a few feet of him.

'Here we go again,' said Jean-Pierre in French and went smartly over to Stephen and, standing directly between the two of them, shook Stephen's hand warmly, declaring in a voice that was intended to carry:

'How are you, Professor Porter? I didn't know you were interested in racing.'

'I'm not really, but I was on my way back from a seminar in London and thought it a good opportunity to see how . . .'

'Professor Porter,' cried Harvey. 'I'm honoured to make your acquaintance, sir, my name is Harvey Metcalfe from Boston, Massachusetts. My good friend, Dr Wiley Barker, who saved my life, told me you'd be here today on your own, and I'm going to make sure you have a wonderful afternoon.'

Jean-Pierre slipped away unnoticed. He could not believe how easy it had been. The telegram had worked like a charm.

'Her Majesty The Queen; His Royal Highness The Duke of Edinburgh; Her Majesty Queen Elizabeth The Queen Mother; and her Royal Highness The Princess Anne are now entering the Royal Box.'

The massed bands of the Brigade of Guards struck up the National Anthem:

'God Save the Queen.'

The crowd of 25,000 rose and sang loyally out of tune.

'We should have someone like that in America,' said Harvey to Stephen, 'to take the place of Richard Nixon. We wouldn't have any Watergate problems then.'

Stephen thought his fellow American was being just a little unfair. Richard Nixon was almost a saint by Harvey Metcalfe's standards.

'Come and join me in my box, Professor, and meet my other guests. The damned box cost me £750, we may as well fill it. Have you had some lunch?'

'Yes, I've had an excellent lunch, thank you,' Stephen lied – something else Harvey had taught him. He had stood by the Members' Enclosure for an hour, nervous and pensive, unable even to manage a sandwich, and now he was starving.

'Well, come and enjoy the champagne,' roared Harvey.

On an empty stomach, thought Stephen.

'Thank you, Mr Metcalfe. I am a little lost. This is my first Royal Ascot.'

'This isn't Royal Ascot, Professor. It's the last day of Ascot Week, but the Royal Family always comes to see the King George and Elizabeth Stakes, so everybody dresses up.'

'I see,' said Stephen timidly, pleased with his deliberate error.

Harvey collared his find and took him back to the box.

'Everybody, I want you to meet my distinguished friend, Rodney Porter. He's a Nobel Prize Winner, you know. By the way, what's your subject, Rod?'

'Biochemistry.'

Stephen was getting the measure of Harvey. As long as he played it straight, the bankers and shippers, and even the journalists, would never doubt that he was the cleverest thing since Einstein. He relaxed a little and even found time to fill himself with smoked salmon sandwiches when the others were not looking.

Lester Piggott won the 2 o'clock on Olympic Casino and the 2.30 on Roussalka, achieving his 3,000th win. Harvey was getting steadily more nervous. He talked incessantly without making much sense. He had sat through the 2.30 without showing any interest in the result and consumed more and more champagne. At 2.50 he called for them all to join him in the Members' Enclosure to look at his famous filly. Stephen, like the others, trailed behind him in a little pseudo-royal entourage.

Jean-Pierre and James watched the procession from a distance.

'He's too deep in to climb out now,' said Jean-Pierre.

'He looks relaxed enough to me,' replied James. 'Let's make ourselves scarce. We can only get under his feet.'

They headed into the champagne bar, which was filled with red-faced men who looked as if they spent more time drinking than they did watching the racing.

'Isn't she beautiful, Professor? Almost as beautiful as my daughter. If she doesn't win today I don't think I'm ever going to make it.'

Harvey left his little clique to have a word with the jockey, Pat Eddery, to wish him luck. Peter Walwyn, the trainer, was giving final instructions before the jockey mounted and left the Enclosure. The ten horses were then paraded in front of the stand before the race, a custom only carried out at Ascot for the King George VI and Queen Elizabeth Stakes. The gold, purple and scarlet colours of Her Majesty The Queen's horse Highclere led the procession, followed by Crown Princess, who was giving Lester Piggott a little trouble. Directly behind her came Rosalie, looking very relaxed, fresh and ready to go. Buoy and Dankaro trotted behind Rosalie, with the outsiders Mesopotamia, Ropey and Minnow bringing up the rear. The crowd rose to cheer the horses and Harvey beamed with pride, as if he owned every horse in the race.

'. . . and I have with me today the distinguished American owner, Harvey Metcalfe,' said Julian Wilson into the BBC TV outside-broadcast camera. 'I'm going to ask him if he'd be kind enough to give me his views on the King George VI and Queen Elizabeth Stakes, for which he has the joint favourite, Rosalie. Welcome to England, Mr Metcalfe. How do you feel about the big race?'

'It's a thrill to be here, just to participate in the race once again. Rosalie's got a great chance. Still, it's not winning that matters. It's taking part.'

Stephen flinched. Baron de Coubertin, who had first made that remark when opening the 1896 Olympics, must have turned in his grave.

'The latest betting shows Rosalie to be the joint favourite with Her Majesty The Queen's horse Highclere. How do you feel about that?'

'I'm just as worried about the Duke of Devonshire's Crown Princess. Lester Piggott is always hard to beat on a great occasion. He won the first two races and he'll be all set for this one – Crown Princess is a fine little filly.'

'Is a mile and a half a good distance for Rosalie?'

'Results this season show it's definitely her best distance.'

'What will you do with the £81,240 prize money?'

'The money is not important, it hasn't even entered my mind.'

It had certainly entered Stephen's mind.

'Thank you, Mr Metcalfe, and the best of luck. And now over for the latest news of the betting.'

Harvey moved back to his group of admirers and suggested that they return to watch the race from the balcony just outside his box.

Stephen was fascinated to observe Harvey at such close quarters. He had become nervous and even more mendacious than usual under pressure – not at all the icy, cool operator they had all feared him to be. This man was human, susceptible and could be beaten.

They all leant over the rails watching the horses being put into the stalls. Crown Princess was still giving a little trouble while all the others waited. The tension was becoming unbearable.

'They're off,' boomed the loudspeaker.

As twenty-five thousand people raised glasses to their eyes, Harvey said, 'She's got a good start – she's well placed,' continuing to give everybody a running commentary until the last mile, when he became silent. The others also waited in silence, intent on the loudspeaker.

'They're into the straight mile – Minnow leads the field around the bend – with Buoy and Dankaro, looking relaxed, just tucked in behind him – followed by Crown Princess, Rosalie and Highclere . . .

'As they approach the six-furlong marker – Rosalie and Crown Princess come up on the stand side with Highclere making a bid . . .

'Five furlongs to go – Minnow still sets the pace; but is beginning to tire as Crown Princess and Buoy make up ground . . .

'Half a mile to go – Minnow still just ahead of Buoy, who has moved up into second place, perhaps making her move too early . . .

'Three furlongs from home – they're quickening up just a little – Minnow sets the pace on the rails – Buoy and Dankaro are now about a length behind – followed by Rosalie, Lester Piggott on Crown Princess and the Queen's filly Highclere all making ground . . .

'Inside the two-furlong marker – Highclere and Rosalie move up to challenge Buoy – Crown Princess is right out of it now . . .

'A furlong to go . . .'

The commentator's voice rose in pitch and volume.

'It's Joe Mercer riding Highclere who hits the front, just ahead of Pat Eddery on Rosalie – two hundred yards to go – they're neck and neck – one hundred yards to go – it's anybody's race and on the line it's a photo finish between the gold, purple and scarlet colours of Her Majesty the Queen and the black-and-green check colours of the American owner, Harvey Metcalfe – M. Moussac's Dankaro was third.'

Harvey stood paralysed, waiting for the result. Even Stephen felt a little sympathy for him. None of Harvey's guests dared to speak for fear they might be wrong.

'The result of The King George VI and The Queen Elizabeth Stakes.' Once again the loudspeaker boomed out and silence fell over the whole course:

'The winner is No. 5, Rosalie.'

The rest of the result was lost in the roar of the crowd and the bellow of triumph from Harvey. Pursued by his guests, he raced to the nearest lift, pressed a pound note into the lift-girl's hand and shouted 'Get this thing moving.' Only half of his guests managed to jump in with him. Stephen was among them. Once they reached the ground floor, the lift gates opened and Harvey came out like a thoroughbred, past the champagne bar, through the rear of the Members' Enclosure into the Winners' Enclosure, and flung his arms round the horse's neck, almost unseating the jockey. A few minutes later he triumphantly led Rosalie to the little white post marked 'FIRST'. The crowd thronged around him, offering their congratulations.

The Clerk of the Course, Captain Beaumont, stood by Harvey's side, briefing him on the procedure that would be followed when he was presented. Lord Abergavenny, the Queen's Representative at Ascot, accompanied Her Majesty to the Winners' Enclosure.

'The winner of The King George VI and The Queen Elizabeth Stakes – Mr Harvey Metcalfe's Rosalie.'

Harvey was in a dream world. Flash-bulbs popped and film cameras followed him as he walked towards the Queen. He bowed and received his trophy. The Queen, resplendent in a turquoise silk suit and matching turban that could only have been designed by Norman Hartnell, said a few words, but for the first time in his life Harvey was speechless. Taking a pace backwards, he bowed again and returned to his place accompanied by loud applause.

Back in his box the champagne flowed and everybody was Harvey's friend. Stephen realised this was not the moment to try anything clever. He must bide his time and watch his quarry's reaction to these changed circumstances. He stayed quietly in a corner, letting the excitement subside, and observed Harvey carefully.

It took another race before Harvey was half back to normal and Stephen decided the time had now come to act. He made as if to leave.

'Are you going already, Professor?'

'Yes, Mr Metcalfe. I must return to Oxford and mark some scripts before tomorrow morning.'

'I always admire the work you boys put in. I hope

you enjoyed yourself?' Stephen avoided Shaw's famous riposte, 'I had to, there was nothing else to enjoy'.

'Yes, thank you, Mr Metcalfe. An amazing achievement. You must be a very proud man.'

'Well, I guess so. It's been a long time coming, but it all seems worthwhile now . . . Rod, it's too bad you have to leave us. Can't you stay on a little longer and join my party at Claridge's tonight?'

'I should have liked that, Mr Metcalfe, but you must visit me at my college at Oxford and allow me to show you the university.'

'That's swell. I have a couple of days after Ascot and I've always wanted to see Oxford, but I never seem to have found the time.'

'It's the university Garden Party next Wednesday. Why don't you join me for dinner at my college on Tuesday evening and then we can spend the following day looking at the university and go on to the Garden Party?' Stephen scribbled a few directions on a card.

'Fantastic. This is turning out to be the best vacation I've ever had in Europe. How are you getting back to Oxford, Professor?'

'By train.'

'No, no,' said Harvey. 'My Rolls Royce will take you. It'll be back well in time for the last race.'

And before Stephen could protest, the chauffeur was called for.

'Take Professor Porter back to Oxford and then return here. Have a good trip, Professor. I'll look forward to seeing you next Tuesday at 8 pm. Great meeting you.'

'Thank you for a wonderful day, Mr Metcalfe, and congratulations on your splendid victory.'

Seated in the back of the white Rolls Royce on his way to Oxford, the car which Robin had boasted he and he alone would travel in, Stephen relaxed and smiled to himself. Taking a small notebook from his pocket he made an entry:

'Deduct 98 pence from expenses, the price of a single second-class ticket from Ascot to Oxford.'

15

'BRADLEY,' said the Senior Tutor, 'you're going a bit grey at the edges, dear boy. Is the office of Junior Dean proving too much for you?'

Stephen had wondered whether any of the Senior Common Room would think the change in the colour of his hair worthy of comment. Dons are seldom surprised by anything their colleagues do.

'My father went grey at an early age, Senior Tutor, and there seems to be no way of defying heredity . . .'

'Ah well, dear boy, you'll look all the more distinguished at next week's Garden Party.'

'Oh yes,' replied Stephen, who had been thinking of nothing else. 'I'd quite forgotten about that.'

He returned to his rooms where the rest of the Team were assembled and waiting for their next briefing.

'Wednesday is the day of the Encaenia and the Garden Party,' began Stephen without as much as a 'Good morning, gentlemen'. His students made no protest. 'Now the one thing we've learnt about our millionaire friend is that when we take him away from his own environment he still continues to assume he knows everything. We've now shown that his bluff can be called, as long as we know what's going to happen next week and he doesn't. It's only the same skill he used when promoting Prospecta Oil – always keeping one step ahead of us. Now, we're going to keep two steps ahead of him by having a rehearsal today and a full dress-rehearsal tomorrow.'

'Time spent on reconnaissance is seldom wasted,' muttered James. It was about the only sentiment he could recall from his Army Cadet days at Harrow.

'Haven't had to spend much time on reconnaissance for your plan, have we?' chipped in Jean-Pierre.

Stephen ignored the interruptions.

'Now, the whole process on the day will take about seven hours for me and four hours for you, which includes the time required for make-up; we'll need an extra session on that from James the day before.'

'How often will you need my two sons?' asked Robin.

'Only once, on the Wednesday. Too many runs at it will make them look stiff and awkard.'

'When do you imagine Harvey will want to return to London?' enquired Jean-Pierre.

'I rang Guy Salmon to check their timetable and they've been instructed to have him back at Claridge's by 7 pm, so I've assumed we have only until 5.30.'

'Clever,' said Robin.

'It's awful,' said Stephen. 'I even think like the man now. Right, let's go over the whole plan once again. We'll take it from the red dossier, halfway down page 16. When I leave All Souls . . .'

On Sunday and Monday they carried out full rehearsals. By the Tuesday they knew every route Harvey could take and where he would be at any given moment of the day from 9 am to 5.30 pm. Stephen hoped he had covered every eventuality. He had little choice. They were only going to be allowed one crack at this one. Any mistakes like Monte Carlo and there would be no second chance. The dress-rehearsal went to a second.

'I haven't worn clothes like this since I was six years old and attending a fancy-dress party,' said Jean-Pierre. 'We're going to be anything but inconspicuous.'

'There'll be red and blue and black all round you on the day,' said Stephen. 'It's like a circus for peacocks. No one will give us a second look, not even you, Jean-Pierre.'

They were all nervous again, waiting for the curtain to go up. Stephen was glad they were on edge: he had no doubt that the moment they relaxed with Harvey Metcalfe, they would be found out.

The Team spent a quiet weekend. Stephen watched the College Dramatic Society's annual effort in Magdalen gardens, Robin took his wife to Glyndebourne and was uncommonly attentive, Jean-Pierre read *Goodbye Picasso* by David Douglas Duncan, and

James took Anne to Tathwell Hall in Lincolnshire, to meet his father, the fifth earl.

Even Anne was nervous that weekend.

'Harry?'

'Doctor Bradley.'

'I have an American guest dining with me in my rooms tonight. His name is Harvey Metcalfe. When he arrives will you see he is brought over to my rooms, please.'

'Certainly, sir.'

'And one small thing. He seems to have mistaken me for Professor Porter of Trinity College. Don't correct the mistake, will you? Just humour him.'

'Certainly, sir.'

Harry retreated into the Porter's Lodge shaking his head sadly. Of course, all academics went dotty in the end, but Dr Bradley had been afflicted at an unusually tender age.

Harvey arrived at eight. He was always on time in England. The head porter guided him through the cloisters and up the old stone staircase to Stephen's rooms.

'Mr Metcalfe, sir.'

'How are you, Professor?'

'I'm well, Mr Metcalfe. Good of you to be so punctual.'

'Punctuality is the politeness of princes.'

'I think you'll find it is the politeness of kings, and, in this particular instance, of Louis XVIII.' For a moment Stephen forgot that Harvey wasn't a pupil.

'I'm sure you're right, Professor.'

Stephen mixed him a large whisky. His guest's eyes took in the room and settled on the desk.

'Gee – what a wonderful set of photographs. You with the late President Kennedy, another with the Queen and even the Pope.'

That touch was due to Jean-Pierre, who had put Stephen in contact with a photographer who had been in jail with his artist friend David Stein. Stephen was already looking forward to burning the photographs and pretending they had never existed.

'Let me give you another to add to your collection.'

Harvey pulled out of his inside coat pocket a large photograph of himself receiving the trophy for the King George VI and Queen Elizabeth Stakes from the Queen.

'I'll sign it for you, if you like.'

Without waiting for a reply, he scribbled an exuberant signature diagonally across the Queen.

'Thank you,' said Stephen. 'I can assure you I will treasure it with the same affection as I do my other photographs. I certainly appreciate you sparing the time to visit me here, Mr Metcalfe.'

'It's an honour for me to come to Oxford, and this is such a lovely old college.'

Stephen really believed he meant it, and he suppressed the inclination to tell Harvey the story of the late Lord Nuffield's dinner at Magdalen. For all Nuffield's munificence to the university, the two were never on entirely easy terms. When a manservant assisted the guest's departure after a college feast, Nuffield took the proffered hat ungraciously. 'Is this mine?' he said, disdainfully. 'I wouldn't know, my lord,' was the rejoinder, 'but it's the one you came with.'

Harvey was gazing a little blankly at the books on Stephen's shelves. The disparity between their subject matter, pure mathematics, and the putative Professor Porter's discipline, biochemistry, happily failed to arrest him.

'Do brief me on tomorrow.'

'Surely,' said Stephen. Why not? He had briefed everyone else. 'Let me first call for dinner and I'll go through what I've planned for you and see if it meets with your approval.'

'I'm game for anything. I feel ten years younger since this trip to Europe – it must've been the operation – and I'm thrilled about being here at Oxford University.'

Stephen wondered if he really could stand seven hours of Harvey Metcalfe, but for another $250,000 and his reputation with the rest of the Team . . .

The college servants brought him shrimp cocktail.

'My favourite,' said Harvey. 'How did you know?'

Stephen would have liked to say, 'There's very little I don't know about you,' but he satisfied himself with, 'A fortunate guess. Now, if we meet up at 10 tomorrow morning we can take part in what is thought to be the most interesting day in the university calendar. It's called Encaenia.'

'What's that?'

'Well, once a year at the end of Trinity Term, which is the equivalent of the summer term in an American university, we celebrate the ending of the university year. There are several ceremonies followed by a magnificent Garden Party, which will be attended by the Chancellor and Vice-Chancellor of the University. The Chancellor is the former British Prime Minister, Harold Macmillan, and the Vice-Chancellor is Mr Habakkuk. I'm hoping it will be possible for you to meet them both, and we should manage to cover everything in time for you to be back in London by 7 pm.'

'How did you know I had to be back by 7?'

'You warned me at Ascot.' Stephen could lie very quickly now. He was afraid that if they did not get their million soon he would end up a hardened criminal.

Harvey enjoyed his meal, which Stephen had planned almost too cleverly, each course featuring one of Harvey's favourite dishes. After Harvey had drunk a good deal of after-dinner brandy (price £7.25 per bottle, thought Stephen) they strolled through the quiet Magdalen Cloisters past the Song School. The sound of the choristers rehearsing a Gabrieli mass hung gently in the air.

'Gee, I'm surprised you allow record players on that loud,' said Harvey.

Stephen escorted his guest to the Randolph Hotel, pointing out the iron cross set in Broad Street outside Balliol College, said to mark the spot on which Archbishop Cranmer was burnt at the stake for heresy in 1556. Harvey forbore to say that he had never even heard of the reverend gentleman.

Stephen and Harvey parted on the steps of the Randolph.

'See you in the morning, Professor. Thanks for a great evening.'

'My pleasure. I'll pick you up at 10 am. Sleep well – you have a full day ahead of you tomorrow.'

Stephen returned to Magdalen and immediately called Robin.

'All's well, but I nearly went too far. The meal was altogether too carefully chosen – I even had his favourite brandy. Still, it'll keep me on my toes tomorrow. We must remember to avoid overkill. See you then, Robin.'

Stephen reported the same message to Jean-Pierre and James before falling gratefully into bed. The same time tomorrow he would be a wiser man, but would he be a richer one?

16

At 5 am the sun rose over the Cherwell, and those few Oxonians who were about that early would have been left in no doubt as to why the connoisseurs consider Magdalen to be the most beautiful college at either Oxford or Cambridge. Nestling on the banks of the river, its perpendicular architecture is easy on the eye. King Edward VII, Prince Henry, Cardinal Wolsey, Edward Gibbon and Oscar Wilde had all passed through its portals. But the only thing that was passing through Stephen's mind as he lay awake that morning was the education of Harvey Metcalfe.

He could hear his own heart-beat, and for the first time he knew what Robin and Jean-Pierre had been through. It seemed a lifetime since their first meeting only three months before. He smiled to himself at the thought of how close they had all become in their common aim of defeating Harvey Metcalfe. Although Stephen, like James, was beginning to have a sneaking admiration for the man, he was now even more convinced that Metcalfe could be outmanoeuvred when he was not on home ground. For over two hours Stephen lay motionless in bed, deep in thought, going over his plan again and again. When the sun had climbed over the tallest tree, he rose, showered, shaved and dressed slowly and deliberately, his mind still on the day ahead.

He made his face up carefully to age himself by fifteen years. It took him a considerable time, and he wondered whether women had to struggle as long in front of the mirror to achieve the opposite effect. He donned his gown, a magnificent scarlet, proclaiming him a Doctor of Philosophy of the University of Oxford. It amused him that Oxford had to be different. Every other university abbreviated this universal award for research work, to PhD. In Oxford, it was DPhil. He studied himself in the mirror.

'If that doesn't impress Harvey Metcalfe, nothing ever will.'

And what's more, he had the right to wear it. He sat down to study his red dossier for the last time. He had read the closely typewritten pages so often that he practically knew them by heart.

He avoided breakfast. Looking nearly fifty, he would undoubtedly have caused a stir amongst his colleagues, though probably the older dons would have failed to observe anything unusual in his appearance.

Stephen headed out of the college into the High, unnoticed among the thousand or so other graduates all dressed like fourteenth-century archbishops. Anonymity on that particular day was going to be easy. That, and the fact that Harvey would be bemused by the strange traditions of the ancient university, were the two reasons why Stephen had chosen Encaenia for his day of battle.

He arrived at the Randolph at 9.55 am and informed one of the younger bell-boys that his name was Professor Porter and that he had come to pick up Mr Metcalfe. Stephen took a seat in the lounge. The young man scurried away and returned moments later with Harvey.

'Mr Metcalfe – Professor Porter.'

'Thank you,' said Stephen. He made a mental note to return and tip the bell-boy. That touch had been useful, even if it was only part of his job.

'Good morning, Professor,' said Harvey, taking a seat. 'So tell me, what have I let myself in for?'

'Well,' said Stephen, 'Encaenia begins officially when all the notables of the university take a breakfast of champagne, strawberries and cream at Jesus College, which is known as Lord Nathaniel Crewe's Benefaction.'

'Who's this Lord Crewe guy? Will he be at the breakfast?'

'Only in spirit; the great man died some three hundred years ago. Lord Nathaniel Crewe was a doctor of the university and the Bishop of Durham, and he left £200 a year to the university as a Benefaction to provide the breakfast and an oration which we shall hear later. Of course, the money he willed no longer covers expenses nowadays, with rising prices and inflation, so the university has to dip into its own pocket to continue the tradition. When breakfast is over there is a procession and parade to the Sheldonian Theatre.'

'What happens then?'

'The parade is followed by the most exciting event of the day. The presentation of the Honorands for degrees.'

'The what?' said Harvey.

'The Honorands,' said Stephen. 'They are the distinguished men and women who have been chosen by the senior members of the university to be awarded Oxford honorary degrees.' Stephen looked at his watch. 'In fact, we must leave now to be sure of having a good position on the route from which to watch the procession.'

Stephen rose and guided his guest out of the Randolph Hotel. They strolled down the Broad and found an excellent spot just in front of the Sheldonian Theatre, where the police cleared a little space for Stephen because of his scarlet gown. A few minutes later the procession wound into sight round the corner from the Turl. The police held up all the traffic and kept the public on the pavement.

'Who are the guys in front carrying those clubs?' enquired Harvey.

'They are the University Marshal and the Bedels. They are carrying maces to safeguard the Chancellor's procession.'

'Jesus; of course it's safe. This isn't Central Park, New York.'

'I agree,' said Stephen, 'but it hasn't always been so over the past three hundred years, and tradition dies hard in England.'

'And who's that behind the Bedel fellows?'

'The one wearing the black gown with gold trimmings is the Chancellor of the University, accompanied by his page. The Chancellor is the Right Honourable Harold Macmillan, who was Prime Minister of Great Britain in the late '50s and early '60s.'

'Oh yes, I remember the guy. Tried to get the British into Europe but De Gaulle wouldn't have it.'

'Well, I suppose that's one way of remembering him. Now, he's followed by the Vice-Chancellor, Mr Habakkuk, who is also the Principal of Jesus College.'

'You're losing me, Professor.'

'Well, the Chancellor is always a distinguished Englishman who was educated at Oxford; but the Vice-Chancellor is a leading member of the university itself and is usually chosen from the heads of one of the colleges.'

'Got it, I think.'

'Now, after him, we have the University Registrar, Mr Caston, who is a fellow of Merton College. He is the senior administrator of the university, or you might look on him as the university's top civil servant. He's directly responsible to the Vice-Chancellor and Hebdomadal Council, who are the sort of cabinet for the university. Behind them we have the Senior Proctor, Mr Campbell of Worcester College, and the

Junior Proctor, the Reverend Doctor Bennett of New College.'

'What's a Proctor?'

'For over 700 years the Proctors have been responsible for decency and discipline in the university.'

'What? Those two old men take care of 9,000 rowdy youths?'

'Well, they are helped by the bulldogs,' said Stephen.

'Ah, that's better, I suppose. A couple of bites from an old English bulldog would keep anyone in order.'

'No, no,' protested Stephen, trying desperately not to laugh. 'The name bulldog is given to the men who help the Proctors keep order. Now, finally in the procession you can observe that tiny crocodile of colour: it consists of heads of colleges who are doctors of the university, doctors of the university who are not heads of colleges and the heads of colleges who are not doctors of the university, in that order.'

'Listen, Rod, all doctors mean to me is pain and money.'

'They are not that sort of doctor,' replied Stephen.

'Forget it. I love everything but don't expect me to understand what it's all about.'

Stephen watched Harvey's face carefully. He was drinking the scene in and had already become quieter.

'The long line will now proceed into the Sheldonian Theatre and all the people in the procession will take their places in the hemicycle.'

'Excuse me, sir, what type of cycle is that?'

'The hemicycle is a round bank of seats inside the theatre, distinguished only by being the most uncomfortable in Europe. But don't you worry. Thanks to your well-known interest in education at Harvard I've managed to arrange special seats for us and there will just be time for us to secure them ahead of the procession.'

'Well, lead the way, Rod. Do they really know what goes on at Harvard here?'

'Why yes, Mr Metcalfe. You have a reputation in university circles as a generous man interested in financing the pursuit of academic excellence.'

'Well, what do you know.'

Very little, thought Stephen.

He guided Harvey to his reserved seat in the balcony, not wanting his guest to be able to see the individual men and women too clearly. The truth of the matter was that the senior members of the university in the hemicycle were so covered from head to toe in gowns and caps and bow-ties and bands, that even their mothers would not have recognised them. The organist played his final chord and the guests settled.

'The organist,' said Stephen, 'is from my own college. He's the Choragus, the leader of the chorus, and Deputy Professor of Music.'

Harvey could not take his eyes off the hemicycle and the scarlet-clad figures. He had never seen a sight like it in his life. The music stopped and the Chancellor rose to address the assembled company in vernacular Latin.

'*Causa hujus convocationis est ut . . .*'

'What the hell's he saying?'

'He's telling us why we're here,' explained Stephen. 'I'll try and guide you through it.'

'*Ite Bedelli*,' declared the Chancellor, and the great doors opened for the Bedels to go and fetch the Honorands from the Divinity School. There was a hush as they were led in by the Public Orator, Mr J. G. Griffith, who presented them one by one to the Chancellor, enshrining the careers and achievements of each in polished and witty Latin prose.

Stephen's translation, however, followed a rather more liberal line and was embellished with suggestions that their doctorates were as much the result of financial generosity as of academic prowess.

'That's Lord Amory. They're praising him for all the work he has done in the field of education.'

'How much did he give''

'Well, he *was* Chancellor of the Exchequer. And there's Lord Hailsham. He has held eight Cabinet positions, including Secretary of State for Education and finally Lord Chancellor. Both he and Lord Amory are receiving the degree of Doctor of Civil Law.'

Harvey recognised Dame Flora Robson, the actress, who was being honoured for a distinguished lifetime in the theatre; Stephen explained that she was receiving the degree of Doctor of Letters, as was the Poet Laureate, Sir John Betjeman. Each was presented with his scroll by the Chancellor, shaken by the hand and then shown to a seat in the front row of the hemicycle.

The final Honorand was Sir George Porter, Director of the Royal Institution and Nobel Laureate. He received his honorary degree of Doctor of Science.

'My namesake, but no relation. Oh well, nearly through,' said Stephen. 'Just a little prose from John Wain, the Professor of Poetry, about the benefactors of the university.'

Mr Wain delivered the Crewian Oration, which took him some twelve minutes, and Stephen was grateful for something so lively in a language they could both understand. He was only vaguely aware of the recitations of undergraduate prize winners which concluded the proceedings.

The Chancellor of the university rose and led the procession out of the hall.

'Where are they all off to now?' asked Harvey.

'They are going to have lunch at All Souls, where they will be joined by other distinguished guests.'

'God, what I would give to be able to attend that.'

'I have arranged it,' replied Stephen.

Harvey was quite overwhelmed.

'How did you fix that, Professor?'

'The Registrar was most impressed by the interest you have shown in Harvard and I think they hope you might find it possible to assist Oxford in some small way, especially after your wonderful win at Ascot.'

'What a great idea. Why didn't I think of that?'

Stephen tried to show little interest, hoping that by the end of the day he would have thought of it. He had learnt his lesson on overkill. The truth was that the Registrar had never heard of Harvey Metcalfe, but because it was Stephen's last term at Oxford he had been put on the list of invitations by a friend who was a Fellow of All Souls.

They walked over to All Souls, just across the road from the Sheldonian Theatre. Stephen attempted, without much success, to explain the nature of All Souls to Harvey. Indeed, many Oxonians themselves find the college something of an enigma.

'Its corporate name,' Stephen began, 'is the College of All Souls of the Faithful Departed of Oxford, and it resonantly commemorates the victors of Agincourt. It was intended that masses should forever be said there for the repose of their souls. Its modern role is unique in academic life. All Souls is a society of graduates distinguished either by promise or achievement, mostly academic, from home and abroad, with a sprinkling of men who have made their mark in other fields. The college has no undergraduates, and generally appears to the outside world to do much as it pleases with its massive financial and intellectual resources.'

Stephen and Harvey took their places among the hundred or more guests at the long table in the noble Codrington Library. Stephen spent the entire time ensuring that Harvey was kept fully occupied and was not too obvious. He was thankfully aware that on such occasions people never remember whom they meet or what they say, and happily introduced Harvey to everyone around as a distinguished American philanthropist. He was fortunately placed some way from the Vice-Chancellor, the Registrar and the Secretary of the University Chest.

Harvey was quite overcome by the new experience and was content just to listen to the distinguished men around him – which surprised Stephen, who had feared he would never stop talking. When the meal was over and the guests had risen, Stephen drew a deep breath and played one of his riskier cards. He deliberately marched Harvey up to the Chancellor.

'Chancellor,' he said to Harold Macmillan.

'Yes, young man.'

'May I introduce Mr Harvey Metcalfe from Boston. Mr Metcalfe, as you will know, Chancellor, is a great benefactor of Harvard.'

'Yes, of course. Capital, capital. What brings you to England, Mr Metcalfe?'

Harvey was nearly speechless.

'Well, sir, I mean Chancellor, I came to see my horse Rosalie run in the King George and Elizabeth Stakes.'

Stephen was now standing behind Harvey and made signs to the Chancellor that Harvey's horse had won the race. Harold Macmillan, as game as ever and never one to miss a trick, replied:

'Well, you must have been very pleased with the result, Mr Metcalfe.'

'Well, sir, I guess I was lucky.

'You don't look to me the type of man who depends on luck.'

Stephen took his career firmly in both hands.

'I am trying to interest Mr Metcalfe in supporting some research we are doing at Oxford, Chancellor.'

'What a good idea.' No one knew better than Harold Macmillan, after seven years of leading a political party, how to use flattery on such occasions. 'Keep in touch, young man. Boston was it, Mr Metcalfe? Do give my regards to the Kennedys.'

Macmillan swept off, resplendent in his academic dress. Harvey stood dumbfounded.

'What a great man. What an occasion. I feel I'm part of history. I just wish I deserved to be here.'

Having completed his task, Stephen was determined to escape before any mistakes could be made. He knew Harold Macmillan would shake hands with and talk to over a thousand people that day and the chances of his remembering Harvey were minimal. In any case, it would not much matter if he did. Harvey was, after all, a genuine benefactor of Harvard.

'We ought to leave before the senior members, Mr Metcalfe.'

'Of course, Rod. You're the boss.'

'I think that would be courtesy.'

Once they were out on the street Harvey glanced at his large Jaeger le Coultre watch. It was 2.30 pm.

'Excellent,' said Stephen, who was running three minutes late for the next rendezvous. 'We have just over an hour before the Garden Party. Why don't we take a look at one or two of the colleges.'

They walked slowly up past Brasenose College and Stephen explained that the name really meant 'brass nose' and that the famous original brass nose, a sanctuary knocker of the thirteenth century, was still mounted in the hall. A hundred yards further on, Stephen directed Harvey to the right.

'He's turned right, Robin, and he's heading towards Lincoln College,' said James, well hidden in the entrance of Jesus College.

'Fine,' said Robin and checked his two sons. Aged seven and nine, they stood awkwardly, in unfamiliar Eton suits, ready to play their part as pages, unable to understand what Daddy was up to.

'Are you both ready?'

'Yes, Daddy,' they replied in unison.

Stephen continued walking slowly towards Lincoln, and they were no more than a few paces away when Robin appeared from the main entrance of the college in the official dress of the Vice-Chancellor, bands, collars, white tie and all. He looked fifteen years older and as much like Mr Habakkuk as possible. Perhaps not quite so bald, thought Stephen.

'Would you like to be presented to the Vice-Chancellor?' asked Stephen.

'That would be something,' said Harvey.

'Good afternoon, Vice-Chancellor, may I introduce Mr Harvey Metcalfe.'

Robin doffed his academic cap and bowed. Stephen returned the compliment in like manner. Robin spoke before Stephen could continue:

'Not the benefactor of Harvard University?'

Harvey blushed and smiled at the two little boys who were holding the Vice-Chancellor's train. Robin continued:

'This is a pleasure, Mr Metcalfe. I do hope you are enjoying your visit to Oxford. Mind you, it's not everybody who's fortunate enough to be shown around by a Nobel Laureate.'

'I've enjoyed it immensely, Vice-Chancellor, and I'd like to feel I could help this university in some way.'

'Well, that is excellent news.'

'Look, gentlemen, I'm staying here at the Randolph Hotel. It would be my great pleasure if you could all have tea with me later this afternoon.'

Robin and Stephen were thrown for a moment. He'd done it again – the unexpected. Surely the man realised that on the day of Encaenia the Vice-Chancellor did not have a moment free to attend private tea parties.

Robin recovered first.

'I'm afraid that would be difficult. One has so many responsibilities on a day like this, you understand. Perhaps you could join me in my rooms at the

Clarendon Building? That would give us a chance to have a more private discussion?'

Stephen immediately picked up the lead:

'How kind of you, Vice-Chancellor. Will 4.30 be convenient?'

'Yes, yes, that will be fine, Professor.'

Robin tried not to look as if he wanted to run a mile. Although they had only been standing there for about five minutes, to him it seemed a lifetime. He had not objected to being a journalist, or an American surgeon, but he genuinely hated being a Vice-Chancellor. Surely someone would appear at any moment and recognise him for the fraud he was. Thank God most of the undergraduates had gone home the week before. He began to feel even worse when a tourist started taking photos of him.

Now Harvey had turned all their plans upside down. Stephen could only think of Jean-Pierre and of James, the finest string to their dramatic bow, loitering uselessly in fancy dress behind the tea tent at the Garden Party in the grounds of Trinity College, waiting for them.

'Perhaps it might be wise, Vice-Chancellor, if we were to invite the Registrar and the Secretary of the University Chest to join us?'

'First-class idea, Professor. I'll ask them to be there. It isn't every day we're visited by such a distinguished philanthropist. I must take my leave of you now, sir, and proceed to my Garden Party. An honour to have made your acquaintance, Mr Metcalfe, and I look forward to seeing you again at 4.30.'

They shook hands warmly, and Stephen guided Harvey towards Exeter College while Robin darted back into the little room in Lincoln that had been arranged for him. He sank heavily into a seat.

'Are you all right, Daddy?' asked his elder son, William.

'Yes, I'm fine.'

'Do we get the ice cream and Coca-Cola you promised us if we didn't say a word?'

'You certainly do,' said Robin.

Robin slipped off all the paraphernalia – the gown hood, bow-tie and bands – and placed them back in the suitcase. He returned to the street just in time to watch the real Vice-Chancellor, Mr Habakkuk, leave Jesus College on the opposite side of the road, obviously making his way towards the Garden Party. Robin glanced at his watch. If they had run five minutes late the whole plan would have struck disaster.

Meanwhile, Stephen had done a full circle and was now heading towards Shepherd & Woodward, the tailor's shop which supplies academic dress for the university. He was, however, preoccupied with the thought of getting a message through to James. Stephen and Harvey came to a halt in front of the shop window.

'What magnificent robes.'

'That's the gown of a Doctor of Letters. Would you like to try it on and see how you look?'

'That would be great. But would they allow it?' said Harvey.

'I'm sure they won't object.'

They entered the shop, Stephen still in his full academic dress as a Doctor of Philosophy.

'My distinguished guest would like to see the gown of a Doctor of Letters.'

'Certainly, sir,' said the young assistant, who was not going to argue with a Fellow of the University.

He vanished to the back of the shop and returned with a magnificent red gown with grey facing and a black, floppy velvet cap. Stephen forged on, brazen-faced.

'Why don't you try them on, Mr Metcalfe? Let's see what you would look like as an academic.'

The assistant was somewhat surprised. He wished Mr Venables would return from his lunch break.

'Would you care to come through to the fitting-room, sir?'

Harvey disappeared. Stephen slipped out on to the road.

'James, can you hear me? Oh hell, for God's sake answer, James.'

'Cool down, old fellow. I'm having a deuce of a time putting on this ridiculous gown, and in any case, our rendezvous isn't for another seventeen minutes.'

'Cancel it.'

'Cancel it?'

'Yes, and tell Jean-Pierre as well. Both of you report to Robin and meet up as quickly as possible. He will fill you in on the new plans.'

'New plans. Is everything all right, Stephen?'

'Yes, better than I could have hoped for.'

Stephen clicked off his speaker and rushed back into the tailor's shop.

Harvey reappeared as a Doctor of Letters; a more unlikely sight Stephen had not seen for many years.

'You look magnificent.'

'What do they cost?'

'About £100, I think.'

'No, no. How much would I have to give . . . ?'

'I have no idea. You would have to discuss that with the Vice-Chancellor after the Garden Party.'

Harvey took a long look at himself in the mirror, and then returned to the dressing-room while Stephen thanked the assistant, asked him to wrap up the gown and cap and send them to the Clarendon building to be left with the porter in the name of Sir John Betjeman. He paid cash. The assistant looked even more bewildered.

'Yes, sir.'

He was not sure what to do, except continue praying for Mr Venables' arrival. His prayers were answered some ten minutes later, but by then Stephen and Harvey were well on their way to Trinity College and the Garden Party.

'Mr Venables, I've just been asked to send the full DLitt. dress to Sir John Betjeman at the Clarendon Building.'

'Strange. We kitted him out for this morning's ceremony weeks ago. I wonder why he wants a second outfit.'

'He paid cash.'

'Well, send it round to the Clarendon, but be sure it's in his name.'

When Stephen and Harvey arrived at Trinity College shortly after 3.30, the elegant green lawns, the croquet hoops having been removed, were already crowded with over a thousand people. The members of the university wore an odd hybrid dress: best lounge suits or silk dresses topped with gowns, hoods and caps. Cups of tea and crates of strawberries and cucumber sandwiches were disappearing rapidly.

'What a swell party this is,' said Harvey unintentionally mimicking Frank Sinatra. 'You certainly do things in style here, Professor.'

'Yes, the Garden Party is always rather fun. It's the main social event of the university year, which as I explained, is just ending. Half the senior members here will be snatching an afternoon off from reading examination scripts. Exams for the final-year undergraduates have only just ended.'

Stephen observed the Vice-Chancellor, the Registrar and the Secretary of the University Chest carefully, and steered Harvey well away from them, introducing him to as many of the older members of the university as possible, hoping they would not find the encounter too memorable. They spent just over three-quarters of an hour moving from person to person, Stephen feeling rather like an aide-de-camp to an incompetent dignitary whose mouth must be kept shut for fear of a diplomatic incident. Despite Stephen's anxious approach, Harvey was clearly having the time of his life.

'Robin, Robin, can you hear me?'

'Yes, James.'

'Where are you?'

'I'm in the Eastgate Restaurant: come and join me here and bring Jean-Pierre.'

'Fine. We'll be there in five minutes. No, make it ten. With my disguise, I'd better go slowly.'

Robin paid his bill. The children had finished their reward, so he took them out of the Eastgate to a waiting car and instructed the driver, who had been hired especially for the day, to return them to Newbury. They had played their part and now could only get in the way.

'Aren't you coming home with us, Dad?' demanded Jamie.

No, I'll be back later tonight. Tell your mother to expect me about seven.'

Robin returned to the Eastgate to find Jean-Pierre and James hobbling towards him.

'Why the change of plan?' asked Jean-Pierre. 'It's taken me over an hour to get dressed and ready.'

'Never mind. You're still in the right gear. We had a stroke of luck. I chatted up Harvey in the street and the cocky bastard invited me to tea with him at the Randolph Hotel. I said that would be impossible, but asked him to join me at the Clarendon. Stephen suggested that you two should be invited along as well.'

'Clever,' said James. 'No need for the deception at the Garden Party.'

'Let's hope it's not too clever,' said Jean-Pierre.

'Well, at least we can do the whole damn charade behind closed doors,' said Robin, 'which ought to make it easier. I never did like the idea of walking through the streets with him.'

'With Harvey Metcalfe nothing is ever going to be easy,' said Jean-Pierre.

'I'll get myself into the Clarendon Building by 4.15,' continued Robin. 'You will appear a few minutes after 4.20, Jean-Pierre, and then you, James, about 4.25 pm. But keep exactly to the same routine, act as if the meeting had taken place, as originally planned, at the Garden Party and we had all walked over to the Clarendon together.'

Stephen suggested to Harvey that they should return to the Clarendon Building, as it would be discourteous to be late for the Vice-Chancellor.

'Sure.' Harvey glanced at his watch. 'Jesus, it's 4.30 already.'

They left the Garden Party and walked quickly down towards the Clarendon Building at the bottom of the Broad, Stephen explaining en route that the Clarendon was a sort of Oxford White House where all the officers and officials of the university had their rooms.

The Clarendon is a large, imposing eighteenth-century building which could be mistaken by a visitor for another college. A few steps lead up to an impressive hallway, and on entering you realise you are in a magnificent old building which has been converted for use as offices, with as few changes as possible.

When they arrived the porter greeted them.

'The Vice-Chancellor is expecting us,' said Stephen.

The porter had been somewhat surprised when Robin had arrived fifteen minutes earlier and told him that Mr Habakkuk had asked him to wait in his room; even though Robin was in full academic dress, the porter kept a beady eye on him, not expecting the Vice-Chancellor or any of his staff to return from the Garden Party for at least another hour. The arrival of Stephen gave him a little more confidence. He well remembered the pound he had received for his guided tour of the building.

The porter ushered Stephen and Harvey through to the Vice-Chancellor's rooms and left them alone, tucking another pound note into his pocket.

The Vice-Chancellor's room was in no way pretentious and its beige carpet and pale walls would have given it the look of any middle-ranking civil servant's office, had it not been for the magnificent picture of a village square in France by Wilson Steer which hung over the marble fireplace.

Robin was staring out of the vast windows overlooking the Bodleian Library.

'Good afternoon, Vice-Chancellor.'

Robin spun round. 'Oh, welcome, Professor.'

'You remember Mr Metcalfe?'

'Yes, indeed. How nice to see you again.' Robin shuddered. All he wanted to do was to go home. They chatted for a few minutes. Another knock and Jean-Pierre entered.

'Good afternoon, Registrar.'

'Good afternoon, Vice-Chancellor, Professor Porter.'

'May I introduce Mr Harvey Metcalfe.'

'Good afternoon, sir.'

'Registrar, would you like some . . .'

'Where's this man Metcalfe?'

The three of them stood, stunned, as a man looking ninety entered the room on sticks. He hobbled over to Robin, winked, bowed and said:

'Good afternoon, Vice-Chancellor,' in a loud, crotchety voice.

'Good afternoon, Horsley.'

James went over to Harvey and prodded him with his sticks as if to make sure he was real.

'I have read about you, young man.'

Harvey had not been called young man for thirty years. The others stared at James in admiration. None of them knew that in his last year at university James had played *L'Avare* to great acclaim. His Secretary of the Chest was simply a repeat performance, and even Molière would have been pleased with it. James continued:

'You have been most generous to Harvard.'

'That's very kind of you to mention it, sir,' said Harvey respectfully.

'Don't call me sir, young man. I like the look of you – call me Horsley.'

'Yes, Horsley, sir,' blurted Harvey.

The others were only just able to keep a straight face.

'Well, Vice-Chancellor,' continued James. 'You can't have dragged me halfway across the city for my health. What's going on? Where's my sherry?'

Stephen wondered if James was overdoing it, but looking at Harvey saw that he was evidently captivated by the scene. How could a man so mature in one field be so immature in another, he thought. He was beginning to see how Westminster Bridge had been sold to at least four Americans in the past twenty years.

'Well, we were hoping to interest Mr Metcalfe in the work of the university and I felt that the Secretary of the University Chest should be present.'

'What's this chest?' asked Harvey.

'Sort of treasury for the university,' replied James,

his voice loud, old and very convincing. 'Why don't you read this?' and he thrust into Harvey's hand an Oxford University Calendar, which Harvey could have obtained at Blackwell's bookshop for £2 as indeed James had.

Stephen was not sure what move to make next when, happily for him, Harvey took over.

'Gentlemen, I would like to say how proud I am to be here today. This has been a wonderful year for me. I was present when an American won Wimbledon, I finally obtained a Van Gogh. My life was saved by a wonderful, wonderful surgeon in Monte Carlo and now here I am in Oxford surrounded by all this history. Gentlemen, it would give me a great deal of pleasure to be associated with this famous university.'

James took the lead again:

'What have you in mind?' he shouted at Harvey, adjusting his hearing-aid.

'Well, sir, I achieved my life's ambition when I received the King George and Elizabeth trophy from your Queen, but the prize money, well, I would like to use that to make a benefaction to your university.'

'But that's over £80,000,' gasped Stephen.

'£81,240 to be exact, sir. But why don't I call it $250,000.'

Stephen, Robin and Jean-Pierre were speechless. James alone was left to command the day. This was the opportunity he had needed to show why his great-grandfather had been one of Wellington's most respected generals.

'We accept. But it would have to be anonymous,' said James. 'I think I can safely say in the circumstances that the Vice-Chancellor would inform Mr Harold Macmillan and Hebdomadal Council, but we would not want a fuss made of it. Of course, Vice-Chancellor, I would ask you to consider an honorary degree.'

Robin was so conscious of James's obvious control of the entire situation that he could only add:

'How would you recommend we go about it, Horsley?'

'Cash cheque, so nobody can trace the money back to Mr Metcalfe. We can't have those bloody men from Cambridge chasing him for the rest of his life. Same way as we did for Sir David – no fuss.'

'I agree,' said Jean-Pierre, not having the vaguest idea what James was talking about. Neither, for that matter, had Harvey.

James nodded to Stephen, who left the Vice-Chancellor's office and made his way to the porter's room to enquire if a parcel had been left for Sir John Betjeman.

'Yes, sir. I don't know why they left it here. I'm not expecting Sir John.'

'Don't worry,' said Stephen. 'He's asked me to pick it up for him.'

Stephen returned to find James holding forth to Harvey on the importance of keeping his donation as a bond between himself and the university.

Stephen undid the box and took out the magnificent gown of a Doctor of Letters. Harvey turned red with embarrassment and pride as Robin placed it on his shoulders, chanting '*De mortuis nil nisi bonum. Dulce et decorum est pro patria mori. Per ardua ad astra. Nil desperandum.*'

'Many congratulations,' bellowed James. 'A pity we could not have organised this to be part of today's ceremony, but for such a munificent gesture as yours we could hardly wait another year.'

Brilliant, thought Stephen, Laurence Olivier could not have done better.

'That's fine by me,' said Harvey, as he sat down and made out a cheque to cash. 'You have my word that this matter will never be mentioned to anyone.'

None of them believed that.

They stood in silence as Harvey rose and passed the cheque to James.

'No, sir.' James transfixed him with a glare.

The others looked dumbfounded.

'The Vice-Chancellor.'

'Of course,' said Harvey. 'Excuse me, sir.'

'Thank you,' said Robin, his hand trembling as he received the cheque. 'A most gracious gift, and you may be sure we shall put it to good use.'

There was a loud knock on the door. They all looked round terrified except for James, who was now ready for anything. It was Harvey's chauffeur. James had always hated the pretentious white uniform with the white hat.

'Ah, the efficient Mr Mellor,' said Harvey. 'Gentlemen, I guarantee he's been watching every move we've made today.'

The four froze, but the chauffeur had clearly made no sinister deductions from his observations.

'Your car is ready, sir. You wanted to be back at Claridge's by 7 pm to be in good time for your dinner appointment.'

'Young man,' bellowed James.

'Yes, sir,' whimpered the chauffeur.

'Do you realise you are in the presence of the Vice-Chancellor of this university?'

'No, sir. I'm very sorry, sir.'

'Take your hat off immediately.'

'Yes, sir.'

The chauffeur removed his hat and retreated to the car, swearing under his breath.

'Vice-Chancellor, I sure hate to break up our party, but as you've heard I do have an appointment . . .'

'Of course, of course, we understand you're a busy man. May I once again officially thank you for your most generous donation, which will be used to benefit many deserving people.'

'We all hope you have a safe journey back to the States and will remember us as warmly as we shall remember you,' added Jean-Pierre.

Harvey moved towards the door.

'I will take my leave of you now, sir,' shouted

James. 'It will take me twenty minutes to get down those damned steps. You are a fine man and you have been most generous.'

'It was nothing,' said Harvey expansively.

True enough, thought James, nothing to you, but everything to us.

Stephen, Robin and Jean-Pierre accompanied Harvey from the Clarendon to the waiting Rolls.

'Professor,' said Harvey, 'I didn't quite understand everything the old guy was saying.' As he spoke he shifted the weight of his heavy robes on his shoulders self-consciously.

'Well, he's very deaf and very old, but his heart's in the right place. He wanted you to know that this has to be an anonymous donation as far as the university is concerned, though, of course, the Oxford hierarchy will be informed of the truth. If it were to be made public all sorts of undesirables who have never done anything for education in the past would come trooping along on the day of Encaenia wanting to buy an honorary degree.'

'Of course, of course. I understand. That's fine by me,' said Harvey. 'I want to thank you for a swell day, Rod, and I wish you all the luck for the future. What a shame our friend Wiley Barker wasn't here to share it all.'

Robin blushed.

Harvey climbed into the Rolls Royce and waved enthusiastically to the three of them as they watched the car start effortlessly on its journey back to London.

Three down and one to go.

'James was brilliant,' said Jean-Pierre. 'When he first came in I didn't know who the hell it was.'

'I agree,' said Robin. 'Let's go and rescue him – he's truly the hero of the day.'

They all three ran up the steps, forgetting that they looked somewhere between the ages of fifty and sixty, and rushed back into the Vice-Chancellor's room to congratulate James, who lay silent in the middle of the floor. He had passed out.

In Magdalen an hour later, with the help of Robin and two large whiskies, James was back to his normal health.

'You were fantastic,' said Stephen, 'just at the point when I was beginning to lose my nerve.'

'You would have received an Academy Award if we could have put it on screen,' said Robin. 'Your father will have to let you go on the stage after that performance.'

James basked in his first moment of glory for three months. He could not wait to tell Anne.

'Anne.' He quickly looked at his watch. 'Six-thirty.

Oh hell, I must leave at once. I'm meant to be meeting Anne at eight. See you all next Monday in Stephen's rooms for dinner. By then I'll try to have my plan ready.'

James rushed out of the room.

'James.'

His face reappeared round the door. They all said in chorus: 'Fantastic.'

He grinned, ran down the stairs and leapt into his Alfa Romeo, which he now felt they might allow him to keep, and headed towards London at top speed.

It took him 59 minutes from Oxford to the King's Road. The new motorway had made a considerable difference since his undergraduate days. Then the journey had taken anything from an hour and a half to two hours through High Wycombe or Henley.

The reason for his haste was that the meeting with Anne was most important and under no circumstances must he be late; tonight he was due to meet her father. All James knew about him was that he was a senior member of the Diplomatic Corps in Washington. Diplomats always expect you to be on time. He was determined to make a good impression on her father, particularly after Anne's successful weekend at Tathwell Hall. The old man had taken to her at once and never left her side. They had even managed to agree on a wedding date, subject, of course, to the approval of Anne's parents.

James had a quick cold shower and removed all his make-up, losing some sixty years in the process.

He had arranged to meet Anne for a drink at Les Ambassadeurs in Mayfair before dinner, and as he put on his dinner-jacket he wondered if he could make it from the King's Road to Hyde Park Corner in 12 minutes: it would require another Monte Carlo. He leapt into his car, revving it quickly through the gears, shot along to Sloane Square, through Eaton Square, up past St George's Hospital, round Hyde Park Corner into Park Lane, and arrived at 7.58 pm.

'Good evening, my lord,' said Mr Mills, the club owner.

'Good evening. I'm dining with Miss Summerton and I've had to leave my car double-parked. Can you take care of it?' said James, dropping the keys and a pound note into the doorman's white-gloved hand.

'Delighted, my lord. Show Lord Brigsley to the private rooms.'

James followed the head porter up the red staircase and into a small Regency room where dinner had been laid for three. He could hear Anne's voice in the next room. She came through, looking even more beautiful than usual in a floating mint-green dress.

'Hello, darling. Come on, I want you to meet Daddy.'

James followed Anne into the next room.

'Daddy, this is James. James, this is my father.'

James went red and then white, and then he felt green.

'How are you, my boy. I've heard so much about you from Rosalie that I can't wait to get acquainted.'

17

'CALL ME HARVEY.'

James stood aghast and speechless. Anne jumped into the silence.

'Would you like a whisky, James?'

James found his voice with difficulty.

'Thank you.'

'I want to know all about you, young man,' continued Harvey, 'what you get up to and why I've seen so little of my daughter in the past few weeks, though I think I can guess the answer to that.'

James drank the whisky in one gulp and Anne quickly refilled his glass.

'You see so little of your daughter because I'm always modelling, which means that I'm very rarely in London.'

'I know, Rosalie . . .'

'James knows me as Anne, Daddy.'

'We christened you Rosalie. It was a good enough name for your mother and me and it ought to be good enough for you.'

'Daddy, whoever heard of a top European model

calling herself Rosalie Metcalfe? All my friends know me as Anne Summerton.'

'What do you think, James?'

'I was beginning to think I didn't know her at all,' replied James, recovering slowly. It was obvious that Harvey did not suspect a thing. He had not seen James face to face at the gallery, he had never seen him at Monte Carlo or Ascot, and James had looked ninety years of age at Oxford earlier in the day. He was beginning to believe he had got away with it. But how the hell could he tell the others at their Monday meeting that the final plan, his plan, would be to outwit not Harvey Metcalfe, but his future father-in-law?

'Shall we go through to dinner?'

Harvey did not wait for a reply. He marched on into the adjoining room.

'Rosalie Metcalfe,' whispered James fiercely, 'you've got some explaining to do.'

Anne kissed him gently on the cheek.

'You're the first person who's given me the chance to beat my father at anything. Can't you forgive me? . . . I do love you . . .'

'Come on, you two. Anyone would think you'd never met before.'

Anne and James joined Harvey for dinner. James was amused by the sight of the shrimp cocktail and remembered how Stephen had regretted that touch at Harvey's Magdalen dinner.

'Well, James, I understand you and Anne have fixed a date for the wedding.'

'Yes, sir, if it meets with your approval.'

'Of course I approve. I was hoping Anne would marry Prince Charles after I'd won the King George and Elizabeth Stakes, but an earl will have to do for my only daughter.'

They both laughed, neither of them thinking it was remotely funny.

'I wish you'd come to Wimbledon this year, Rosalie. Imagine, me there on Ladies' Day and the only company I had was a boring old Swiss banker.'

Anne looked at James and grinned.

The waiters cleared the table and wheeled in a trolley bearing a crown of lamb in immaculate cutlet frills, which Harvey studied with great interest.

'Still,' said Harvey, chattering on, 'it was thoughtful of you to ring me at Monte Carlo, my dear. I really thought I was going to die, you know. James, you wouldn't have believed it. They removed a gall stone the size of a baseball from my stomach. Thank God, the operation was performed by one of the greatest surgeons in the world, Wiley Barker, the President's surgeon. He saved my life.'

Harvey promptly undid his shirt and revealed a 4-inch scar across his vast stomach.

'What do you think of that, James?'

'Remarkable.'

'Daddy, really. We're having dinner.'

'Stop fussing, honey. It won't be the first time James has seen a man's stomach.'

It's not the first time I've seen that one, thought James.

Harvey pushed his shirt back into his trousers and continued:

'Anyway, it was really kind of you to phone me.' He leant over and patted her hand. 'I was a good boy too. I took your advice and kept that nice Doctor Barker on for another week in case any complications arose. Mind you, the price these doctors . . .'

James dropped his wine glass. The claret covered the tablecloth with a red stain.

'I'm so sorry.'

'You all right, James?'

'Yes, sir.'

James looked at Anne in silent outrage. Harvey was quite unperturbed.

'Bring a fresh tablecloth and some more wine for Lord Brigsley.'

The waiter opened a fresh bottle of claret and James decided it was his turn to have a little fun. Anne had been laughing at him for three months. Why shouldn't he tease her a little, if Harvey gave him the chance? Harvey was still talking.

'You a racing man, James?'

'Yes, sir, and I was delighted by your victory in the King George VI and Queen Elizabeth Stakes – for more reasons than you realise.'

In the diversion caused by the waiters clearing the table, Anne whispered *sotto voce*:

'Don't try to be too clever, darling – he's not as stupid as he sounds.'

'Well, what do you think of her?'

'I beg your pardon, sir?'

'Rosalie.'

'Magnificent. I put £5 each way on her.'

'Yes, it was a great occasion for me and I was sorry you missed it, Rosalie, because you would have met the Queen and a nice guy from Oxford University called Professor Porter.'

'Professor Porter?' enquired James, burying his face in his wine glass.

'Yes, Professor Porter, James. Do you know him?'

'No, sir, I can't say I do, but didn't he win a Nobel Prize?'

'He sure did and he gave me a wonderful time at Oxford. I enjoyed myself so much I ended up presenting the university with a cheque for $250,000 to be used for research of some kind, so he should be happy.'

'Daddy, you know you're not meant to tell anybody about that.'

'Sure, but James is family now.'

'Why can't you tell anyone else, sir?'

'Well, it's a long story, James, but it was quite an honour for me. You do understand this is highly confidential, but I was Professor Porter's guest at Encaenia. I lunched at All Souls with Mr Harry Macmillan, your dear old Prime Minister, and then I attended the Garden Party, and afterwards I had a meeting with the Vice-Chancellor in his private rooms along with the Registrar and the Secretary of the University Chest. Were you at Oxford, James?'

'Yes, sir. The House.'

'The House?' queried Harvey.

'Christ Church, sir.'

'I'll never understand Oxford.'

'No, sir.'

'You must call me Harvey. Well, as I was saying, we all met at the Clarendon and they stammered and stuttered and they were totally lost for words, except for one funny old guy, who was ninety if he was a day. The truth is that those people just don't know how to approach millionaires for money, so I put them out of their embarrassment and took over. They'd have gone on all day about their beloved Oxford, so eventually I had to shut them up and simply wrote out a cheque for $250,000.'

'That was very generous, Harvey.'

'I'd have given them $500,000 if the old boy had asked. James, you've gone quite white. Do you feel all right?'

'I'm sorry. Yes, I'm fine. I was quite carried away with your description of Oxford.'

Anne joined in:

'Daddy, you made an agreement with the Vice-Chancellor that you would keep your gift as a bond between the university and yourself, and you must promise never to repeat that story again.'

'I think I shall wear the robes for the first time

when I open the new Metcalfe library at Harvard in the fall.'

'Oh, no sir,' stammered James a little too quickly, 'that wouldn't be quite the thing. You should only wear full robes in Oxford on ceremonial occasions.'

'Gee, what a shame. Still, I know what sticklers you English are for etiquette. Which reminds me, we ought to discuss your wedding. I suppose you two will want to live in England?'

'Yes, Daddy, but we'll visit you every year and when you make your annual trip to Europe you can come and stay with us.'

The waiters cleared the table again and reappeared with Harvey's favourite strawberries. Anne tried to steer the conversation to domestic issues and stop her father returning to what he'd been up to during the past two months, while James did everything to get him back on the subject.

'Coffee or liqueur, sir?'

'No, thank you,' said Harvey. 'Just the check. I thought we'd have a drink in my suite at Claridge's, Rosalie. I have something to show you both. It's a bit of a surprise.'

'I can't wait, Daddy. I love surprises. Don't you, James?'

'Normally yes, but I think I've had enough for one day.'

*

James left them and drove the Alfa Romeo to Claridge's garage so that Anne could have a few moments alone with her father. They strolled along Curzon Street, arm in arm.

'Isn't he wonderful, Daddy?'

'Yeah, great guy. Didn't seem too bright to begin with but he cheered up as the meal went on. And fancy my little girl turning out to be a genuine English lady. Your Momma's tickled pink and I'm pleased that we've patched up our silly quarrel.'

'Oh, you helped a lot, Daddy.'

'I did?' queried Harvey.

'Yes, I managed to get things back into perspective during the last few weeks. Now tell me, what is your little surprise?'

'Wait and see, honey. It's your wedding present.'

James rejoined them at the entrance to Claridge's. He could tell from Anne's look that Harvey had given him the seal of parental approval.

'Good evening, sir. Good evening, my lord.'

'Hi there, Albert. Could you fix some coffee and a bottle of Rémy Martin to be sent up to my suite?'

'Right away, sir.'

James had never seen the Royal Suite before. Off the small entrance room, there is a master bedroom on the right and a sitting-room on the left. Harvey took them straight to the sitting-room.

'Children, you are about to see your wedding present.'

He threw the door open in dramatic style and there on the far wall, facing them, was the Van Gogh. They both stared, quite unable to speak.

'That's exactly how it left me,' said Harvey. 'Speechless.'

'Daddy.' Anne swallowed. 'A Van Gogh. But you've always wanted a Van Gogh. You've dreamed of possessing one for years. I couldn't possibly deprive you of it now, and anyway I couldn't think of having anything as valuable as that in my house. Think of the security risk – we don't have the protection you have.' Anne stammered on. 'We couldn't let you sacrifice the pride of your collection, could we, James?'

'Absolutely not,' said James with great feeling. 'I wouldn't have a moment's peace with that on the premises.'

'Keep the painting in Boston, Daddy, in a setting worthy of it.'

'But I thought you'd love the idea, Rosalie.'

'I do, I do, Daddy, I just don't want the responsibility, and in any case Mother must have the chance to enjoy it too. You can always leave it to James and me if you like.'

'What a great idea, Rosalie. That way we can both enjoy the painting. Now I shall have to think of another wedding present. She nearly got the better of me then, James, and she hasn't done that in twenty-four years.'

'Well, I've managed it two or three times lately, Daddy, and I'm still hoping I shall do it once more.'

Harvey ignored Anne's remark and went on talking.

'That's the King George and Elizabeth trophy,' he said, pointing to a magnificent bronze sculpture of a horse and jockey with his hoop and quartered cap studded with diamonds. 'The race is so important they present a new trophy every year – so it's mine for life.'

James was thankful that the trophy at least was genuine.

The coffee and brandy arrived and they settled down to discuss the wedding in detail.

'Now, Rosalie, you must fly over to Lincoln next week and help your mother with the arrangements, otherwise she'll panic and nothing will get done. And, James, you let me know how many people you'll have coming over and I'll put them up at the Ritz. The wedding will be in Trinity Church, Copley Square, and we'll have a real English-style reception afterwards back in my home in Lincoln. Does all that make sense, James?'

'Sounds wonderful. You're a very well organised man, Harvey.'

'Always have been, James. Find it pays in the long run. Now, you and Rosalie must get the details sewn up before she comes over next week; you may not have realised it, but I'm returning to America tomorrow.'

Page 38A of the blue dossier, thought James.

James and Anne spent another hour chatting

about the wedding arrangements and left Harvey just before midnight.

'I'll see you first thing in the morning, Daddy.'

'Goodnight, sir.'

James shook hands and left.

'I told you he was super.'

'He's a fine young man and your mother will be very pleased.'

James said nothing to Anne in the lift on the way down because two other men stood beside them in silence, also intent on reaching the ground floor. But once they were in the Alfa Romeo he took Anne by the scruff of her neck, threw her across his legs, and spanked her so hard that she didn't know whether to laugh or cry.

'What's that for?'

'Just in case you ever forget after we're married who's the head of this household.'

'You male chauvinist pig, I was only trying to help.'

James drove at furious speed to Anne's flat.

'What about all your so-called background – "My parents live in Washington and Daddy's in the Diplomatic Corps",' James mimicked. 'Some diplomat.'

'I know, darling, but I had to think of something once I'd realised who it was you were up against.'

'What in hell's name am I going to tell the others?'

'Nothing. You invite them to the wedding, explain that my mother is American and that's why we're getting married in Boston. I'd give the earth to see their faces when they discover who your father-in-law is. In any case, you still have a plan to think of and you can't possibly let them down.'

'But the circumstances have changed.'

'No, they haven't. The truth of the matter is that they've all succeeded and you've failed, so you be sure you think of a plan by the time you reach America.'

'It's obvious now that we wouldn't have succeeded without your help.'

'Nonsense, darling. I had nothing to do with Jean-Pierre's scheme. I just added some background colour here and there – Promise you'll never spank me again?'

'Certainly I will, every time I think of that picture, but now, darling . . .'

'James, you're a sex maniac.'

'I know, darling. How do you think we Brigsleys have reared tribes of little lords for generations?'

Anne left James early the next morning to spend some time with her father, and they both saw him off at the airport on the midday flight to Boston. Anne could not resist asking in the car on the way back what James had decided to tell the others. She could get no response other than:

'Wait and see. I'm not having it changed behind my back. I'm only too glad you're off to America on Monday.'

18

MONDAY WAS A double hell for James. First, he had to see Anne off on the morning TWA flight for Boston, and then he had to spend the rest of the day preparing for the Team meeting in the evening. The other three had now completed their operations and would be waiting to hear what he had come up with. It was twice as hard now he knew that the victim was to be his father-in-law, but he realised that Anne was right and he could not put that forward as an excuse. Nevertheless, he still had to relieve Harvey of $250,000. To think he could have done it with one sentence at Oxford. That was another thing he could not tell the rest of the Team.

As Oxford had been Stephen's victory, the Team dinner was at Magdalen College and James travelled out of London just after the rush hour, past the White City Stadium and on down the M40 to Oxford.

'You're always last, James,' said Stephen.

'Sorry, I've been up to my eyes . . .'

'Preparing a good plan, I hope,' said Jean-Pierre.

James didn't answer. How well they all knew each other now, he thought. In twelve weeks James felt he had come to know more about these three men than any of the so-called friends he'd known for twenty years. For the first time he understood why his father continually referred back to friendships formed during the war with men he normally would never have met. He began to realise how much he was going to miss Stephen when he returned to America. Success was, in fact, going to split them up.

James would have been the last to go through the agony of another Prospecta Oil, but it had certainly had its compensations.

Stephen could never treat any occasion as a celebration, and as soon as the servants had brought in the first course and left, he banged the table with a spoon and declared that the meeting was in progress.

'Make me a promise,' said Jean-Pierre.

'What's that?' asked Stephen.

'When we have every last penny back, I can sit at the top of the table and you won't speak until you're spoken to.'

'Agreed,' said Stephen, 'but not until we do have every last penny. The position at the moment is that we've received \$777,560. Expenses on this operation have totalled \$5,178, making a grand total of \$27,661.24. Therefore, Metcalfe still owes us \$250,101.24.'

Stephen handed round a copy of the current balance sheet.

'These sheets are to be added to your own folders as pages 63C. Any questions?'

'Yes, why were the expenses so high for this operation?' asked Robin.

'Well, over and above the obvious things,' said Stephen, 'the truth is that we've been hit by the floating exchange rate of sterling against the dollar. At the beginning of this operation you could get $2.44 to the pound. This morning I could only get $2.32. I'm spending in pounds but charging Metcalfe in dollars at the going rate.'

'Not going to let him off with one penny, are you?' said James.

'Not one penny. Now, before we go on I should like to place on record . . .'

'This gets more like a meeting of the House of Commons every time,' said Jean-Pierre.

'Stop croaking, frog,' said Robin.

'Listen, you Harley Street pimp.'

Uproar broke out. The college scouts, who had seen some rowdy gatherings in their time, wondered if they would have to be called in to help before the evening was completed.

'Quiet,' the sharp, senatorial voice of Stephen brought them all back to order. 'I know you're in high spirits, but we still have to get $250,101.24.'

'We must on no account forget the 24 cents, Stephen.'

'You weren't as noisy the first time you had dinner here, Jean-Pierre:

The man that once did sell the lion's skin
While the beast liv'd, was killed with hunting him.'

The table was silent.

'Harvey still owes the Team money and it'll be just as hard to acquire the last quarter as it was with the first three-quarters. Before I hand over to James, I'd like to place on record that his performance at the Clarendon was nothing less than brilliant.'

Robin and Jean-Pierre banged the table in appreciation and agreement.

'Now, James, we're all ears.'

Once again the room fell into silence.

'My plan is nearly complete,' began James.

The others looked disbelieving.

'But I have something to tell you, which I hope will allow me a short respite before we carry it out.'

'You're going to get married.'

'Quite right, Jean-Pierre, as usual.'

'I could tell the moment you walked in. When do we meet her, James?'

'Not until it's too late for her to change her mind, Jean-Pierre.'

Stephen consulted his diary.

'How much reprieve are you asking for?'

'Well, Anne and I are getting married on August 3rd, in Boston. Anne's mother is American,' explained James, 'and although Anne lives in England, it would please her mother if she was married at home. Then there'll be the honeymoon and after that we anticipate returning to England on August 25th. My plan for Mr Metcalfe ought to be carried out on September 15th, the closing day of the Stock Exchange account.'

'I'm sure that's acceptable, James. All agreed?'

Robin and Jean-Pierre nodded.

James launched into his plan.

'I shall require a telex and seven telephones. They'll need to be installed in my flat. Jean-Pierre will have to be in Paris at the Bourse, Stephen in Chicago on the commodity market and Robin in London at Lloyds. I will present a full blue dossier as soon as I return from my honeymoon.'

They were all struck dumb with admiration and James paused for dramatic effect.

'Very good, James,' said Stephen. 'We'll await the details with interest. What further instructions do you have?'

'First, Stephen, you must know the opening and closing price of gold in Johannesburg, Zürich, New York and London each day for the next month. Jean-Pierre, you must know the price of the Deutschmark, the French franc and the pound against the dollar every day during the same period, and Robin must master a telex machine and PBX 8-line switchboard by September 2nd. You must be as competent as an international operator.'

'Always get the easy jobs, Robin, don't you?' said Jean-Pierre.

'You can . . .'

'Shut up, both of you,' said James.

Their faces registered surprise and respect.

'I've made notes for all of you to work on.'

James handed two typewritten sheets to each member of the Team.

'You add these to your dossiers as pages 74 and 75 and they should keep you occupied for at least a month. Finally, you're all invited to the wedding of Miss Anne Summerton to James Brigsley. I shan't bother issuing you with formal invitations at such short notice, but I've reserved seats for us on a 747 on the afternoon of August 2nd and we're all booked in at the Ritz in Boston for the night. I hope you'll honour me by being ushers.'

Even James was impressed by his own efficiency. The others received the plane tickets and instructions with astonishment.

'We'll meet at the airport at 3 pm and during the flight I shall test you on your dossier notes.'

'Yes, sir,' said Jean-Pierre.

'Your test, Jean-Pierre, will be in both French and English, as you'll be required to converse in two languages over a trans-Atlantic telephone, and appear expert on foreign currency exchange.'

There were no more jokes about James that evening, and as he travelled back up the motorway he felt a new man. Not only had he been the star of the Oxford plan; now he had the other three on the run. He would come out on top and do his old pa yet.

19

For a change James was the first to arrive at a meeting and the others joined him at Heathrow. He had gained the upper hand and was determined not to lose it. Robin arrived last, clutching an armful of newspapers.

'We're only going to be away for two days,' said Stephen.

'I know, but I always miss the English papers, so I've brought enough for tomorrow as well.'

Jean-Pierre threw his arms up in Gallic despair.

They checked their luggage through the No. 3 Terminal and boarded the British Airways 747 flight to Logan International Airport.

'It's more like a football ground,' said Robin, stepping for the first time inside a jumbo jet.

'It holds 350 people. About the size of the crowds most of your English clubs deserve,' said Jean-Pierre.

'Cut it out,' said James sternly, not realising that they were both nervous passengers and were only trying to relieve the tension. Later, during take-off, they both pretended to read, but as soon as the plane reached 30,000 feet and the little white light that says 'fasten seat-belts' switched off, they were back in top form.

The Team chewed its way stolidly through a plastic dinner of cold chicken and Algerian red wine.

'I do hope, James,' said Jean-Pierre, 'that your father-in-law will feed us a little better.'

After the meal James allowed them to watch the film, but insisted that as soon as it was over they must prepare to be tested one by one. Robin and Jean-Pierre moved back fifteen rows to watch *The Sting*. Stephen stayed in his seat to be grilled by James.

James handed Stephen a typewritten sheet of forty questions on the price of gold all over the world and the market movements during the past four weeks. Stephen completed it in twenty-two minutes, and it came as no surprise to James to find that every answer was correct: Stephen had always been the backbone of the Team, and it was his logical brain that had really defeated Harvey Metcalfe.

Stephen and James dozed intermittently until Robin and Jean-Pierre returned, when they were given their forty questions. Robin took thirty minutes over his and scored 38 out of 40. Jean-Pierre took twenty-seven minutes and scored 37.

'Stephen got 40 out of 40,' said James.

'He would,' said Jean-Pierre.

Robin looked a little sheepish.

'And so will you by September 2nd. Understood?'

They both nodded.

'Have you seen *The Sting*?' asked Robin,

'No,' replied Stephen. 'I rarely go to the cinema.'

'They're not in our league. One big operation, and they don't even keep the money.'

'Go to sleep, Robin.'

The meal, the film and James's quizzes had taken up most of the six-hour flight and they all nodded off in the last hour, to be woken suddenly by:

'This is your captain speaking. We are approaching Logan International Airport and our flight is running twenty minutes late. We expect to land at 7.15 in approximately ten minutes. We hope you have enjoyed your flight and will travel again with British Airways.'

Customs took a little longer than usual as they all three had brought presents for the wedding and did not want James to know what they were. They had considerable trouble in explaining to the customs officer why one of the two Piaget watches had inscribed on the back: 'Part of the illicit profits from Prospecta Oil – the three who had plans.'

When they finally escaped the customs official, they found Anne standing at the entrance by a large Cadillac waiting to chauffeur them to the hotel.

'Now we know why it took you so long to come up with something: you were genuinely distracted. Congratulations, James, you're entirely forgiven,' said Jean-Pierre, and threw his arms round Anne as only a Frenchman could. Robin introduced himself and kissed her gently on the cheek. Stephen shook hands with her rather formally. They bustled into the car, Jean-Pierre sitting next to Anne.

'Miss Summerton,' stuttered Stephen.

'Do call me Anne.'

'Will the reception be at the hotel?'

'No,' replied Anne, 'at my parents' house, but there'll be a car to pick you up and take you there after the wedding. Your only responsibility is to see that James gets to the church by 3.30. Other than that you have nothing to worry about. While I think of it, James, your father and mother arrived yesterday and they're staying with my parents. We thought it might not be a good idea for you to spend this evening at home because Mother's flapping about everything.'

'Anything you say, darling.'

'If you should change your mind between now and tomorrow,' said Jean-Pierre, 'I find myself available. I may not be blessed with noble blood, but there are one or two compensations we French can always offer.'

Anne smiled to herself. 'You're a little late, Jean-Pierre. In any case, I don't like beards.'

'But I only . . .' began Jean-Pierre.

The others glared at him.

At the hotel they left Anne and James alone while they went to unpack.

'Do they know, darling?'

'They haven't the slightest idea,' replied James. 'They're going to get the surprise of their life tomorrow.'

'Is your plan ready?'

'Wait and see.'

'Well, I have one,' said Anne. 'When's yours scheduled for?'

'September 13th.'

'I win then – mine's for tomorrow.'

'What, you weren't meant to . . .'

'Don't worry. You just concentrate on getting married . . . to me.'

'Can't we go somewhere?'

'No, you terrible man. You can wait until tomorrow.'

'I do love you.'

'Go to bed, you silly thing. I love you too, but I must go home, otherwise nothing'll be ready.'

James took the lift to the seventh floor and joined the others for coffee.

'Anyone for blackjack?'

'Not with you, you pirate,' said Robin. 'You've been tutored by the biggest crook alive.'

The Team were in top form and looking forward to the wedding. In spite of the transatlantic time dislocation they didn't depart for their separate rooms until well after midnight. Even then, James lay awake for some time, turning over the same question in his mind:

'I wonder what's she's up to this time?'

20

Boston in August is as beautiful a city as any in America, and the Team enjoyed a large breakfast in James's room.

'I don't think he looks up to it,' said Jean-Pierre. 'You're the captain of the Team, Stephen. I volunteer to take his place.'

'It'll cost you $250,000.'

'Agreed,' said Jean-Pierre.

'You don't have $250,000,' said Stephen. 'You have $187,474.69, being one quarter of what's been raised so far, so my decision is that James must be the bridegroom.'

'It's an Anglo-Saxon plot,' said Jean-Pierre, 'and when James has successfully completed his plan and we have the full amount, I shall re-open negotiations.'

They sat talking and laughing for a long time over the toast and coffee. Stephen regarded them fondly, regretting how rarely they would meet once, *if*, he corrected himself sternly, James's operation were accomplished successfully. If Harvey Metcalfe had ever had a team like this on his side instead of against him, he would have been the richest man in the world.

'You're dreaming, Stephen.'

'Yes, I'm sorry. I mustn't forget that Anne has put me in charge.'

'Here we go again,' said Jean-Pierre. 'What time shall we report, Professor?'

'One hour from now, fully dressed to inspect James and take him to the church. Jean-Pierre, you will go and buy four carnations – three red ones and one white. Robin, you will arrange for the taxi and I shall take care of James.'

Robin and Jean-Pierre left, singing the *Marseillaise* lustily in two different keys. James and Stephen watched them depart.

'How are you feeling, James?'

'Great. I'm only sorry that I didn't complete my plan before today.'

'Doesn't matter at all. September 13th will be quite early enough. In any case, the break will do us no harm.'

'We'd never have managed it without you. You know that, don't you, Stephen? We'd all be facing ruin and I wouldn't even have met Anne. We all owe you so much.'

Stephen stared fixedly out of the window, unable to reply.

*

'Three red and one white,' said Jean-Pierre, 'as instructed, and I presume the white one is for me.'

'Pin it on James. Not behind his ear, Jean-Pierre.'

'You look fantastic, but I still fail to see what the lady sees in you,' said Jean-Pierre. Although the four of them were ready to leave, they still had half an hour to kill before the taxi was due. Jean-Pierre opened a bottle of champagne and they toasted James's health, the Team's health, Her Majesty The Queen, the President of the United States, and finally, with simulated reluctance, the President of France. Having finished the bottle, Stephen thought it wise for them to leave immediately and dragged the other three down to the waiting taxi.

'Keep smiling, James. We're with you.'

And they bundled him into the back.

The taxi took only a few minutes to reach Trinity Church, Copley Square, and the driver was not unhappy to be rid of the four of them.

'Three-fifteen pm. Anne will be very pleased with me,' said Stephen.

He escorted the bridegroom to the front pew on the right-hand side of the church, while Jean-Pierre made eyes at the prettiest of the girls. Robin helped hand out the wedding sheets while one thousand overdressed guests waited for the bride.

Stephen had just come to Robin's aid on the steps of the church and Jean-Pierre had joined them, suggesting they took their seats, when the Rolls Royce arrived. They were riveted to the steps by the beauty of Anne in her Balenciaga wedding gown. Her father stepped out behind her. She took his arm and proceeded to climb the steps.

The three stood motionless, like sheep in the stare of a python.

'The bastard.'

'Who's been conning who?'

'She must have known all along.'

Harvey beamed vaguely at them as he walked past with Anne on his arm. They proceeded down the aisle.

'Good God,' thought Stephen. 'He didn't recognise any of us.'

They took their places at the back of the church, out of earshot of the vast congregation. The organist stopped playing when Anne reached the altar.

'Harvey can't know,' said Stephen.

'How do you work that out?' asked Jean-Pierre.

'Because James would never have put us through this unless he'd passed the test himself at some earlier date.'

'Good thinking,' whispered Robin.

'I require and charge you both, as ye will answer at the dreadful day of judgment when the secrets of all hearts shall be disclosed . . .'

'I'd like to know one or two secrets right now,' said Jean-Pierre. 'To start with, how long has she known?'

'James Clarence Spencer, wilt thou have this

woman to thy wedded wife, to live together after God's ordinance in the Holy estate of Matrimony? Wilt thou love her, comfort her, honour and keep her, in sickness and in health and, forsaking all other, keep thee only unto her, so long as ye both shall live?'

'I will.'

'Rosalie Arlene, wilt thou have this man to thy wedded husband, to live . . .'

'I think,' said Stephen, 'we can be sure that she's a fully fledged member of the Team; otherwise we could never have succeeded at Monte Carlo or Oxford.'

'. . . so long as ye both shall live?'

'I will.'

'Who giveth this woman to be married to this man?'

Harvey bustled forward and took Anne's hand and gave it to the priest.

'I, James Clarence Spencer, take thee, Rosalie Arlene, to my wedded wife . . .'

'And what's more, why should he recognise us when he's only seen each of us once, and not as we really are,' continued Stephen.

'And thereto I plight thee my troth.'

'I, Rosalie Arlene, take thee, James Clarence Spencer, to my wedded husband . . .'

'But he must have a chance of working it out if we hang around,' said Robin.

'Not necessarily,' said Stephen. 'No need to panic. Our secret has always been to catch him off home ground.'

'But now he's on home ground,' said Jean-Pierre.

'No, he isn't. It's his daughter's wedding day and it's totally strange to the man. Naturally, we avoid him at the reception, but we don't make it too obvious.'

'You'll have to hold my hand,' said Robin.

'I will,' volunteered Jean-Pierre.

'Just remember to act naturally.'

'. . . and thereto I give thee my troth.'

Anne was quiet and shy, her voice only just reaching the astonished three at the back. James's was clear and firm:

'With this ring I thee wed, with my body I thee worship, and with all my worldly goods I thee endow . . .'

'And with some of ours too,' said Jean-Pierre.

'In the name of the Father, and of the Son and of the Holy Spirit. Amen.'

'Let us pray,' intoned the priest.

'I know what I'm going to pray,' said Robin. 'To be delivered out of the power of our enemy and from the hands of all that hate us.'

'O Eternal God, Creator and Preserver of all mankind . . .'

'We're near the end now,' said Stephen.

'An unfortunate turn of phrase,' offered Robin.

'Silence,' said Jean-Pierre. 'I agree with Stephen. We've got the measure of Metcalfe, just relax.'

'Those whom God hath joined together let no man put asunder.'

Jean-Pierre continued mumbling to himself, but it didn't sound like a prayer.

The blast of Handel's Wedding March from the organ brought them all back to the occasion. The ceremony was over and Lord and Lady Brigsley walked down the aisle watched by two thousand smiling eyes. Stephen looked amused, Jean-Pierre envious, and Robin nervous. James smiled beatifically as he passed them.

After a ten-minute session for the photographers on the steps of the church, the Rolls Royce carried the newly married couple back to the Metcalfes' house in Lincoln. Harvey and the Countess of Louth took the second car, and the Earl and Arlene, Anne's mother, took the third. Stephen, Robin and Jean-Pierre followed some twenty minutes later, still arguing the pros and cons of bearding the lion in his own den.

Harvey Metcalfe's Georgian house was magnificent, with an oriental garden leading down to a lake, great beds of roses and in the conservatory his pride and joy, his collection of rare orchids.

'I never thought I'd see this,' said Jean-Pierre.

'Nor me,' said Robin, 'and now that I have, I'm not too happy.'

'Let's run the gauntlet,' said Stephen. 'I suggest that we join the receiving line at well-separated intervals. I'll go first. Robin, you come second, at least twenty places behind, and Jean-Pierre, you come third, at least twenty places behind Robin, and *act naturally*. We're just friends of James's from England. Now, when you take your places in the queue, listen to the conversation. Try and find someone who's a close friend of Harvey's and jump immediately in front of them. When it comes to your turn to shake hands, Harvey's eyes will already be on the next person because he won't know you and will want to talk to them. That way we should escape.'

'Brilliant, Professor,' said Jean-Pierre.

The queue seemed interminably long. A thousand people shuffled past the outstretched hands of Mr and Mrs Metcalfe, the Earl and Countess of Louth, and Anne and James. Stephen eventually made it and passed with flying colours.

'So glad you could come,' said Anne.

Stephen did not reply.

'Good to see you, Stephen.'

'We all admire your plan, James.'

Stephen slipped into the main ballroom and hid behind a pillar on the other side of the room, as far as he could be from the multi-storey wedding cake in the centre.

Robin was next and avoided looking Harvey in the eyes.

'How kind of you to come all this way,' said Anne.

Robin mumbled something under his breath.

'Hope you've enjoyed yourself today, Robin?'

James was obviously having the time of his life. After being put through it in the same way by Anne, he was relishing the Team's discomfiture.

'You're a bastard, James.'

'Not too loud, old fellow. My mother and father might hear you.'

Robin slipped through to the ballroom and, after a search behind all the pillars, found Stephen.

'Did you get through all right?'

'I think so, but I don't want to see him ever again. What time is the plane back?'

'Eight pm. Now don't panic. Keep your eye out for Jean-Pierre.'

'Bloody good thing he kept his beard,' said Robin.

Jean-Pierre shook hands with Harvey, who was already intent on the next guest as Jean-Pierre had, by shameless queue-barging, managed to secure a place in front of a Boston banker who was obviously a close friend of Harvey's.

'Good to see you, Marvin.'

Jean-Pierre had escaped. He kissed Anne on both cheeks, whispered in her ear, 'Game, set and match to James,' and went off in search of Stephen and Robin. He forgot his original instructions when he found himself face to face with the chief bridesmaid.

'Did you enjoy the wedding?' she asked.

'Of course. I always judge weddings by the bridesmaids, not the bride.'

She blushed with pleasure.

'This must have cost a fortune,' she continued.

'Yes, my dear, and I know whose,' said Jean-Pierre, slipping his arm around her waist.

Four hands grabbed a protesting Jean-Pierre and unceremoniously dragged him behind the pillar.

'For God's sake, Jean-Pierre. She's not a day over seventeen. We don't want to go to jail for rape of a juvenile as well as theft. Drink this and behave yourself.' Robin thrust a glass of champagne into his hand.

The champagne flowed and even Stephen had a little too much. They were all clinging to their pillar for support by the time the toast-master called for silence.

'My lords, ladies and gentlemen. Pray silence for the Viscount Brigsley, the bridegroom.'

James made an impressive speech. The actor in him took over and the Americans adored it. Even his father had a look of admiration on his face. The toast-master then introduced Harvey, who spoke long and loud. He cracked his favourite joke about marrying off his daughter to Prince Charles, at which the assembled guests roared heartily as they always do at weddings, even for the weakest joke. He ended by calling the toast for the bride and groom.

When the applause had died down, and the hubbub of chatter had struck up again, Harvey took an envelope from his pocket and kissed his daughter on the cheek.

'Rosalie, here's a little wedding present for you, to

make up for letting me keep the Van Gogh. I know you'll put it to good use.'

Harvey passed her the white envelope. Inside there was a cheque for $250,000. Anne kissed her father with genuine affection.

'Thank you, Daddy, I promise you James and I will use it wisely.'

She hurried off in pursuit of James, whom she found besieged by a group of American matrons:

'Is it true you're related to the Queen . . .?'

'I never met a real live lord . . .'

'I do hope you'll invite us over to see your castle . . . ?'

'There are no castles in the King's Road,' said James relieved to be rescued by Anne.

'Darling, can you spare me a minute?'

James excused himself and followed Anne, but they found it almost impossible to escape the crowd.

'Look,' she said. 'Quickly.'

James took the cheque.

'Good God – $250,000.'

'You know what I'm going to do with it, don't you?'

'Yes, darling.'

Anne hunted for Stephen, Robin and Jean-Pierre, which was not an easy task as they were still hidden behind a pillar in the far corner. She was eventually guided to the spot by the subdued but spirited rendering of 'Who Wants to be a Millionaire?' issuing from behind it.

'Can you lend me a pen, Stephen?'

Three pens shot out for her use.

She took the cheque from the middle of her bouquet and wrote on its back, 'Rosalie Brigsley – pay Stephen Bradley'. She handed it to him.

'Yours, I believe.'

The three of them stared at the cheque. She was gone before they could even comment.

'What a girl our James has gone and married,' said Jean-Pierre.

'You're drunk, you frog,' said Robin.

'How dare you, sir, suggest that a Frenchman could get drunk on champagne. I demand satisfaction. Choose your weapons.'

'Champagne corks.'

'Quiet,' said Stephen. 'You'll give yourselves away.'

'Well now, tell me, Professor, what's the latest financial position?'

'I'm just working it out now,' said Stephen.

'What?' said Robin and Jean-Pierre together, but they were too happy to argue.

'He still owes us $101 and 24 cents.'

'DISGRACEFUL,' said Jean-Pierre. 'Burn the place down.'

Anne and James left to change, while Stephen, Robin and Jean-Pierre forced down some more champagne. The toast-master announced that the bride and groom would be leaving in approximately fifteen minutes and requested the guests to gather in the main hall and courtyard.

'Come on, we must watch them go,' said Stephen. The drink had given them new confidence and they took their places near the car.

It was Stephen who heard Harvey say, 'God damn it. Do I have to think of everything?' and watched him look round his guests until his eyes fell on the trio. Stephen's legs turned to jelly as Harvey's finger beckoned him.

'Hey, you, weren't you an usher?'

'Yes, sir.'

'Rosalie is going to leave at any moment and there are no flowers for her. God knows what's happened to them, but there are no flowers. Grab a car. There's a florist half a mile down the road, but hurry.'

'Yes, sir.'

'Say, don't I know you from somewhere?'

'Yes, sir, I mean, no sir. I'll go and get the flowers.'

Stephen turned and fled. Robin and Jean-Pierre, who had been watching horrified, thinking that Harvey had at last rumbled them, ran after him. When he reached the back of the house, Stephen came to a halt and stared at the most beautiful bed of roses. Robin and Jean-Pierre shot straight past him, stopped, turned round and staggered back.

'What the hell are you up to – picking flowers for your own funeral?'

'It's only Metcalfe's wishes. Somebody forgot the flowers for Anne and I have five minutes to get them, so start picking.

'*Mes enfants*, do you see what I see?'

The others looked up. Jean-Pierre was staring rapturously at the conservatory.

Stephen rushed back to the front of the house, the prize orchids in his arms, followed by Robin and Jean-Pierre. He was just in time to pass them over to Harvey before James and Anne came out of the house.

'Magnificent. They're my favourite flowers. How much were they?'

'$100,' replied Stephen, without thinking.

Harvey handed over two $50 bills. Stephen retreated sweating, to join Robin and Jean-Pierre.

James and Anne fought their way through the crowd. No man in the gathering could take his eyes off her.

'Oh Daddy, orchids, how beautiful.' Anne kissed Harvey. 'You've made this the most wonderful day in my life . . .'

The Rolls Royce moved slowly down the drive away from the large crowd on its way to the airport, where James and Anne were to catch the flight to San Francisco, their first stop on the way to Hawaii. As the car glided round the house, Anne stared at the empty conservatory and then at the flowers in her arms. James did not notice. He was thinking of other things.

'Do you think they'll ever forgive me?' he said.

'I'm sure they'll find a way, darling. But do let me into a secret. Did you really have a plan?'

'I knew you wouldn't be able to resist asking me that, and the truth is . . .'

The car purred effortlessly along the highway and only the chauffeur heard his reply.

Stephen, Robin and Jean-Pierre watched the guests dispersing, most of them saying their goodbyes to the Metcalfes.

'Don't let's risk it,' said Robin.

'Agreed,' said Stephen.

'Let's invite him out to dinner,' said Jean-Pierre.

The other two grabbed him and threw him into a taxi.

'What's that you have under your morning coat, Jean-Pierre?'

'Two bottles of Krug *dix-neuf cent soixante-quatre*. It seemed such a shame to leave them there on their own. I thought they might get lonely.'

Stephen instructed the driver to take them back to the hotel.

'What a wedding. Do you think James ever had a plan?' asked Robin.

'I don't know, but if he has it will only have to bring in $1.24.'

'We should have retrieved the money he made from his win on Rosalie at Ascot,' mused Jean-Pierre.

After packing and signing out of the hotel, they took another taxi to Logan International Airport and, with considerable help from the British Airways staff, managed to board the plane.

'Damn,' said Stephen. 'I wish we hadn't left without the $1.24.'

21

ONCE ON BOARD, they drank the champagne Jean-Pierre had captured at the wedding. Even Stephen seemed content, although he did occasionally revert to the theme of the missing $1.24.

'How much do you imagine this champagne cost?' teased Jean-Pierre.

'That's not the point. Not a penny more, not a penny less.'

Jean-Pierre decided he would never understand academics.

'Don't worry, Stephen. I've every confidence that James's plan will bring in $1.24.'

Stephen would have laughed, but it gave him a headache.

'To think that girl knew everything.'

On arrival at Heathrow, they had little trouble in clearing customs. The purpose of the trip had never been to bring back gifts. Robin made a detour to W. H. Smiths and picked up *The Times* and the *Evening*

Standard. Jean-Pierre bargained with a taxi-driver about the fare to central London.

'We're not some bloody Americans who don't know the rate or the route and can be easily fleeced,' he was saying, still not yet sober.

The taxi-driver grumbled to himself as he nosed his black Austin towards the motorway. It was not going to be his day.

Robin read the papers happily, one of those rare people who could read in a moving car. Stephen and Jean-Pierre satisfied themselves with watching the passing traffic.

'Jesus Christ.'

Stephen and Jean-Pierre were startled. They had rarely heard Robin swear. It seemed out of character.

'God Almighty.'

This was too much for them, but before they could enquire, he began to read out loud:

'"BP announced a strike in the North Sea which is likely to produce 200,000 barrels of oil a day. The strike is described by their Chairman, Sir Eric Drake, as a major find. The British Petroleum Forties Field is one mile from the so far unexplored Prospecta Oil field and rumours of a bid by BP have sent Prospecta Oil shares to a record high of $12.25 at the close of business."'

'Nom de Dieu,' said Jean-Pierre. 'What do we do now?'

'Oh well,' said Stephen. 'I suppose we'll have to work out a plan for how to give it all back.'

extracts reading groups
competitions books new
discounts extracts
competitions
books new
events books
extracts new reading groups
interviews
events extracts
discounts
new books events
events new
discounts extracts discounts
www.panmacmillan.com
extracts events reading groups
competitions books extracts new